panda-monium

Also by Stuart Gibbs

The FunJungle series
Belly Up
Poached
Big Game

The Spy School series
Spy School
Spy Camp
Evil Spy School
Spy Ski School

The Moon Base Alpha series
Space Case
Spaced Out

The Last Musketeer

STUART GIBBS

panda-monium

A **funjungle** NOVEL

Simon & Schuster Books for Young Readers

New York London Toronto Sydney New Delhi

SIMON & SCHUSTER BOOKS FOR YOUNG READERS
An imprint of Simon & Schuster Children's Publishing Division
1230 Avenue of the Americas, New York, New York 10020

SIMON & SCHUSTER BOOKS FOR YOUNG READERS
is a trademark of Simon & Schuster, Inc.
For information about special discounts for bulk purchases, please contact Simon & Schuster Special Sales at 1-866-506-1949 or business@simonandschuster.com.
The Simon & Schuster Speakers Bureau can bring authors to your live event. For more information or to book an event, contact the Simon & Schuster Speakers Bureau at 1-866-248-3049 or visit our website at www.simonspeakers.com.
Endpaper art by Ryan Thompson
The text for this book was set in Adobe Garamond Pro.
Manufactured in the United States of America
0217 FFG
First Edition
10 9 8 7 6 5 4 3 2 1
Library of Congress Cataloging-in-Publication Data
Names: Gibbs, Stuart, 1969– author.
Title: Panda-monium : a Funjungle novel / Stuart Gibbs.
Description: First Edition. | New York : Simon & Schuster Books for Young Readers, 2017. | Sequel to: Big game. | Summary: Teddy Fitzroy must solve the crime of the kidnapped rare and expensive panda, Li Ping.
Identifiers: LCCN 2016002113| ISBN 9781481445672 (hardcover) | ISBN 9781481445696 (eBook)
Subjects: | CYAC: Mystery and detective stories. | Zoos—Fiction. | Pandas—Fiction. | Zoo animals—Fiction.
Classification: LCC PZ7.G339236 Pan 2017 | DDC [Fic]—dc23
LC record available at https://lccn.loc.gov/2016002113

For all the people who work in animal conservation, fighting to protect endangered species and habitats. Thanks for everything you do.

Contents

THE THIEF

I almost missed all the mayhem with the giant panda because a dolphin stole my bathing suit.

The dolphin was a male Atlantic bottlenose named Snickers, and I was swimming in the Dolphin Adventure tank at FunJungle Wild Animal Park. Snickers was known for being extremely playful, but up until that point, he'd never swiped anyone's clothing before. Fortunately for me, it happened at eight in the morning on a Sunday, an hour before the park opened, so there were only two other people around when I got pantsed. Unfortunately, both of those other people were girls.

One of them was my girlfriend, Summer McCracken, the fourteen-year-old daughter of the owner of FunJungle. The other was Olivia Putney, the dolphin trainer. Olivia was twenty-three, but she behaved in such a youthful, enthusiastic way that I often forgot she was ten years older than me.

Dolphin Adventure was an enormous saltwater tank where tourists could pay to interact with the park's eight dolphins. Some less reputable dolphin encounters allowed tourists to ride on the animals, but FunJungle only let guests swim close by, feed the dolphins some fish, and pet them gently. Everyone loved it. The sessions were expensive—and that was in addition to the steep price of park admission—but Dolphin Adventure sold out almost every day.

Summer and I had been swimming with the dolphins a lot lately. We had come for the first time a month before, when Summer had surprised me with a private swim for my birthday. Normally, guests swam in groups, but since we did it after official park hours, the two of us and Olivia had the dolphins all to ourselves. It was supposed to be a one-time event, but then Olivia had invited us to come back whenever we wanted—so we had. Usually, we visited after the park closed; even though it was only April, central Texas could still be awfully hot in the evenings and the dolphin tank was refreshingly cool. No one ever charged us, even though Summer could easily afford it. It was one of the perks of being the owner's daughter. The trainers claimed it wasn't a big deal; one of them always had to be there before opening and after closing anyhow, and they said the stimulation we provided was good for the dolphins. They even gave us our own employee lockers to store bathing suits and towels, so we didn't have to lug our stuff home and back each time.

We hadn't really meant to go swimming that morning. We had *really* come to FunJungle to see Li Ping. The five-year-old panda's arrival was a huge deal. Most animals were owned by their zoos, but every panda in the world was owned by the country of China, which only loaned them to a few select zoos around the world. Other animals could attract crowds, but nothing else on earth was as rare, adorable, and beloved as a giant panda. The fact that one was coming to FunJungle had boosted ticket presales for the entire summer.

Li Ping was supposed to be there at 8:00 a.m., but Summer and I had arrived much earlier. That wasn't a big deal for me, since my family actually lived at FunJungle. (Both of my parents worked for the park—Mom was the head primatologist, while Dad was the official photographer—so we lived in employee housing beyond the back fence.) Summer lived twenty miles away, but she and her father weren't about to miss something this momentous. Unfortunately, the truck with Li Ping got stuck in a major traffic jam on I-10, delaying the panda's arrival at least an hour. Even that early in the morning, it was already hot, so Summer had said that, instead of just sitting around, we might as well go see the dolphins.

A few months before, J.J. McCracken would have had

a bodyguard tail Summer to the dolphin tank, but Summer had always chafed at this. Having enormous men constantly following her made it difficult to have a normal social life. So she'd begged her father to stop hiring them, pointing out that, so far, the guards had actually caused more problems than they'd solved. (The last one had been complicit in a crime at FunJungle.) J.J. had reluctantly agreed on a trial basis, which had worked out so far.

When Summer and I reached Dolphin Adventure, we found Olivia on duty, feeding the dolphins a breakfast of raw squid and herring. She was wearing her standard Dolphin Adventure bathing suit and her hair was wet, indicating that she'd already been in the tank. Olivia didn't even bother asking if we wanted to swim. She simply said, "Hop on in, kids! The water's fine!"

"Sounds good," Summer replied, then told me, "Last one in is a sea cucumber!" and bolted for her locker. We quickly changed into our bathing suits, grabbed scuba masks, and hit the water. Summer beat me by five seconds. A bit earlier in the year, we might have needed neoprene suits to keep warm, but it was hot enough that day to go in without them.

The dolphin tank was an oval pool twelve feet deep and a quarter mile in circumference. It was divided into two sections: one for the dolphins to interact with guests and a much larger area to be on their own. The interaction area was fronted by a long man-made beach built with sand that had been trucked in from South Padre Island. A floating catwalk separated the two areas on the surface, with a small island in the center of the tank. Under the surface, though, there were no barriers. The dolphins were always free to go wherever they wanted. If they felt like ignoring us—or any guests— they could simply swim away.

Two of them, Snickers and his sister, Twix, raced right over to us, eager to play. Bottlenose dolphins are extremely social and the siblings knew us well. They swam all around us, leaping over our heads and corkscrewing through the water below. Snickers kept rolling onto his back, eager to have his belly rubbed, like a 400-pound aquatic poodle.

"Want to see something cool?" Olivia asked us, after we'd been in long enough for our fingers to start pruning. "I've taught Twix a new behavior. Check this out." She stepped onto the floating catwalk and blew into a small silver whistle she kept on a chain around her neck. Twix zipped over to her.

Dolphins' personalities are as varied as humans' are. Twix was much more acrobatic than the others, able to do all sorts of amazing tricks, like double flips with a twist. Snickers was far more impish, always looking for ways to steal fish from the trainers. Their mother, Skittles, had the most vocalizations of any dolphin at FunJungle; in addition to whistles, grunts, clicks, and clacks, she could make an incredible variety of farting noises with her blowhole.

Olivia blew her whistle again.

Twix bobbed upright with her head out of the water.

Olivia then clenched her hand into a fist.

Twix promptly spit a mouthful of water over the wall.

"Cool!" Summer exclaimed. "Can I try it?"

"Sure." Olivia tossed a handful of squid into Twix's mouth. "I'd like to see if she'll do it for other people." She blew into her whistle once more and pointed toward us.

Twix shot back through the tank to where we were treading water and came to a sudden stop in front of Summer, sticking her head above the surface.

"Okay, Twixie," Summer said. "When I give you the signal, spit at Teddy."

"Hey!" I protested.

"One," Summer counted. "Two . . ."

Before she could get to three, I raised my hand and made a fist. Twix promptly spit a mouthful of water into Summer's face instead of mine.

Most people assumed I liked Summer because she was rich, beautiful, and famous. They were wrong. I liked Summer because she was the coolest, smartest, most down-to-earth girl I'd ever met. (Although her being rich, beautiful, and famous were all nice perks.) For example, a lot of girls might have been upset to have a giant marine mammal spit on them. But Summer thought it was funny. She spluttered a bit, laughing the whole time—then pounced on me and tried to dunk me. "You're going down for that!" she warned.

I caught her arms in mid-attack and we ended up wrestling, each trying to shove the other one under the water. Snickers seemed to feed off our energy, spiraling around us in the pool. He even nudged us a few times, like he wanted to join in the fun.

And then, he grabbed my bathing suit in his teeth and dove, yanking it right off me.

I was suddenly buck naked except for my scuba mask. Needless to say, this caught me by surprise. I forgot all about wrestling. Summer, who hadn't noticed I'd been stripped, promptly dunked me. She shoved me under and crowed victoriously.

Below the surface, I spotted Snickers speeding to the farthest end of the tank, my bathing suit clenched firmly in his mouth. It didn't look like I was going to get it back anytime soon.

I promptly cupped my hands over my privates and bobbed back to the surface.

"I got you gooood," Summer taunted, still unaware of what had happened. "And you are not getting me back."

"You're right," I agreed. "I'm not."

Summer cocked her head at me curiously. "You're gonna let me get away with that?"

"Um, yes. I'm feeling very chivalrous."

"You weren't so chivalrous when you made Snickers spit in my face," Summer told me. "What's going on?"

"Nothing," I said, a bit too quickly.

Summer might have pressed on suspiciously if her cell phone hadn't rung. She'd left it on the fake beach with her towel, and it now chimed loudly with the specific ringtone that indicated her father was calling.

"That's Daddy!" Summer exclaimed, then checked her watch. "Oh man, we've been here longer than I thought! I'll bet Li Ping's almost here!" She swam for the beach.

I stayed right where I was, trying to figure out how to get out of the pool without revealing I was naked.

Now Olivia grew suspicious too. Thankfully, from where she was standing on the catwalk, she couldn't see too well below the surface of the water, so she hadn't noticed my nakedness yet either. "You're not going to see the panda?" she asked.

"I thought I'd take a little extra time with the dolphins," I replied.

"You can swim with the dolphins whenever you want," Olivia pointed out. "A giant panda doesn't show up every day."

Normally, this would have been a good point. However,

even though I was excited to see Li Ping, I *wasn't* excited for the two girls to see me naked. Or to even learn that I *was* naked.

Only, that was getting harder and harder to keep a secret. Summer had now reached the beach. As she checked the message from her father, she realized I was still back in the pool. "What are you doing?" she demanded. "Daddy says Li Ping will be here in fifteen minutes! We've gotta bolt."

"You go ahead," I said. "I'll catch up."

"I'm not going without you," Summer insisted, then asked, "Why are you treading water so funny?"

"What are you talking about?" I asked innocently.

Summer's jaw dropped as she finally realized why my hands were cupped over my privates. "Oh my gosh. Did you lose your bathing suit?"

"No," I lied.

At which point, Snickers ambushed me from below. He'd returned from hiding my bathing suit and was still in a rambunctious mood. Dolphins are surprisingly powerful. With only a few strokes of their tails, they can launch their entire bodies ten feet out of the water. Or plow into a great white shark hard enough to kill it. Or, it turned out, fling a thirteen-year-old boy fifteen feet through the air. Snickers drove his head right under my rear end and flicked me upward. The next thing I knew, I was flying. In my surprise, I let go of my privates and windmilled my arms in the air, allowing Summer and Olivia ample opportunity to see that I was completely naked. Then I belly flopped back into the water.

When I resurfaced, Summer and Olivia were laughing hysterically. So was Snickers. The dolphin's laughter sounded more like rapid-fire clicking, but I definitely got the sense that he knew what he'd done was funny. To everyone but me, at least.

"What happened to your suit?" Summer asked, though she was laughing so hard she could barely speak.

"That jerk stole it!" I exclaimed, pointing at Snickers.

Snickers apparently didn't like being insulted. He promptly flipped his tail, dousing me with a wave of water.

Summer laughed even harder.

"It's not funny," I said.

"Yes it is," she informed me. "In fact, it's *very* funny. And I guarantee you, if I'd lost *my* bathing suit in there, you'd be laughing."

I didn't reply to that, because it was probably true. Instead, I said, "Could you two turn away so I can get my towel?"

Summer and Olivia both averted their eyes. Snickers hit me with another wave of water.

I clambered out onto the beach and quickly wrapped my towel around me.

Summer started for the women's changing room, where

she'd left her dry clothes. "Let's move it. Li Ping's gonna be here soon."

"I'm drying off as fast as I can," I told her.

The changing rooms were to the side of the beach, next to a small building where guests checked in for their dolphin swims. Both structures had thatched roofs to give the impression that we were on some tropical island, rather than two hundred miles from the ocean. The walls of the changing room didn't even go all the way up to the thatch, so we could easily talk back and forth between them. As I rinsed off the salt water in the men's shower, Olivia called to me from outside the door. "Teddy! How did Snickers get your swimsuit off?"

"He just grabbed on to it with his teeth and yanked it down!" I yelled back. "Then he swam away with it."

"Hmmm," Olivia said, like something was bothering her.

"Is something wrong?" I asked.

"He's never done that before," Olivia said. "And none of the other dolphins have either, so he couldn't have learned it from them. I wonder where he got the idea."

I turned off the water and grabbed my towel. "He couldn't have figured it out himself?"

"It's possible," Olivia replied, "but it's highly unlikely. There are two types of dolphin behaviors: natural ones and learned ones. A natural one would be something with a purpose, like leaping out of the water—while one that's learned is more of a trick, like doing a backflip. Stealing someone's bathing suit doesn't seem like it'd have much natural purpose to a dolphin, and it's a little complicated, so my guess is it was learned."

"Hold on," Summer said from the women's room. "Are you saying one of the trainers *taught* Snickers to do that?"

"I hope not," Olivia said. "But I don't think I can let Snickers interact with the public for the time being. If he strips the suit off a paying guest, we could get sued."

I yanked on my dry clothes and exited the changing room. "How could someone else have taught the dolphins to do anything? No one has access to the dolphins *except* the trainers, right?"

"No one else is *supposed* to have access," Olivia corrected. "But maybe someone does."

"And you're worried they'll teach all the dolphins to strip the guests?"

"Actually, I'm more worried that someone's been in with the dolphins without authorization. Maybe they didn't really try to teach Snickers to pants people, but it still happened somehow."

"How?"

"Dolphins pick up behaviors all the time without necessarily being taught them. They can learn things just by interacting with guests. When the trainers are here, we can try to make sure they don't pick up any bad habits. But if someone sneaks in here when we're not around . . ."

"The dolphins could learn some bad behaviors?" I finished.

"Yes. But even more importantly, the dolphins could get hurt. Like if someone didn't know what they were doing and tried to ride one of them." Olivia turned to me. "Teddy, you're tight with security . . ."

"I wouldn't say that, exactly . . ."

"Well, you've solved a couple crimes around here. So you know Chief Hoenekker pretty well. Could you ask him to check the security feeds from the last few days for me?"

"Only the last few days?"

"If the dolphins learned this behavior more than a few days ago, I think we would have already seen them do it."

"Sure," I said. "I can ask Hoenekker."

Summer exited the changing room, wearing one of her standard all-pink outfits. That was her trademark when she appeared in public, and there were going to be lots of TV cameras around that day. (Summer didn't actually like pink that much; she'd chosen it as her trademark color so that, when she didn't wear it, most people wouldn't recognize her.) Her blond hair was still wet, making it look darker, and she was pulling it back into a ponytail. "Hoenekker's gonna be awfully busy with the panda today," she told Olivia. "You might want to call security yourself."

"I will," Olivia said. "But I'm worried they might not take me seriously. Having a dolphin stealing bathing suits probably won't seem like a very high priority to them. So I figure every little bit helps."

"Good point," Summer admitted, then checked her watch. "Teddy, we have to motor or we'll miss Li Ping."

"I'm ready," I said, tossing my towel into my locker.

Summer did the same thing, and we ran for the front gates of FunJungle.

If I had known how big a disaster the panda's arrival was going to be, I would have stayed in the pool.

THE BIG EVENT

Most people didn't know Summer was my girl-
friend. Even our closest friends. Because Summer was
the daughter of a billionaire and a famous model, she'd
been in the public eye since the day she was born. Gossip
websites and trashy magazines were always running stories about her, most of which were completely wrong. A
few weeks before, she had been in the audience at a boy
band concert in San Antonio, and the next day, the rumor
machine announced she was dating the lead singer. (One
website even claimed they were engaged, despite the fact
that neither was old enough to drive.) In truth, Summer
had never had a boyfriend before me, and she worried all
the magazines and websites would go nuts if they found
out about us.

"Our friends aren't going to tell the press that we're dating," I'd argued.

"No, but they'll tell *someone*," she'd countered. "And those people will tell other people, who'll tell other people, who'll tell other people. Sooner or later, the media will find out about it, and the next thing you know, there'll be TV crews camped out on your lawn."

"We don't have a lawn," I pointed out. "We live in your dad's crummy trailer park." We were *supposed* to have a lawn, along with landscaping and a communal swimming pool and all sorts of other nice stuff, but J.J. McCracken appeared to have forgotten about putting it all in. All we had was a murky sinkhole that excelled at breeding mosquitoes.

"You know what I mean," Summer said. "Trust me, the longer we can keep this a secret, the better."

I figured she knew more about being in the public eye than I did, so I didn't tell anyone we were dating—except for my parents. I didn't like lying to them, and they would have figured it out anyhow; I'd suddenly been spending a lot more time with Summer.

Summer and I never really spent much time at my house, because even though we had a new double-wide trailer, courtesy of J.J., it was still smaller than Summer's mother's closet. Sometimes we went to the McCrackens' ranch, because they had a pool and tennis courts and stables with horses and a chef who'd studied in Paris. But most of the time, we just hung out at FunJungle. Because Summer was J.J.'s daughter, she could arrange lots of cool things in addition to swimming with dolphins, like getting to sneak onto rides without having to wait in line like everyone else. Although Summer didn't live at FunJungle like I did, she still considered it her second home. The park had been her idea, back when she was a little girl, and she'd spent much of her life watching it all come together. Since she loved animals, she'd been extremely involved in the development, making plenty of suggestions her father had actually used. So she knew the park as well as I did, maybe even better. As we raced through FunJungle from Dolphin Adventure, we both knew every shortcut, agreeing on the fastest route without even needing to discuss it. We dodged between Shark Encounter and the Petting Zoo, circled Monkey Mountain, and cut right through the underwater section of Hippo River until we arrived at the entry plaza.

It was a madhouse. To our surprise, even though it was still a half hour before the park opened, hundreds of people were gathered at the front gates.

While Li Ping's arrival at FunJungle was huge news, J.J. McCracken had still hoped to keep the actual moment a secret. Over the past year, almost every time FunJungle had tried to hold a big media event, it had ended in disaster: At the gala opening of Carnivore Canyon, someone had let a tiger loose; when the park had made a big deal about getting a koala, it had been stolen; and when a formal funeral was attempted after Henry the Hippo died, the crane holding the coffin had dropped it, splattering the front row of dignitaries with hippo guts. So J.J. was worried about tempting fate yet again.

Pete Thwacker, FunJungle's head of public relations, had decided to use the secrecy of the event to sell the story. Pete didn't actually know that much about animals—he'd recently stated on live television that the primary food source for coyotes was roadrunners—but he knew how to work the media. Instead of getting the public excited about the exact day the panda would arrive, he made the whole thing a huge mystery: Li Ping was coming . . . but when? He advertised on billboards, TV, and radio stations around the country. ("The first person to see Li Ping the Panda could be *you*!") It worked like gangbusters. The story trended on every social media platform. Guests flocked to FunJungle, hoping they might be lucky enough to be there the day the panda arrived.

Of course, J.J. and Pete had known the exact delivery date all along. It had all been planned out months ahead of time with the rigor of the D-Day invasion. The idea was to have Li Ping arrive in late April so that she would grab even more media attention, diverting tourists from other theme parks, like Disney World or Universal Studios, and enticing them to plan their summer vacations at FunJungle. But up until that moment, everything was supposed to be shrouded in secrecy. Almost no one was told the actual arrival date. Even Summer was kept in the dark. She had only learned the night before, then promptly called me to share the news.

Li Ping was being shipped to FunJungle from the San Diego Zoo, where she'd been born, in a custom-made, climate-controlled semi truck. A male panda, Shen Ju, would be flown out from China later in the summer, with the hope that they'd breed. Originally, Pete had hoped to make an event of Li Ping's transit across the country. He'd wanted to christen the truck "The Panda Express," splash Li Ping's picture all over it, and have it stop for photo ops in every town along the way. But J.J., fearing disaster, had made him scrap all that. Li Ping's delivery was to be far more clandestine. The truck was specially designed for the panda on the inside, but on the outside, it was made to look like every other truck on the highway: a bland, easy-to-ignore gray.

However, it was now evident that all attempts at secrecy had failed. Word had gotten out, and the panda fanatics had arrived in full force. When FunJungle had displayed a koala the previous winter, I'd been surprised by how many fans those animals had—but that was nothing compared to how crazy people were for pandas. Pandas, it seemed, were the rock stars of the animal world, right down to having groupies. (The people who worked at FunJungle had already taken to calling them "PandaManiacs.") Maybe it was because pandas were cute; maybe it was because they were rare. Probably it was a combination of the two. Whatever the case, panda fans were more intense than those for any other animal.

For starters, they dressed up. Almost everyone gathered outside the front gates had worn a combination of black and white. Many were merely in panda-themed T-shirts, but a surprising number wore panda costumes or had painted their faces. Almost everyone had a set of "Li Ping ears," which had been available for purchase at FunJungle for weeks. (They were quite similar to the Mickey Mouse ears at Disney World, except the ears themselves were a lot smaller, which allowed J.J. McCracken to avoid accusations of copyright infringement *and* save on production costs.) Instead of looking like a large group of pandas, however, the big mass of black and white really looked more like an Antarctic penguin colony.

Meanwhile, the press had come out in full force as well. News trucks from every local TV station, along with a few national ones, were parked outside the gates, cameras at the ready.

Inside the park, at the far edge of the entry plaza, stood a much smaller, considerably less enthusiastic contingent of people.

J.J. McCracken was there, in his customary jeans and cowboy boots, looking infuriated about the crowds. Pete Thwacker stood beside him, dressed in a fancy three-piece suit. Then came Chief Hoenekker, FunJungle's head of security, in a freshly starched khaki outfit that looked more like something a five-star general might wear. After that came my father, ready to document the panda's arrival with three separate cameras (two digital SLRs and one video recorder) dangling from straps around his neck. The last person was Mom, who was helping Dad out that morning, with two camera bags slung over her shoulder. She and Dad were the only ones in the group who'd had the sense to wear shorts and T-shirts in the heat.

"It'd be bad enough to have all the panda freaks out there," J.J. was grumbling as Summer and I arrived. "But how the heck did all the news stations get wind of this? What holy idiot tipped them off?"

"Er . . . ," Pete squeaked, looking embarrassed.

J.J. wheeled on him. He was nearly a foot shorter than Pete, even with lifts in his cowboy boots, but J.J.'s personality was so big, he somehow seemed just as tall. "*You* told them?"

"Not *all* of them," Pete mewled. "But I thought it'd be a good idea to offer exclusive access to a few stations."

"Jack's the only one who was supposed to have exclusive access!" J.J. snapped, pointing at my father. "So *we* could control the story this time! If you offer exclusive access to a bunch of people, then it's not really exclusive anymore, is it?"

"No," Pete admitted, "but the news stations all get more excited when they *think* they have exclusive access. Only, it looks like the few I told must have blabbed to all the others . . ."

"As well as half the county," Hoenekker muttered, nodding to the crowds.

"And that crowd's gonna get real angry when they find out the panda's not even going on display for a month," J.J. said.

"A month?!" Pete echoed, going pale. "What do you mean?"

"The panda has to go into quarantine at the hospital," J.J. explained. "Just like any other animal that shows up here. We have to isolate it to make sure it doesn't have any diseases that'll infect the rest of my animals. You know the drill, Thwacker."

"Yes," Pete whined. "But I figured, since the panda would be on display by itself, that would count the same as being quarantined."

"No dice," J.J. replied. "Federal regulations state it has to be done in an official quarantine facility for thirty days. And Doc says it could be even longer."

"Longer?" Pete gasped, looking like he might pass out.

The men were all so focused on the issue, no one noticed Summer and me arriving except Mom. She stepped away to greet us, ran her fingers through my wet hair, and smelled them. "Salt water," she observed. "Someone's been swimming with the dolphins again."

"Wow, Mrs. Fitzroy," Summer said, impressed. "I see where Teddy gets the detective genes from."

"You did go with permission, right?" Mom asked.

"Yes," I groaned, even though Mom's suspicions were probably justified. Summer and I had snuck into exhibits before, though never merely for fun. We had only done it to investigate crimes. "Olivia Putney was with us the whole time."

"So what am I supposed to do here?" Dad was asking the other men. "Am I filming Li Ping's arrival—or are all the news crews?"

"*You* are," J.J. replied, cutting Pete off before he could answer. "You're the only one I trust around the panda. When that truck gets here, I want you front and center. You go inside the trailer to document Li Ping, and you stay with her until she gets transferred to quarantine." He turned to Pete. "That's what *exclusive* means. The news will just have to be happy with filming the truck."

"They won't even get to see the panda?" Pete asked, aghast. "They won't be happy about that."

"Well then, you better go change their minds about it," J.J. told him. "Flash that big old smile of yours, put a good spin on this, and make sure that crowd doesn't turn into an angry mob." He checked his watch, then added, "And do it quick. Li Ping's coming in hot."

"All right," Pete said. He was obviously annoyed at J.J., but as he turned toward the news crews, his standard, confident on-camera personality took over. A smile bloomed on his face. He straightened his tie and strode purposefully toward the front gates.

The moment the crowd saw him coming, their excitement grew. Everyone started asking when Li Ping was going to arrive.

"I assure you all, the long wait for Li Ping is nearly over!" Pete announced, and a cheer went up from the crowd.

Hoenekker sighed. "Sometimes Thwacker can be such a moron, I'm surprised he can walk in a straight line."

"He looks good on TV, though," J.J. said. "Often, that's all that matters. Are these crowds gonna cause us any trouble?"

"I think we'll be all right," Hoenekker replied. "I assigned extra security starting at oh-600 this morning in case of an eventuality such as this." No one at the park but J.J. knew what Hoenekker had done before he had taken over security, but everyone suspected he'd worked for some branch of the military, or possibly the CIA; the way he spoke was a big reason why.

"Any word from Marge?" Mom asked.

"Officer O'Malley last reported in at oh-800," Hoenekker replied. "Ever since they got past that traffic jam, the trip has gone without a hitch."

"Wait," I said, concerned. "Large Marge is with the panda?"

Mom gave me a sharp stare, displeased with my choice of words.

"I mean, Marge O'Malley is with the panda?" I corrected.

"She is tasked with providing security for Li Ping en route to FunJungle," Hoenekker explained.

"Really?" I asked, unable to hide my shock. "Of all the people in security, you sent *Marge?*"

Since the day I'd first arrived at FunJungle, Marge had been a thorn in my side. She had instantly decided I was trouble, her thought process being: 1) I was a young boy and 2) all young boys were trouble. In her determination to prove this, she had often ignored the actual misbehavior of park guests— for example, littering, banging on the glass of the exhibits, or throwing food to the animals—in order to catch me at crimes she merely *suspected* I was committing. Eventually, I had played a few pranks on her to get her to back off, but they had produced the opposite effect I'd hoped for. Every time I had glued Marge's shoes to the floor or left a gorilla poop in her locker, it had only made her even more determined to bust me.

As a result, Marge had mistakenly tried to pin two major crimes at FunJungle on me, rather than looking for the real culprits. The first was the theft of Kazoo the Koala, and Marge's failure to solve it had resulted in her getting demoted from chief of security in favor of Hoenekker. The second was a rash of thefts at candy and ice cream shops around FunJungle. Once Marge had realized I wasn't responsible for those, either, she'd had a small nervous breakdown. She'd cried and admitted that she'd never be able to prove I was as bad as she thought, so she might as well give up. Unfortunately, I was the only person who witnessed this. Afterward, Marge pretended like it had never happened. In fact, she even seemed a bit angrier at me for witnessing her moment of weakness. She was still always bad-mouthing me, giving me the stink-eye, and trying to pin anything that went wrong at FunJungle on me.

All of which was proof to me that Marge wasn't a very competent member of the security team. I would never have trusted her to guard a piggy bank, let alone something as important as a giant panda. But then, I wasn't chief of security.

"I know you've had your differences with Officer O'Malley before . . . ," Hoenekker said to me.

"Differences?" Mom echoed. "She tried to send Teddy to juvenile hall! Twice!"

". . . but when it comes to keeping an eye out for crime,"

Hoenekker continued, "she's the most vigilant member of my entire team. And I needed someone vigilant on this mission to be alert for any signs of trouble."

I sighed, aware there was some truth to this. FunJungle was so large, it actually qualified as an incorporated city, which meant the security division was a licensed police force—but sadly, it wasn't exactly Scotland Yard. Working security at a zoo usually wasn't a very exciting job, and so it mostly tended to attract guys who'd barely finished high school and who couldn't make the cut for the real police. Which explained why an overzealous bonehead like Marge could be considered one of the most competent members of the force.

"What kind of trouble were you expecting?" Summer asked.

"Any kind," Hoenekker replied. "That panda's worth millions, and technically, she's not even ours. She's property of the Chinese government. So I needed someone to sit with the driver of the truck and be alert for the whole trip, and O'Malley was the right one for the job."

"She was also probably the only one who wanted to do it," Summer whispered to me.

"She's only in the cab of the truck?" Dad asked. "Not in the back with the panda?"

"There's no windows in the back of the truck," J.J.

explained. "You couldn't see any trouble coming from there. And besides, I needed Doc in the back, keeping an eye on Li Ping."

That part I knew. Doc Deakin was the head vet at Fun-Jungle and one of the finest zoo vets in the world. I had heard he'd wanted to send one of the vets who worked under him in the truck instead—traveling in the back of a semi didn't sound like a very enjoyable way to cross the country—but J.J. had staunchly refused, insisting that where the panda was concerned, he needed the best man he had.

"So Doc's been riding in the back of a truck for a whole day?" I asked.

"It's not as bad as you'd think," J.J. told me. "In fact, we fixed things up pretty darn nice for both Doc and Li Ping. I had the entire interior of the truck customized. Doc has a couch, a bed, and a TV with a DVD player. It's nicer than a lot of hotel rooms I've seen. And Li Ping has her own separate area and all the bamboo she can eat. Frankly, it's probably been like a vacation for the both of them."

I caught Mom and Dad sharing a look. It appeared they didn't think Doc would have considered this a vacation at all. But neither said anything to J.J.

My phone buzzed in my pocket. I heard Summer's do the same thing, which meant someone was trying to reach both of us at once. I had a pretty good idea who it was before I even checked my phone.

As I'd suspected, it was Xavier Gonzalez, my best friend. Xavier was an animal fanatic. He was creating his own zoo at home; his room was filled with aquariums holding lizards and snakes he'd caught in the woods, as well as fish and assorted small rodents. Every week, he spent his entire allowance on pet food. He idolized field biologists—like my mother—the way other kids idolized professional athletes.

The text said: *I'm at the front gates!*

Summer and I both turned around. Sure enough, Xavier was at the gates, pressed up against the bars. Like almost everyone else, he was wearing black and white and Li Ping ears, though to my surprise, his outfit was a tuxedo. He waved to us excitedly and shouted something, though I couldn't hear it over the crowd. Xavier's mother stood next to him, obviously there against her will; the look on her face clearly said she would rather be back home in bed.

"Xavier's here," I told my mother. "Can I go say hi?"

"Of course." Mom spotted Xavier and waved to him.

"I'm gonna stay over here," Summer told me.

"You don't want to talk to Xavier?" I asked.

"Sure I do, but . . ."

A few PandaManiacs near Xavier looked to see who he was waving to, spotted Summer, and shrieked. They seemed even more excited to see her than the panda. Word quickly rippled through the crowd that Summer was around, and soon everyone had whipped out their cell phones and started taking pictures—even though they were all so far away from Summer, she would probably only be a dot in their photos.

"That's why," Summer finished.

"Oh. Right," I said.

"Say hi to him for me." Summer gave the crowd a friendly wave, which resulted in a roar of approval. Then she slipped behind some landscaping so they couldn't see her anymore, which sparked a chorus of disappointed groans.

I headed over to see Xavier, feeling bad for Summer. She knew she was lucky to be so rich, but there were many times when her fame caused her trouble. She rarely had the chance to do anything normal, like eat lunch in a restaurant or play catch in the park, without total strangers accosting her. Instead, she had to either disguise herself or keep herself cloistered.

As I approached the gates, I felt the residual effects of her fame. People started shouting at me, simply because I'd been near her: "Who are you?" "Are you Summer's boyfriend or something?" "Can you get her to come over here?" "Tell her I love her!"

I did my best to ignore them and focus on Xavier.

"I've been trying to get your attention for five minutes!" he chided as I approached.

"Sorry," I said. "We didn't see you."

"I've been right here, waving!"

I pointed toward his black-and-white outfit. "Well, you sort of blended in with the crowd."

Xavier grew offended. "These people are wearing T-shirts. This is a tuxedo! I rented it just for this occasion! Do you have any idea how hard it is to find a tuxedo in my size? I had to go all the way to San Antonio to get it!"

"It's still black and white." I avoided mentioning that, despite all the trouble he'd gone through to find it, it still didn't fit him very well. But then, they probably didn't make a lot of tuxedos in Xavier's size. Not only was he a kid, but he was short and overweight, with a big belly and stubby legs. While the waistband of the tuxedo pants strained over his stomach, the sleeves and legs were bunched loosely around his wrists and ankles.

Before Xavier could say anything else about his formal wear, his mother spoke, sounding exasperated. "Teddy, do you know when this panda is actually going to get here?"

Several other people in the crowd echoed this question.

"Soon," I said.

"How soon?" Xavier's mother pressed.

The blast of an air horn echoed in the distance, and a

semi rolled into the far end of the parking lot. The entire crowd turned toward it expectantly.

"How about now?" I asked.

A rumble of excitement began. The crowd surged toward the truck.

As everyone moved away from the gates, I got a clearer version of Li Ping's ride. It looked like almost every other tractor-trailer I'd ever seen. If it had passed me on the highway, I probably wouldn't have looked twice at it.

I looked back toward my parents and saw that they, along with Summer, J.J., and Hoenekker, were now on the move, crossing the entry plaza. Mom waved for me to join them quickly. I started after them.

"Wait!" Xavier yelled to me. "Is there any way you can let me and my mom in to see the panda?"

"*I* don't even get to see the panda yet," I informed him, although I was secretly hoping that might not be the case. "They're limiting her contact with people so she doesn't get sick."

Xavier frowned, like I was being a bad friend somehow. It made me feel guilty, even though I'd never promised him anything. "Sorry," I said, then ran after everyone else.

The crowd was now so amped up, I could feel the energy rolling off it. The PandaManiacs began to chant, "Li Ping! Li Ping! Li Ping!" TV cameramen clambered on top of their news vans to film the semi's arrival.

I passed by the gate where Pete Thwacker was holding court in front of a throng of reporters. "As you can see," he was telling them, mustering as much gravitas as he could, "Li Ping has finally reached the end of her epic journey, and with her arrival, a wonderful new era in FunJungle's history begins."

The semi veered away from the main gates, heading onto the service road that led to the employee area of the park. It suddenly dawned on the PandaManiacs that, despite all the trouble they'd gone through to greet Li Ping, they probably weren't going to see her at all. The chants of "Li Ping!" faded and were replaced by booing. The crowd angrily returned to the front gates and shook the bars. Someone threw a bottle into the entry plaza.

Hoenekker got on his radio and spoke to his men outside the gates. "Looks like things are getting ugly out there. Do what you can to calm the crowds, but do not—I repeat, do not—use force against anyone. There are news cameras everywhere, and the last thing we need is footage of a Fun-Jungle employee roughing up someone dressed as a panda."

As the FunJungle security forces moved in on the crowds, J.J., Summer, Hoenekker, Mom, Dad, and I passed into FunJungle's employee area and headed for the animal hospital. Instead of going inside it, though, we looped around to the loading docks. The semi was already there, beeping a warning as it backed up to the building.

Dad filmed some footage of this.

Marge O'Malley was leaning out the passenger window of the truck's cab, telling the driver how to back up, even though he'd certainly done it many times before without her help. "Take it slowly now," Marge was saying. "Easy . . . easy . . ."

"Mission status?" Hoenekker called to her.

"A-okay!" Marge reported. "It all went exactly as planned, Chief."

The semi stopped with the rear doors right at the edge of the loading dock. There was a hiss from the air brakes, and then the truck shuddered as the engine cut off.

"That's perfect!" Marge told the driver, even though the truck had already stopped. "Park her right here!"

J.J. hopped up onto the loading dock. Despite being a bit older than my parents, he was spry as an eight-year-old—not to mention as excited as one. He rapped on the double doors at the rear of the trailer and called out, "Good news, Doc! You made it! How's our panda doing?"

There was no answer from inside. I figured maybe I couldn't hear Doc's reply—or maybe he was asleep. He'd been on the road for nearly eighteen hours straight.

J.J. seemed concerned, though. He banged on the rear of the truck again. Harder now. "Doc! Answer me! If you think this is funny, it's not!"

Now everyone started to grow worried. Summer nervously bit her lower lip. Mom gave me an anxious glance. Dad kept on filming.

Hoenekker called out to Marge again. "You're sure Doc's back there?"

"Of course I'm sure," Marge said confidently, hopping out of the cab. "Where else could he be? He got in the trailer after our pit stop in Las Cruces and we've been driving ever since."

J.J. banged on the doors one last time, then reached for the handles. It was only now that he—and the rest of us—noticed something was wrong with the lock. There should have been a standard, key-operated dead bolt, but instead, there was only a hole with scorch marks around it. J.J. yanked on the handles and the doors swung open.

The rest of us couldn't see inside the truck yet, as we weren't on the loading dock. J.J. could, though, and what he saw made him gasp in shock. The color drained from his face.

"Daddy?" Summer asked, really worried now. "What's wrong?"

J.J. was so stunned, he didn't even answer. It was one of the first times I'd ever seen him speechless. He simply stared into the back of the truck, as though he couldn't believe his eyes.

The rest of us scrambled up onto the loading dock as well.

Li Ping's cage and all of Doc's furniture were in the back of the truck, exactly where they should have been.

But both Doc and the panda were gone.

SCENE OF THE CRIME

Within fifteen minutes, the semi was a full-scale crime scene. Although FunJungle Security was mostly staffed by nitwits, Chief Hoenekker himself was extremely competent. At his behest, three officers had brought him a criminal investigation kit and then been posted around the loading dock to keep unauthorized personnel away. J.J. wanted to keep the panda's disappearance a secret, even from his employees, so the guards told any potential onlookers that they were to steer clear of the loading dock in order to protect Li Ping's safety. Meanwhile, Hoenekker went to work searching the interior of the trailer for clues.

Only two other people were allowed in the trailer with him. One was my father. Instead of documenting the arrival of the panda, he was now recording the scene for the investigation.

The other person was me. Hoenekker hadn't been pleased about this, but J.J. had insisted. And when J.J. had his mind set on something, there was no talking him out of it. Especially when he could fire you. "Teddy's had a hand in solving every major crime that's taken place here," he'd declared. "I'm not keeping him on the sidelines when my top vet and my panda are missing."

The way he said it, I didn't have much choice in the matter either. I definitely wanted to help find Doc and Li Ping, but even though I'd had some success solving crimes at Fun-Jungle before, I was still only a kid. Being asked—or really *told*—to aid Hoenekker in his investigation was daunting. And yet, it didn't seem like a good idea to say no.

So Hoenekker let me into the crime scene—although he warned me to give him space and not touch anything. Then he slipped on a pair of linen gloves and went to work.

Meanwhile, Marge desperately wanted to be a part of the investigation. Only, she was in the doghouse for letting Li Ping and Doc disappear in the first place. She stood off to the side of the loading dock while Pete Thwacker went ballistic on her. Pete didn't lose his cool very often—staying calm under pressure was part of his job—but now it appeared that every bit of frustration he'd bottled up over the past few weeks was spewing out of him. There were probably other things he should have been doing, but at the moment, he was flipping out. "How could you lose the panda?" he screamed.

"This wasn't my fault," Marge said defensively.

"Then whose fault was it?" Pete demanded. "You were the only security officer on duty. This wasn't a sightseeing trip! You had a job to do: make sure the panda got here. And guess what? There's no panda!"

"I'm aware of that," Marge said.

"Are you aware of how much time, energy, and money it has taken to arrange for a panda to come to FunJungle?" Pete yelled. His normally perfect complexion was now mottled red from rage. He looked like a tomato with teeth. "Are you aware how angry the Chinese are going to be? They don't hand out pandas like they're fortune cookies! It took us five years to negotiate getting this animal! *Five years!* J.J. had to call in a thousand favors. He put his reputation on the line. We spent millions building a special panda facility! And more millions on advertising and promotion. All of which doesn't mean squat if we don't have a freaking panda!"

Marge glanced toward J.J. McCracken, as though hoping he might come to her aid. But J.J. wouldn't even make eye contact with her, which indicated he was as angry with Marge as Pete was. He was simply letting Pete do the dirty work. I could understand why. Pete wasn't exaggerating what J.J. had gone through to get Li Ping. Summer had told me about the whole process. J.J. had a lot of business interests in China, and he'd had to use every one of them as leverage with the Chinese government. He'd made plenty of back-room deals and promises, and now that the panda was miss-ing, each of those could come back to haunt him.

Even so, Marge looked so beaten down by Pete's anger that I almost felt bad for her. Almost, but not quite. Because Marge had berated me plenty of times—and I had never really deserved it. Meanwhile, she had really messed up big now, letting the panda—and Doc—vanish on her watch. I was pretty upset with her about that myself.

Everyone else seemed equally annoyed. My mother and Summer lingered outside the truck, glaring at Marge. Dad was mostly hidden behind his camera, but I could tell he was upset too. And Hoenekker wasn't even trying to hide his anger as he poked around the crime scene.

"How on earth did she miss all this?" he muttered.

"Miss what?" Dad asked.

"This, for starters." Hoenekker pointed to where the lock had been on the rear doors of the semi. While the hole had been rather small on the outside of the doors, on the inside it was much larger, the size of a baseball. The metal was peeled back and scorched as though a meteor had blasted through it. "The thieves used an explosive to blow the lock off. Probably C-4, but I won't know until we get it analyzed by a lab. I have no idea how they did it on a moving truck, but I can guarantee you, it wouldn't have been quiet. And yet, Marge didn't have a clue that it happened."

Dad snapped a few photos of the hole.

On the loading dock, Mom tried calling Doc's cell phone, which she'd been doing every two minutes since learning he'd disappeared. I could tell from the look on her face that this call, like all the others, had gone straight to Doc's voicemail. "Still no answer on Doc's phone," she reported.

"You're wasting your time," Hoenekker told her. "Whoever snatched him weren't amateurs. We're not gonna hear squat from Doc until they want us to."

He moved on to the panda's cage, which was set along the driver's-side wall at the rear of the truck, where it would have been easiest to get Li Ping in and out. The cage was twelve feet long and six feet wide, which would have given Li Ping plenty of room, although this only left us a two-foot gap to squeeze past it along the opposite wall.

Transporting a panda—or any zoo animal—was a complicated task. You couldn't explain to an animal that it was going to be in an unfamiliar confined space, like a truck or an airplane, for hours, if not days. So if you simply tried to move the animal without any preparation, it would stress out. (Sometimes they could even die from the anxiety.) To prevent this, the keepers had to prepare the animals for travel.

In Li Ping's case, this had taken six months of training.

The first step had been to get Li Ping used to being in a cage. The keepers in San Diego had trained her to go inside one for increasingly long periods of time by rewarding her with treats like apples and yams. Then they practiced lifting her in the cage with a forklift and moving it to a simulation of the truck, where she would be transferred to the somewhat larger cage inside. The actual truck was sent to San Diego a month ahead of the move, and Li Ping spent that time getting used to it.

However, once Li Ping was comfortable in the truck, there was still plenty left to coordinate. The timing of her delivery had been planned down to the minute. It was no mistake that the drive had been done overnight; the idea was to be on the roads when the fewest other drivers were—and thus, the least chance of an accident. Plus, it would also be significantly cooler in the truck at night than during the day. (Giraffes were particularly tricky to deliver, since they were so tall; they needed special trucks with holes in the roof to stick their necks through, and the routes they took had to be carefully planned to avoid any low bridges.)

By all accounts, though, Li Ping had handled her truck training perfectly. Short of the traffic delay at the end, the trip had gone exactly as planned.

Except for the part where the panda and Doc had vanished.

The panda cage was empty, save for a scattering of bamboo bits and a large plastic ball, which Li Ping had probably been given to keep herself stimulated.

The gate of the cage was aimed toward the rear doors of the trailer. It had been locked with another dead bolt and then wrapped with a padlocked chain for good measure. The chain now dangled loosely, two of the thick links snapped open, while the dead bolt had been ripped apart. "Looks like the thieves used bolt cutters and a crowbar," Hoenekker observed. He didn't seem to be sharing information with me so much as talking things through to himself, trying to make sense of how the crime had played out. "Quieter than blowing the bolt off, but it would have taken quite a bit longer. Maybe a few minutes."

"So why didn't they just blow it open, the same as the back door?" I asked.

Hoenekker gave me a disappointed look. "You can't figure that one out yourself, Sherlock?"

I thought about it, then came up with an idea. "Because blowing stuff up is dangerous?"

"That's one reason. The back of this truck is an enclosed space. Not a great place for an explosion, no matter how controlled it is. Our kidnappers didn't want to hurt themselves."

"Or the panda," I suggested.

Hoenekker considered that, then shrugged noncommittally and turned to my father. "Jack, can you get some photos of this?"

"Sure thing," Dad agreed. "Just the gate?"

"Start with that and then, heck, you might as well get anything that seems of interest. There's no such thing as too many crime-scene photos."

Dad nodded in agreement, then set to work. The inside of the truck flickered with the blasts of his flash.

Back on the loading dock, Marge was still pleading her case to Pete. "I don't see why everyone's so angry at *me*. What about the drivers? They were right there with me the whole time."

"Their job was to drive the truck," Pete informed her. "Your job was to protect it."

"Even so, they didn't hear anything either," Marge pointed out. "I'm not the only one."

This was a somewhat valid point. There had been two other people in the cab so that the drive could be made in one shot; a single driver would have to stop to sleep. There was a space in the back of the truck's cab for whoever wasn't driving to sleep or relax. It was eight feet long and four feet wide, with a narrow bed and a little TV with a DVD player and headphones.

Both drivers were sitting on the edge of the loading dock.

Greg Jefferson, who'd driven the first shift, was a big, bearded bear of a man. Juan Velasquez, who'd driven the second half, was small and wiry. Both looked considerably more upset about the missing panda and veterinarian than Marge did. Now that Marge had pointed the finger at both of them, they had very different reactions. Juan grew even more upset, as though he blamed himself. He nodded and said, "That's true. We didn't hear anything."

Meanwhile, Greg got angry at Marge. "We had other things on our minds," he snarled. "Driving this truck ain't as easy as you think. And we had an awful tight schedule to follow. *You* were supposed to be keeping an eye out for any trouble, not us."

"I *was* keeping an eye out for trouble," Marge said, getting her dander up. "I'm just saying, there were three of us, and none of us sensed anything was wrong. So I don't understand why I'm the one getting raked over the coals here."

"Because you screwed up!" Pete screamed. "In the history of epic fails, this is up there with steering the *Titanic* into an iceberg! We have spent the last three months telling the entire world to come here to see our panda and now we don't have a panda for them to see!"

"We're also missing a *person*," Mom pointed out quietly.

"Yes!" Pete said quickly, in a way that indicated he had actually forgotten Doc was missing too. "There's that as well.

Do you have any idea how upset his family is going to be?"

"Speaking of which, has anyone told them?" J.J. asked.

There was an uncomfortable silence as we all realized no one had.

J.J. looked to Pete. "As our head of PR, perhaps it'd be best if you took care of that. Pronto. I believe by now Marge is aware of how badly she's screwed up."

Pete realized this wasn't a suggestion so much as an order. He took a few deep breaths to calm himself, then found the closest reflective surface—a window—and smoothed his hair and tightened the knot on his tie. "You're right, J.J. Something of this nature needs to be handled by someone competent." He gave Marge one last nasty look and stormed off.

Behind his back, Marge made a face at him.

Hoenekker moved farther into the trailer of the semi, past the panda cage. Dad and I followed him, Dad snapping pictures the whole way.

Just beyond the cage was a full-size refrigerator. While the truck had been driving, the refrigerator had run off the electrical system, but even now it hummed, powered by a separate generator.

Hoenekker snapped on a pair of surgical gloves and opened it.

There was bamboo inside. Several sheaves of it.

"They have to refrigerate the bamboo?" I asked.

"To keep it from wilting," Dad explained. "From what I understand, Li Ping was a picky eater. They wanted to keep her as content as possible en route."

Hoenekker closed the refrigerator and we moved on. Since we were far from the rear doors now, there was less light, though we could still see all right. Doc's quarters were much nicer than I'd expected. The space was about twelve feet long and eight feet wide. On the wall of the semi farthest from the rear doors—the reverse side of the truck's cab—a flat-screen TV was mounted with a couch facing it. To the side of the couch was a small table with a lamp bolted to the top so it wouldn't topple off if the truck made a sharp turn. Between the couch and the panda cage was a twin bed. The furniture was better quality than ours back home and seemed comfortable enough.

The only thing that looked unusual was the bed. The sheets weren't merely rumpled; they were twisted up and partly pulled off the mattress.

"Looks like Doc was yanked out of the bed," I observed.

Hoenekker gave me a sidelong glance. It seemed like he might have been either annoyed or impressed by my statement, but I couldn't tell which. "Why do you say that?"

"Er . . . ," I hemmed, now on the spot. "Because most people don't kick the sheets off like that when they sleep. Or

I don't, at least. But if Doc was sleeping in there and someone pulled him out, maybe the sheets might have come off too."

Hoenekker gave the tiniest of nods. "It does appear he was forcibly removed. Although, given the state of the rest of the surroundings, it doesn't look like he put up much of a fight." He knelt by the bed, then carefully ran his gloved hands over the sheets.

"Are you looking for something?" Dad asked.

"This," Hoenekker said suddenly. He removed a white washcloth from the snarl of sheets and stood, holding it at arm's length from his face. I got a faint whiff of something kind of like alcohol from it.

Dad quickly snapped some photos of it.

"What's that?" I asked.

"Chloroform," Hoenekker replied. "It appears that whoever took Li Ping drugged Doc in his sleep, then made off with him, too." Hoenekker removed a large plastic evidence bag from his jacket pocket, dropped the cloth inside, and sealed it.

Dad swept in to get some photos of the bed. I stepped back, taking everything in.

Hoenekker was right; there didn't seem to be any signs of struggle. Doc had been moved out as easily as a sack of laundry. Besides the rumpled sheets, nothing was upset or overturned. The TV area looked as though Doc had barely used it. Someone had provided plenty of brand-new DVDs for him to watch during the long ride, but the only one he'd unwrapped was a National Geographic documentary about lions in the Okavango Delta.

In the glare of a camera flash, I spotted an oddly shaped hunk of metal on the floor near the TV. Then the light faded and the object was swallowed by shadows again. "There's something over there," I told Hoenekker, pointing.

The next flash illuminated it again. Hoenekker saw it, then flipped on a flashlight so we could get a better look.

It was a few interlocked pieces of metal, charred and twisted, about the size of my fist.

"It's the dead-bolt lock from the rear doors," Hoenekker said.

"What's left of it, at least," Dad added.

"The explosive blew it all the way over here?" I asked.

"That's not too surprising," Hoenekker told me. "C-4 is awfully powerful. Even a small bit could have sent that lock a dozen yards."

I looked down the length of the truck, toward the rear doors. "Would an explosion like that be dangerous?"

"It could be," Hoenekker agreed. "But the explosive would have been on the other side of the doors. The biggest threat to them would have probably been getting hit by the lock as it flew out."

"Would it have been loud?"

"Of course." Hoenekker sounded like he was getting annoyed with my questions. "What's your point?"

"They grabbed Doc out of bed," I explained. "Why didn't the explosion wake him up?"

Hoenekker and Dad looked to each other, like they were surprised they hadn't thought of this. "Maybe Doc had earplugs in," Dad suggested. "It probably would have been awfully loud in here while the truck was moving."

"Or maybe . . . ," Hoenekker began, but then seemed to think better of finishing the sentence.

"Maybe what?" I pressed.

Hoenekker mulled over whether to share his idea with us for a few moments. Finally, he said, "Maybe Doc knew the explosion was coming."

"You mean, you think Doc was involved in the crime?" Dad asked, incredulous.

"No way," I said. "Doc would never do anything like this!"

Hoenekker held up his hands, signaling us to calm down. "I didn't say he did. I'm just thinking out loud. That's all."

"It *sounded* like you were accusing him," I said. I would have gone on, but Dad put a hand on my shoulder, indicating I shouldn't.

"I'm not accusing anyone," Hoenekker told me. "Not yet. However, the evidence clearly indicates that whoever committed this crime had inside information. This truck was designed to look like ten thousand others. The timing of the delivery was kept top secret. And yet, our thieves knew exactly what truck to hit, when to hit it, and how to hit it. There weren't very many people with that information, and Doc was one of them."

"So was Marge," I pointed out.

To my surprise, Hoenekker didn't defend her. Instead, he simply admitted, "She was."

"I still can't imagine Doc being involved," Dad said. "Why on earth would he help steal a panda?"

"Why would anyone steal a panda, period?" Hoenekker's voice trailed off as he noticed something in the beam of his flashlight. A white envelope poked out from beneath the couch. It looked like it had been placed on the small table but had slid off while the truck was driving.

Dad knelt and took some pictures of it.

Then Hoenekker carefully picked up the envelope. It hadn't been sealed, so the flap hung open, revealing a single sheet of paper inside. Hoenekker removed it, read it, then said, "Guess this answers my question."

He then held it out so my father and I could read the message typed on it:

Dear J.J. McCracken,

If you want your panda back alive, it will cost you ten million dollars. Cash.

Start getting it together.

More details to come.

THE SECOND BATHING SUIT

The moment FunJungle's front gates opened that morning, hundreds of PandaManiacs, unaware that Li Ping was missing, surged through and stampeded for the panda exhibit, each hoping to be the first to see her. It looked like a black-and-white tidal wave coursing through the park. In their rush, the fanatics flattened thousands of freshly planted flowers, knocked over a hot dog cart, and nearly trampled an unfortunate groundskeeper. (Luckily, he was able to avoid being crushed by climbing a jacaranda tree.)

The new exhibit was called Panda Palace, and it was modeled after the Forbidden City in Beijing, with red walls, intricate decoration, and a curved tile roof. The PandaManiacs overwhelmed the two guards stationed there for crowd control and crammed into the viewing rooms, severely violating the official capacity and piling up thirty deep against the glass. Then they began chanting for Li Ping again.

Pete Thwacker knew he couldn't let this go on all day: After a few hours without a panda, the crowd would get angry, and an angry crowd was a mob. So he reluctantly went out to the exhibit to face the PandaManiacs.

I was still at the crime scene, but I watched the whole thing with Summer on her phone. The local news stations all had cameras in position and were live-streaming the event.

Inside the truck, Hoenekker was dusting for fingerprints. I was with Summer because, frankly, watching someone dust for fingerprints was boring. No one quite knew what to make of the ransom note yet. J.J. McCracken had gone off to his office to discuss it with his lawyers.

Pete couldn't even get inside Panda Palace. Instead, he had to speak to the hundreds of people crowded outside, still waiting to enter the exhibit. He stared them all down—and lied to their faces. It would have been horrible PR to reveal that the panda had been stolen—and J.J. probably would have killed him. So instead, he told them what *would* have been the truth, had Li Ping actually arrived as planned. "Hello, panda fans!" he said cheerfully, doing an incredible job of acting as though nothing had gone wrong. "We at FunJungle are thrilled to see so many of you here today to welcome Li Ping. However, federal law mandates that, for her safety—as well as the safety of all the other beloved animals here—Li Ping must remain under quarantine at our medical facility for the next thirty days."

This was met with a chorus of boos, and then Pete was pelted with everything from balled-up napkins to stuffed panda toys.

"It's for the health of the panda!" Pete added, somewhat desperately. "You don't want Li Ping to get sick, do you?"

This was followed by a lot of disgruntled muttering as most of the crowd realized Pete had a point. "Why'd you even announce that the panda was here if you weren't going to put her on display today?" someone shouted.

"We *didn't* announce the panda would be here!" Pete protested indignantly, even though it was partly his fault that word had leaked out. "You all just showed up! However, to show our appreciation for all of you, everyone here today is entitled to a free large soft drink *and* a commemorative Li Ping cup."

To my surprise, this appeared to quell most of the crowd. They were still upset, but most of them quickly made a beeline for the closest soda stands.

"That actually worked?" I asked Summer. "What's a large soda cost your father? Five cents?"

"If that," Summer said. "Including the cup. But he charges $7.99 for it normally, so everyone probably thinks they just got a great deal. Daddy always says the quickest way to win over your enemies is to make them think they suckered you out of something."

I was suddenly aware of a commotion around the corner of the building. One of Hoenekker's guards was telling someone they couldn't approach the loading dock. "It's for the safety of the panda," he insisted. "Li Ping has had a very long trip and she needs her privacy."

"I'm not *trying* to approach the loading dock," the other person said. "I need to talk to Teddy Fitzroy."

I recognized the voice. Olivia Putney.

"Hey, Olivia!" I called. "Hold on!" I jumped off the loading dock and ran around the corner. Summer came with me.

There was a wide alley between the veterinary hospital and the administration building, the seven-story tower where all of FunJungle's administrators and lawyers—and J.J. McCracken—had their offices. I recognized the guard with Olivia. His name was Kevin Wilks, he was young, and he wasn't exactly the sharpest member of the force. In fact, there were probably several animals at the park that were smarter than Kevin. He stood directly in Olivia's path, legs and arms splayed, to keep her from getting past him.

If I hadn't heard Olivia first, I might not have recognized her. I saw Olivia in her swimsuit so often, she looked strange in regular clothes. I'd also never seen her with dry hair. It was lighter than I'd realized, and it was frizzed out from the humidity. She was carrying a plastic gift bag from the Fun-Jungle Emporium.

"What's going on?" Summer asked.

Kevin seemed starstruck by Summer. "Er . . . Ah . . . This woman claims she knows Teddy."

"She knows both of us," Summer told him.

"Oh," Kevin said, looking embarrassed. "Sorry. But Chief Hoenekker told me to keep all unauthorized personnel away from the loading dock."

"I wasn't trying to cause any trouble," Olivia said, then looked to me. "I needed to talk to you about the dolphins and I heard you were over here. How's Li Ping, anyway?"

She tried to make this last question sound casual, like it had only occurred to her at that moment, but she didn't quite pull it off. Which made me suspect that Olivia was using the dolphins as an excuse to find out what was going on with Li Ping. After all, if she had *really* needed to talk to me, she could have called me.

I also noticed that Olivia wasn't the only curious FunJungle employee around. Despite Hoenekker's attempts to keep the panda's disappearance under wraps, it appeared people were beginning to suspect that something was wrong. By now, it must have been clear to all the employees at the hospital that neither Li Ping nor Doc was anywhere to be seen.

Behind Olivia, at the far corner of the administration building, a small crowd of employees milled about, trying to act casual, but obviously intrigued by what was going on. It was an odd assortment of people: a few keepers, some members of the janitorial staff, two lawyers (they were the only people at FunJungle who wore suits besides Pete), and three actors dressed as mascots. Or, at least, partially dressed as mascots; the ones who played Eleanor Elephant and Zelda Zebra had popped their heads off. Meanwhile, the actor dressed as Li Ping remained fully suited up, probably to avoid damaging the brand-new costume. They were all paying close attention to us, as though hoping for news about the real panda.

I wasn't going to be the one to spill the beans about what had happened, though. A glance from Summer indicated she wasn't going to either. Instead, both of us played dumb.

"Li Ping's fine," we both said at once.

"Really?" Olivia asked. "Then why's there so much security around?"

"They're just here to keep everyone away from the panda," Summer said quickly. "Pandas aren't like dolphins. They get sick really easily around people."

Olivia seemed unsure whether or not to believe that. But before she could pose any more questions, I asked her, "What'd you need to talk to me about?"

Olivia seemed to realize she couldn't press the panda

issue any more. "We got your bathing suit back." She dug my wet suit out of the plastic bag. "Sorry, but it's a little chewed up. It took me a while to get Snickers to give it up."

"A little chewed up" was an understatement. Thanks to Snickers, my suit now had more holes than a golf course. "Thanks," I said.

"That was your big emergency?" Summer asked skeptically. "You could have just texted Teddy about that."

"There's also this." Olivia pulled a second wet bathing suit out of the plastic bag. This one was blue. She dangled it from a finger, as though she really didn't want to touch it. "Is it yours, Teddy?"

I shook my head. "Nope."

Olivia gave me a suspicious stare. "You barely even looked at it."

"I only have one other bathing suit," I told her. "And it's green." I took the blue suit off her finger and examined it. It was a souvenir from FunJungle: board shorts with a piece of one leg purposefully missing, cut so that it looked as if it had been bitten off by a shark. On the rear end, written in letters designed to look like dripping blood, it said, "I survived Shark Encounter at FunJungle!"

I'd seen similar suits on sale at the Shark Encounter gift shop, which had always seemed to be very poor taste. After all, Shark Encounter was supposed to be teaching tourists that sharks actually weren't very dangerous, while this bathing suit reinforced the stereotype that they were. Plus, *I* had barely survived Shark Encounter once, when the underwater viewing tunnel had collapsed, so the idea of a shark attack didn't seem very funny to me.

"Yuck," Summer said under her breath. "Who would wear something like that?"

"Hey!" Kevin exclaimed. "I have that exact same bathing suit!"

"Why?" Summer asked, not bothering to hide her disgust.

"It's pretty sick," Kevin said proudly, failing to realize Summer wasn't impressed. "And as a FunJungle employee, I get a ten percent discount on all merchandise!"

I held the bathing suit up against my own waist to check the size. It was way too big for me. "I think this is an adult's bathing suit, not a kid's," I pointed out.

Summer, who knew a lot more about clothes than I did, simply checked the tag on the inside of the elastic waistband. "Men's medium," she read. "What size pants do you wear, Teddy?"

"Uh . . . I don't know," I said.

Summer looked at me like I'd said I didn't know my own hair color. "How could you not know your pant size?"

I shrugged. "My mom buys all my clothes for me."

Summer rolled her eyes and returned her attention to Olivia. "Teddy's obviously too small to wear these. If you'd just checked the tag, you wouldn't have had to come all the way over here."

"I didn't think of it," Olivia said. "One of the other trainers found them in the dolphin tank, and we didn't know who else's they could be." She looked to me. "You're the only one who Snickers has pantsed and the only kid who's normally here after park hours, so . . ."

"You jumped to a conclusion?" Summer finished.

"Yes," Olivia admitted. "Sorry, Teddy."

"It's okay," I told her. "Where in the tank was this?"

"Down at the bottom," Olivia replied. "On the far side from the beach. There's some pipes there to recirculate the water, and the bathing suit was jammed under one. Sometimes the dolphins like to hide things there."

"The dolphins hide things?" Kevin asked, surprised. "How? They don't even have hands!"

"They use their mouths," Olivia said slowly, as though she was talking to a child. "And yes, sometimes if they find something unusual, they'll try to hide it where we might not notice it."

"Does that happen a lot?" Summer asked.

"Well, we try to control what goes into the tank," Olivia replied. "Although we do give them lots of toys to play with to keep them stimulated. Plastic rings and balls and such. And sometimes we'll put food inside something to see if they can figure out how to get it out. Like a plastic box with a latch. Or we'll freeze it in ice."

"The same thing Mom does with the primates," I pointed out.

"Yes," Olivia said. "Both species are very smart and need lots of stimulation."

"Wow," Kevin gasped. "I didn't know there were fish as smart as monkeys."

Olivia glared at him. "Dolphins aren't fish. They're mammals. And they're *smarter* than monkeys. Or even some apes. They have complex communication, use tools, and work as teams. For all we know, they're smarter than we are."

Kevin laughed disdainfully. "Yeah, right. If they're so smart, then why don't they invent things like airplanes and television?"

"They also don't kill each other," Olivia pointed out. "So they've got that on us."

"I'm just saying, *we* put *them* in shows," Kevin pressed. "If they were the smart ones, we'd be balancing balls on our noses for *them,* right?"

"Can you pinpoint a fish two hundred yards away in the darkness using only sound waves?" Olivia asked.

"Uh . . . no," Kevin said.

"Well, a dolphin can," Olivia replied curtly. "We each have our talents." Kevin started to protest, but Olivia held up a hand to silence him. "I'm not going to discuss intelligence with someone who can't even remember to zip his fly," she said.

Kevin glanced down and realized that his fly was, in fact, unzipped. Plus, his shirt was poking out through it. He turned bright red and quickly spun around to fix things. "Oops!"

While he was distracted, we all slipped away from him so we could finish our conversation in peace. We headed away from the loading dock, toward the front of the hospital.

"What were we talking about before that doofus interrupted?" Olivia asked.

"The dolphins finding things in the tank," Summer told her.

"Right," Olivia agreed. "We give them things to stimulate them and try to keep other stuff out, but every once in a while, something gets in. Some idiot tourist throws in a toy from the gift shop or drops a soda bottle over the rail—or maybe a bird feather or a plastic bag blows in. Well, if a dolphin gets ahold of something like that and wants to keep it, they'll hide it someplace."

"How good is this hiding place?" I asked. "Could the bathing suit have been in the tank for a few days?"

Olivia stopped walking to think about this. "Uh . . . maybe. We do our best to check the tank every night to make sure the dolphins haven't gotten ahold of something dangerous. We don't want them choking on garbage or anything. But they're clever. This suit was wedged under the pipe so it was almost impossible to see. So I suppose it could have been in the tank more than a day."

"Then whoever it belongs to could have been in the tank well before last night," Summer said.

"Well, not much more before last night," Olivia countered. "Only a few days, max. I'm sure this suit hasn't been down there longer than that. Someone would have noticed it."

We were now quite close to the group of FunJungle employees who'd been milling around. I realized they were all eavesdropping on our conversation. They were trying to act inconspicuous, but that was hard to do when three of them were dressed like an elephant, a zebra, and a giant panda.

I was about to suggest we find a more private place to talk when Olivia asked me, "Teddy, did you ever ask Hoenekker to check the camera feeds from the dolphin exhibit?"

"Er . . . no," I admitted. Given all the excitement with Li Ping's disappearance, I'd forgotten. And now Hoenekker was certainly too busy to check the feeds, although I couldn't tell Olivia *why*. So I had to bend the truth. "I didn't get a chance.

He's been really swamped this morning, with all the crowds and everything."

Olivia seemed to suspect that I wasn't giving her the full story, but before she could press the point, Summer wrinkled her nose and said, "That bathing suit smells funny."

I held it up to examine it again. "I don't smell anything."

"Well, your nose probably isn't as good as mine. Trust me, something's funky about it." Summer took the suit from me and sniffed it closer. Then, seeming to sense something, she shifted it around to sniff different parts of it.

I started laughing.

"What's so funny?" Summer demanded.

"You look like a bloodhound," I said.

Summer stuck her tongue out at me, then went right back to smelling the suit. She took another few sniffs, then gave a triumphant shout. "Aha!" She inverted one of the pockets and a chunk of something grayish and flaky fell out onto the ground at our feet.

"Is that tuna fish?" I asked.

"Definitely," Summer replied. "It totally smells like tuna."

The FunJungle employees nearby were no longer even trying to pretend that they weren't eavesdropping on us. They all craned forward, wondering what was going on.

"Why would somebody put tuna fish in the pockets of their bathing suit?" I asked.

"For a snack while swimming?" suggested the woman half-dressed as Zelda Zebra.

Before anyone could suggest a better answer, a helicopter roared overhead, catching us all by surprise. J.J. McCracken had made sure airspace over FunJungle was severely restricted; both the guests and the animals could find the sound of aircraft irritating. In addition, this helicopter came in extremely low, close enough to the ground that I could have hit it with a rock. It then banked sharply and started lowering behind the animal hospital. There was a helipad back there, in case a severe emergency required a human—or an animal—to be airlifted out, but as far as I knew, it had never been used.

Summer instantly darted that way, eager to see what was going on. I dropped in behind her. So did Olivia. We raced back to the area behind the hospital.

Kevin had abandoned his post to watch the helicopter as well. He was standing with Hoenekker, Marge, and my parents, a safe distance from the helipad, where they wouldn't be hit by debris kicked up by the rotors. Hoenekker appeared more annoyed than I'd ever seen him—and that was really saying something. He was annoyed a lot.

Summer had to shout to be heard over the incoming copter. "Who's that?"

"The FBI!" Kevin shouted back.

"The FBI?" I repeated, incredulous. "Why?"

Kevin started to answer me, but Hoenekker gave him a look that said he'd be better off keeping his mouth shut.

It was almost impossible to talk over the helicopter anyhow. The noise was earsplitting as it touched down. Before the rotors had stopped spinning, the chopper's passenger door opened and a tall woman in a suit and sunglasses hopped out. Three other people got out behind her, but I barely noticed them because the tall woman was so striking. She had red hair so bright, it almost looked like her head was on fire, and though her eyes were hidden behind dark sunglasses, she was extremely beautiful—although there was also something strangely familiar about her too.

"Oh no," Marge groaned.

The red-haired woman strode directly up to Hoenekker and flashed her official badge. "Agent Molly O'Malley, FBI. I'm here to take over the investigation into the disappearance of Li Ping."

"Agent O'Malley?" Summer echoed next to me, as surprised by the name as I was. Both of us turned to see Marge shrinking away in embarrassment.

Agent O'Malley noticed her as well. She looked to Marge and flashed a cocky smile.

"Hey, little sister," she said.

THE FEDS

While the rest of us reeled from the surprise that Marge had a sister—and one who was an FBI agent, no less—the three other people who'd been on the helicopter gathered behind Molly O'Malley. There were two men and a woman, and they all appeared to be FBI agents as well. They all dressed exactly the same, in dark suits and sunglasses. They hung back from us, though, allowing Molly to run the show.

I was looking back and forth between Marge and Molly. I had never seen two sisters who looked so different. Molly was tall and skinny, while Marge was squat and round. Molly was impeccably dressed, while Marge looked as though she had slept in her clothes, then rolled around in the garbage for good measure; there were a dozen food stains on her uniform, ranging from chili to Cheez Whiz. Molly stood upright and radiated intelligence and confidence. Marge slouched—and the only thing she radiated was body odor.

Everyone else from FunJungle was looking from one O'Malley to the other as well—except Chief Hoenekker. He kept his gaze riveted on Molly, his eyes narrowed in anger. "We can handle this investigation on our own," he told her. "We don't need the FBI."

"This isn't a negotiation," Molly informed him. "It's a done deal. That panda isn't the property of FunJungle. It's the property of the country of China, which makes its theft an international incident. The nation's best law enforcement agency needs to be on this case, not a group of security guards."

"We are a fully operational police force," Hoenekker growled.

"J.J. McCracken doesn't seem to think so," Molly said with a smirk. "He's the one who tipped us off."

Hoenekker's eyes widened in surprise.

"Furthermore, this case doesn't even fall within your jurisdiction," Molly went on. "It didn't occur at FunJungle. It happened somewhere en route between San Diego and here, which means the panda crossed state lines, which makes this a federal crime. Which, once again, mandates the presence of the FBI to investigate."

Hoenekker didn't respond. He still appeared stunned that J.J. had called in the FBI.

Molly gave him a smug smile, knowing she'd won this round. "So then, if you will hand over any evidence you have uncovered so far and disclose any discoveries you have made to my agents, I'd like to get started with this investigation right away." With that, she brushed past Hoenekker, heading for the panda truck.

Hoenekker shook off his stupor and raced after her. "Now, hold on. My team has a right to be a part of this. The theft of that panda was a crime committed against Fun-Jungle, for which we are the official law-enforcement arm."

"Then perhaps you should have worked harder to prevent the crime in the first place," Molly told him. She hopped onto the loading dock and strode purposefully toward the truck.

Hoenekker looked ready to explode. But before he could say anything, J.J. McCracken raced around the corner and intervened, desperate to keep the peace.

"Whoa there, Chief. Let's not say anything we're gonna regret." J.J. was slightly out of breath, as though he'd run the whole way from his office. Several lawyers trailed behind him, like they'd been caught in his wake and sucked out of the administration building with him.

"She's the one with the attitude problem, not me,"

Hoenekker muttered to J.J. "Cocky feds. Why on earth did you call them?"

"Because the Chinese insisted on it." Before Hoenekker could protest, J.J. held up a hand, silencing him. "I know, it stinks. But I couldn't keep Li Ping's disappearance a secret from China. I've got billions of dollars in business interests over there, and I can't afford not to be a straight shooter with them. So if they want the feds involved, the feds are involved. Frankly, I probably would've had to bring them in sooner or later anyhow."

Hoenekker's frown grew even deeper, but he didn't say anything. He and J.J. followed Molly O'Malley up onto the loading dock, and the rest of us dropped in behind them.

Molly was now examining the panda delivery truck from the outside. She seemed amused by Hoenekker's criminal investigation kit, which was still sitting on the dock. "That's cute," she said mockingly, then asked, "So what have you found here?"

Hoenekker didn't answer right away, still annoyed by how everything was playing out.

Molly groaned theatrically. "Please tell me you're not going to get territorial over this. If I have to, I can get the US ambassador to China on the phone, but I really think she has better things to do with her time."

Hoenekker sighed heavily, realizing he was beat, and

coughed up what he knew. "It appears the truck was attacked while en route to FunJungle sometime last night. The attackers blew the lock off the rear door with what we believe was C-4 putty explosive, then entered the truck, cut the chains on the panda's cage with bolt cutters, and forcibly removed both the panda and Doc Deakin, the veterinarian."

"All while the truck was moving?" Molly asked, sounding incredulous.

"That appears to be the case," Hoenekker replied. "I had someone stationed in the cab of the truck throughout the trip—"

"That'd be you, Marge?" Molly interrupted, looking at her sister and raising an eyebrow.

"Er . . . yes," Marge said. Normally, she was full of bluff and bravado, but it had all vanished in front of her sister.

"Looks like someone removed Marge's spine," Summer whispered to me.

"According to Officer O'Malley," Hoenekker went on, "the truck made a pit stop at midnight near Las Cruces, New Mexico. At that time, Doc Deakin and Li Ping were still inside the trailer, alive and well. Everyone took a bathroom break, and afterward, Doc was locked back in with the panda. The truck did not stop again until it arrived here shortly before oh-900 this morning, when the disappearance of both Doc and Li Ping was discovered."

Molly O'Malley made a face like she'd sucked on a lemon, as if she didn't like any of what she was hearing. "And what evidence have you discovered in the truck?"

"Trace amounts of explosive," Hoenekker reported. "No fingerprints as of yet."

"Fibers?" Molly asked.

"Quite a lot," Hoenekker replied. "But there's a good chance most of them are panda fur. We haven't had a chance to analyze them yet."

"We'll handle that," Molly told him. "And I understand there was a ransom note?"

"I have my own people doing analysis on that . . . ," Hoenekker began.

"Not anymore," Molly said brusquely. "We'll handle that as well. Any ideas who it might be from?"

"None yet," Hoenekker replied.

"Really?" Molly taunted. "You don't have *one* idea? For example, exotic animal traffickers, someone with a grudge against the Chinese government, a radical animal rights group like the Nature Freedom Force . . ."

Hoenekker laughed dismissively at this. "The NFF is a rinky-dink group of radicals. They hand out anti-zoo pamphlets at our front gates and picket construction sites. They don't have the know-how to pull off a complex job like this."

"I wouldn't be so quick to dismiss them," Molly said coolly. "You'd be surprised what they're capable of. And we've picked up some chatter from them over the past few weeks. . . ."

"Chatter?" I asked.

Molly suddenly swiveled toward me. I couldn't read her expression behind her sunglasses, but it didn't appear she was happy to be interrupted. And by a kid, no less.

It occurred to me that the rules had changed. The last time there'd been a crime at FunJungle, I'd been allowed to ask questions. (Hoenekker might not have appreciated it, but it had been allowed.) Now it seemed that I had spoken out of turn.

Molly removed her glasses, allowing me to see her eyes for the first time. They were a piercing green, the same color as the skin of an emerald tree boa, and they seemed to be boring right through me. "You must be Theodore Roosevelt Fitzroy," she said. "I've heard quite a lot about you from my sister. She says you're a real troublemaker."

"Your sister is wrong," I replied.

"It wouldn't be the first time." Molly looked to Marge again and gave her another cruel smile.

"Anything you've heard about Teddy being troublesome is erroneous information," J.J. said quickly. "Your sister—and all of us at FunJungle—have found him to be of great help in solving several cases here. He might only be a boy, but he's a regular Encyclopedia Brown. It wouldn't be a bad idea to have him around."

Molly laughed. "At the FBI, we don't need children to help us solve our crimes. We're fully capable of handling them on our own."

The three FBI agents laughed at this as well.

No one who worked at FunJungle thought it was funny. Even Marge. Her annoyance at her sister seemed to even trump her usual annoyance at me.

"Speaking of which," Molly went on, then turned to face me and Summer. "This is a crime scene, children. You need to leave it. Now." She then shifted her attention to all the adults. "That goes for the rest of you too. This area is restricted to FBI personnel—unless I request your presence. And at the moment, the only person I need is Chief Hoenekker."

With that, she turned her back on everyone, as though we had suddenly ceased to exist, and stepped inside the panda truck.

On the loading dock, the other three FBI agents formed a human blockade between us and the crime scene.

Hoenekker started to say something, but J.J. caught his arm before he could. "I know you're not happy about this,"

J.J. told him, "but there's no point in arguing it. You're not gonna win. So just be a good soldier, play ball, and help get Doc and my panda back."

J.J. then turned to me, looking genuinely sorry. "Looks like you're gonna have to sit this one out, Teddy. I'm sure we can trust the feds to handle it. C'mon, folks. We've all got better things to do than milling around here all day." He headed back down off the loading dock.

There was nothing to do but follow him. I glanced at Marge as we all left. She was glaring back at the panda truck. It occurred to me she'd only spoken two words to her sister.

"I can't believe this," Summer protested to her father. "How can they just come in here and kick all of us out like this?"

"Their job is to solve the crime," J.J. explained. "How they do it is up to them."

"Well, if they want to solve the crime, why boot Teddy? He's the best crime-solver we have!"

"I'm not as good as the FBI," I pointed out. "I'm only thirteen."

"And barely thirteen, at that," Mom added. "To be honest, Summer, I'm glad this happened. I know Teddy has solved some other cases here, but he always ended up in danger as a result. You did too, last time. I'd prefer that not happen again. Plus, it's not only an animal whose life is at stake this time; it's Doc, too. So I'm happy to leave this in the hands of the professionals for once."

At this, she gave J.J. a glance. It was quick, but it was loaded with meaning; Mom was still angry at him for forcing me to help investigate the last case at FunJungle.

"Okay, Mrs. Fitzroy," Summer said. "I get it." But then, she leaned in close to me and whispered, "They're still making a mistake. I'll bet you could solve this with your eyes closed."

I grinned, pleased by Summer's faith in me, although I was secretly relieved to be kicked off the case. Mom was right. In the past year, while investigating the various crimes at FunJungle, I'd been stranded in a room with a venomous snake (which had yet to be found), plunged into a shark tank, left face-to-face with an escaped tiger, barely avoided being trampled by elephants, gaurs, and Cape buffalo—and dangled above a pit full of man-eating crocodiles.

Plus, I wasn't as sure of my crime-solving abilities as Summer was. I might have cracked a few cases, but maybe that had just been luck. I had no idea how someone could have kidnapped Doc and Li Ping from a moving truck without Large Marge or the drivers noticing, and I feared that, maybe this time, I wouldn't figure it out. Which would let everyone down—and leave Doc and Li Ping in danger.

So as we left the crime scene behind, I actually felt fine. Yes, I was annoyed with how dismissive Molly O'Malley had been about me, but overall, I was happy that a professional organization like the FBI had been brought in to solve the crime and that, for once, an investigation was going to take place without me.

Only, things didn't work out that way at all.

THE THREAT

"I can't believe Marge has a sister like *that*," Summer said.

"Neither can I," I agreed. Even though a lot of strange things had happened that morning—Li Ping and Doc vanishing, a dolphin stealing my bathing suit—the fact that Marge and Molly O'Malley were sisters was the hardest to believe.

"All this time we've known Marge and she never mentioned a sister once," Summer said.

"Why would she?" I asked. "Marge has barely said anything to me except 'You're in trouble now, Teddy.'"

"Or"—Summer did her best Marge impression, scowling—"I'll get you this time, you little pipsqueak!"

I laughed, so she kept going. "You're a bad egg, Teddy

Fitzroy! Sure, our animals are getting killed and stolen, but you put a whoopie cushion on the seat of my car! As far as I'm concerned, you're public enemy number one and I won't rest until you're behind bars!"

Summer's impression was startlingly good, and very funny. I was laughing so hard, I had to steady myself against the railing of the polar bear exhibit.

We were inside the Polar Pavilion, because it was the coldest exhibit at FunJungle. Since Li Ping was missing and we'd been kicked off the investigation, we now had the day free at FunJungle. It was nasty hot, though. At 10:00 a.m., it was already ninety-five degrees, and so humid, it felt like we were swaddled in wet towels. So we'd come to the fake Arctic.

Other zoos had heavily air-conditioned exhibits for polar bears, but FunJungle was the only place that refrigerated the entire building. This allowed guests to see the bears in their natural habitat—or at least, a facsimile of it—without glass in between them. The bears had a big, icy area the size of a baseball diamond, surrounded by a moat of frigid water that they loved to swim in, and the guests could watch it all from a pathway that looped the moat. (A safety railing canted out a foot beyond the viewing wall to keep anyone from accidentally falling in.) On occasion, FunJungle even made it snow *inside* the building, using a specially designed machine that blew ice flakes out of vents in the ceiling. The bears and the guests all enjoyed this, although on several occasions, park security had to stop guests from pelting the polar bears—or other people—with snowballs. Keeping such a big building so cold made the Polar Pavilion the most expensive exhibit to maintain at FunJungle, costing thousands of dollars a month for air-conditioning alone.

There were also other cold-weather animals in the pavilion: walruses, leopard seals, crabeater seals, and beluga whales, all of which could be seen above and below water. And of course, there were penguins: a huge colony of emperors, Adélies, gentoos, macaronis, chinstraps, Humboldts, and jackasses. (Some guests had actually complained about the names of the last ones, but "jackass" was the official appelation; they were called that because their braying cries sounded somewhat like donkeys.) The penguins were still kept behind glass, though. They weren't dangerous; they just smelled terrible. Three dozen penguins produced a tremendous amount of penguin poop, and the entire exhibit reeked of partially digested fish.

Normally, a day as hot as this one would have been far more crowded in the Polar Pavilion, but the crowds were still mobbing the Panda Palace. While news had quickly spread about Li Ping's arrival that morning, lots of guests had missed the update that the panda wasn't on display yet.

So now they were pouring into the park and racing straight to the empty panda exhibit. Since that was on the far side of FunJungle from the Polar Pavilion, most people hadn't come back our way yet. By afternoon, however, the pavilion would probably be packed wall to wall with people seeking a break from the heat.

There were still a few guests around, though, so Summer was taking care to avoid being recognized. She had changed out of her usual pink clothes, tucked her long hair up underneath a FunJungle sunhat, and was now wearing sunglasses even though she was indoors.

"Molly must be way smarter than Marge, right?" Summer asked me. "I mean, she's FBI."

"I guess," I agreed. "She *seemed* smart."

"But not very nice."

"No. Especially not to Marge."

"Do you think she might have been right, then?" Summer lowered her voice, to make sure no one around us would overhear her. "About her suspects for stealing Li Ping?"

"I don't know. I guess it could be animal traffickers or someone with a grudge against the Chinese government. But I'm not sure about that animal rights group." I tried to remember the name she'd mentioned. "The Nature Freedom Foundation?"

"Freedom *Force*," Summer corrected. "Daddy's always

complaining about them. They splintered off from the Animal Liberation Front, and they're even *more* determined to get FunJungle shut down. They've been picketing out along the road that leads here, and Daddy thinks they might have sabotaged some of the construction equipment for the new rides."

"Really?" I asked. It made sense that I might have missed the picketers, as I always came into the park through the rear employee entrance near my house, but I was surprised I hadn't heard about something as big as sabotage. "What happened?"

"One of the cranes building the Black Mamba Coaster broke down a few weeks ago. The electrical panel or something. No one could figure it out, but Daddy's sure the NFF messed with it. They *hate* this park. No matter how well we treat the animals, they still act like this is just some giant prison. So, yeah, I could see them taking Li Ping."

I shook my head, not liking this idea. "When Henry the Hippo was murdered, everyone thought the Animal Liberation Front was behind it, and they were wrong."

"That doesn't mean the NFF didn't do this."

"If the NFF is against animals being held captive in zoos, why would they take one captive themselves?"

"For ten million dollars. That could fund an awful lot of enviro-activism."

"There are ways to get ten million dollars that don't involve stealing a panda."

"Maybe. But this one might work."

I stared out at the polar bears, thinking about that. There were two bears on display at the moment, pacing around on the ice. Both were enormous. Polar bears are the largest predators on land; each weighed nearly half a ton and was as big as a rhino when on all fours.

"Is your father really going to pay up?" I asked.

Summer shrugged. "I don't know. I don't think the FBI wants him to. But he has to get that panda back. It'll be a disaster for the park if he doesn't."

I frowned. "I still don't think it's the NFF. Like you said, they mostly picket the park. Even if they sabotaged a crane, that doesn't make them a bunch of commandos. I doubt they'd know how to steal something from a moving truck."

"Well, it couldn't be animal traffickers either," Summer said. "If they're going to sell the panda, why would they leave a ransom note?"

"To make us *think* it was the NFF," I suggested. "Or some other animal rights group. And while the FBI is distracted, they deliver Li Ping to their buyer. I'll bet there's plenty of rich people who'd love to have a panda."

"Maybe," Summer said, though she didn't seem so convinced. "I have to go to the bathroom. Wait here for me?"

"All right," I said.

Summer headed to the women's room. I returned my attention to the polar bears.

They were now sniffing the air, like they were on the hunt. FunJungle often pumped scents into the room to keep the bears stimulated. Their sense of smell was far more keen than humans'—in the wild, they had been known to detect a carcass from twenty miles away—so FunJungle used scents so faint that humans couldn't even detect them. Which was good news when the smell being pumped into the room was that of a rotting seal. The guests never knew it was being done; as far as they were concerned, the bears were just putting on a show.

One bear inhaled deeply and reared up on its hind legs. It was nearly ten feet tall like this, taller than almost any other animal on earth. The guests around me gasped in amazement.

I sniffed the air myself, trying to pick up on the scent. This time, I thought I caught a hint of something rank. Only, it smelled more like bad body odor than I expected.

Marge O'Malley suddenly leaned against the rail next to me.

I fanned my nose in disgust. On a hot day like this, Marge sweated a great deal and could overwhelm even the most powerful deodorant.

"I need to talk to you," she said.

I tried to run, because that was generally a good move whenever Marge came looking for me. But she grabbed my wrist before I could get away.

"I wasn't doing anything!" I told her. "I was just standing here."

"I know," she said. "I'm not here to bust you."

"Really?" I asked suspiciously.

"Really."

"Then let go of me."

Marge did. She released my wrist and held her hands up, palms open, signaling she meant no harm. Unfortunately, with her arms raised, the stench from her armpits was even worse. Even the polar bears seemed bothered by it. The one on its rear legs dropped down and covered its nose with its paws, as though trying to block Marge's body odor from entering its nostrils.

"What do you want?" I asked.

Marge grimaced, like what she was about to say was going to cause her physical pain. "I need your help."

The statement was so startling, I thought I hadn't heard her correctly. "What?"

"I need your help," Marge repeated, through gritted teeth this time.

"Doing what?"

"Putting my big-shot, know-it-all sister in her place."

"You mean, like playing a prank on her?"

"No, doofus. I want to find this panda before she can. And prove that Molly's not as smart as she thinks she is."

I gave Marge a wary look. "I can't do that. Your sister told me to stay away from the investigation."

"Because she's afraid of a little competition."

"No. Because she wants me to stay away. And disobeying her is against the law."

"There's no law that says we can't investigate this crime too."

"Actually," I said, "I think there is. . . ."

"Well then, we'll just have to make sure she doesn't know we're doing it."

I looked around to see if any other guests were eavesdropping on us. Everyone seemed too distracted by the bears, though. And they were keeping their distance to get away from Marge's stench. I said, "Every time there's been a crime at this park, you've accused me of committing it and ignored all my attempts to find the actual criminal. And now you're asking me to investigate a crime even though the FBI has ordered me not to?"

"Yes," Marge said, completely ignorant of the irony. "You're always trying to prove what a brilliant kid you are. So now I'm giving you the chance to do it."

"But I don't want to do it."

"Well, you're going to do it anyhow."

"No I'm not." I tried to slip away.

Once again, Marge moved faster than I had expected, as though she'd anticipated this. She grabbed my arm and shoved me up against the railing. "You don't understand what it was like, being her sister." There was anger in Marge's voice, though I couldn't tell if it was directed at me or Molly. "She was always so good at everything: school, sports, dating, you name it. She was the valedictorian *and* the homecoming queen. And she rubbed every last bit of it in my face. My whole life, she's been telling me she's better than I am. And now, as if that wasn't enough, she shows up on my turf, claiming jurisdiction over *my* case, acting like the panda's disappearance is my fault somehow."

"Marge, it *is* kind of your fault. . . ."

"It is not!" Marge's shout was so loud, the polar bears lifted their heads, startled. The other tourists turned our way, curious.

I lowered my voice so they couldn't hear me. "But you were supposed to be guarding Li Ping in the truck when someone stole her."

"I was on the alert every minute of that ride," Marge said defensively. "I didn't drop my guard for one moment."

"Then how'd someone steal the panda?"

"If I knew that, I wouldn't be coming to you for help,

would I?" Marge backed off a tiny bit, allowing me to pull away from the cold railing.

"You were on guard for eighteen hours straight?" I asked dubiously. "You didn't fall asleep?"

"Never."

"Not even in the middle of the night?"

"I was drinking coffee the whole time. I'm telling you, whoever took Leaf Spring was no ordinary criminal."

"Li Ping," I corrected.

"Whatever. Point is, we're gonna find these criminals before my sister does—and we're gonna make her look like a fool."

"If *you* want to do that, that's fine with me," I said, edging away slowly. "But you can't make *me* do it."

"Yes I can."

"How? By accusing me of another crime I didn't commit? You've done that too many times. No one's ever going to believe you."

"Who said I was gonna accuse *you* of a crime?" Marge asked. There was a devious glint in her eyes.

I suddenly got a feeling like I was a seal in the water with the polar bears. "What are you talking about?"

"Your girlfriend isn't as perfect as everyone thinks."

"Summer's not my girlfriend."

"Yeah, right. I've been watching you two," Marge told

me. "You're together every chance you get, hanging out, eating all your meals together . . . making fun of me."

I swallowed hard, realizing Marge had probably been watching us the whole time we'd been in the Polar Pavilion, waiting for the chance to get me alone. If so, there was a good chance she'd overheard us imitating her. "Summer wasn't making fun of you. . . ."

"It just so happens, I have recovered security footage of Miss Fancy-Pants shoplifting at the FunJungle Emporium. Multiple times."

My stomach clenched with anxiety. I knew exactly what Marge was talking about. Because I'd seen it happen. The Emporium was an enormous store by the entry plaza that sold everything from snacks to T-shirts to athletic equipment. Quite often, when Summer was hungry, she would simply walk inside and take whatever she wanted: candy, Popsicles, sodas. She had always claimed that it wasn't really shoplifting, because her father had paid for everything in the first place, and since the clerks all knew her, they never raised a fuss.

"It's not stealing," I said as confidently as I could, hoping I was right. "Not if she's only taking things from her father."

"Doesn't matter," Marge replied. "What's important is, it'll *look* like stealing to everyone else."

"How?"

"Let's say these security tapes happened to end up at some of those websites that post embarrassing videos of celebrities. Footage of a girl as famous as Summer shoplifting would probably get a couple million hits, easy. And those viewers won't realize she's only taking merchandise from her daddy. They'll think she's breaking the law. Suddenly, Summer won't be America's Sweetheart anymore. She'll be just another spoiled rich girl with a load of skeletons in her closet." Marge smiled cruelly as she said this, relishing the thought of it.

My jaw was clenched so tight in anger, it was almost hard to speak. "If you do that, J.J. will fire you."

"Not if he doesn't find out it was me."

"I'll tell him it was you."

"You'll never be able to prove it. I already have the footage. I can get it to these sites without leaving any trace I did it. All I have to do is drop it in a mailbox. In two days it'll be all over the Web. And Summer's reputation will be dirt."

I didn't reply. I didn't know what to say. I knew Marge was probably right about how the world would respond. I was pretty sure that, in my middle school alone, there were plenty of people who would quickly turn on Summer the moment she appeared to have broken the law. Summer had often told me how cautious she was to never do anything embarrassing in public for fear of it being recorded. But it had obviously never occurred to her that she could be so easily undone by her own father's security system.

"If you go to J.J., or your parents, or anyone else, and tell them about this—or do anything else to get me in trouble—then I'll mail the footage," Marge warned. Then she stepped back, letting go of me and acting nice and friendly, as though she hadn't just threatened my girlfriend. "But we can avoid all that messiness if you just agree to help me. And I know, deep down inside, Teddy, that you want to find whoever stole that panda as bad as I do. So what do you say? Are we partners?"

Marge was wrong. While I wanted *someone* to find Li Ping and Doc, I didn't feel that it had to be me. I trusted her sister and the rest of the FBI to do it, and I didn't want to cross them up or get on their bad side.

But I also didn't want Summer's reputation ruined. And I was willing to do whatever it took to protect her. There might have been some way to undermine Marge's plan, but I had no idea what it was. Until I came up with something, I was going to have to at least *act* like I was helping Marge.

"What do you need me to do?" I asked.

Marge smiled again, extremely pleased with herself. "Just do what you always do. Stick your nose where it doesn't belong." She noticed that Summer was on her way back from the bathroom, then said, "I'll be in touch."

With that, she slipped away, heading off toward the walruses.

I shivered as I watched her go, but it had nothing to do with the temperature of the room.

In the exhibit, one of the polar bears dove into the water. It swam with surprising grace and speed for a land animal the size of a car. The guests oohed and aahed.

Summer resumed her place beside me at the railing. "Sorry it took so long. There was only one toilet working and some gross woman was hogging it forever." She looked down the hall and asked, "Was that Marge?"

"Yes."

"Was she accusing you of stealing Li Ping?"

"No."

"What, then? Plotting to murder the polar bears? Fondling penguins? Walrus trafficking?"

"She wanted me to help her investigate Li Ping's disappearance."

Summer stopped joking and gaped at me. "Marge O'Malley asked for *your* help?"

"Yes. She wants to find Li Ping and Doc before her sister can."

Summer's eyes lit up with excitement. "Sounds like fun. When do we start?"

EAVESDROPPING

"The best place to begin our investigation," Summer told me as we headed out of the Polar Pavilion, "is by finding out what the FBI has learned."

"How?" I asked.

"We spy on *their* investigation."

"And how are we supposed to do that?"

"Just leave it to me." Summer grinned proudly. "I have a plan."

We passed through the exit doors and were walloped by the heat. It was like being transported from Antarctica to Texas in an instant.

Even though Summer was doing exactly what Marge wanted us to do, I still felt I should be the voice of caution. It was one thing to snoop around a bit to get Marge off my back.

But I knew we could get in a lot of trouble by crossing the FBI.

"Molly warned us not to interfere with her investigation," I said.

"Because she wants all the glory of solving this for herself and the FBI. Which is really selfish. She's not thinking about Doc or Li Ping. She's only thinking of herself."

"So is Marge. She only wants to show up her sister."

"At least she asked for our help. And for once, she's right. You're smarter than the whole FBI, Teddy."

"No, I'm not."

"Sure you are. You've solved every case you've ever had. If anyone can crack this case, it's you. Man, it's hot. Want a frozen fruit bar or something?"

FunJungle Emporium, the site of Summer's "shoplifting," loomed ahead. I'd allowed Summer to treat me to a snack there dozens of times, but now things had changed.

"I've been thinking," I said, "maybe you shouldn't just grab food at the Emporium whenever you want. Someone might think you're stealing it."

"But I'm not. Daddy already paid for everything. If some dumb security guard tries to bust me, I can just call my father."

"I didn't mean a security guard. I meant a tourist. What if someone recognizes you and films you grabbing food without paying for it and posts it online? That would look pretty bad."

A frown spread across Summer's face as my point sank in. "What if we were really stealth?" she suggested. "If no one sees us, no one can film me."

"What if we just paid for our snacks like normal people? I'm sure you can afford it."

"Not right now," Summer groused. "I'm not carrying any money. Are you?"

"No. Doesn't your father have an account in the park? Could you just take the stuff to the register?"

"I could, but then I'd have to call attention to myself, and I'd get stuck taking selfies with tourists for the next twenty minutes instead of figuring out who took Doc and Li Ping. Speaking of which, we should get on that." Summer cast a longing look at FunJungle Emporium, probably imagining the aisles of frozen treats inside, then turned her back on it and launched into a long diatribe about how spying on the FBI was really the *right* thing to do. The gist was that if we all really wanted to rescue Doc and Li Ping, then the more people looking for them, the better, and if Molly O'Malley couldn't share like a decent person, then we owed it to Doc and Li Ping to find out what she knew. I realized there'd be no chance of talking Summer out of this. Once she got an idea in her head, you couldn't dislodge it with dynamite.

So I tailed along after her, figuring the worst that could happen was that Molly O'Malley would get annoyed at us and tell us to beat it. (My chances of getting in trouble were always diminished when Summer was around, because no one wanted to risk J.J. McCracken's wrath by punishing his daughter.) This way, I could at least claim to Marge that I was *trying* to help her out—and it gave me something to do with Summer besides going around FunJungle for the thousandth time.

We passed into the employee section and headed to the administration building. Most people needed a special ID badge to enter Admin, but Summer simply waved to the guards and breezed right through the security area. Since I was with her, no one batted an eye at me. We then rode the elevators up to the top floor, where J.J. had let the FBI set up camp in the conference room next to his office.

There was a large reception area outside J.J.'s office. Usually, lots of people were gathered there, waiting to meet with him. J.J. owned lots of companies, which did everything from making laundry detergent to building bridges, although FunJungle was now his main priority. Most of his businesses were headquartered in San Antonio, but since J.J. was the boss, any time he had to be in a meeting, everyone came to him. Today, however, the reception area was almost empty. J.J. had cancelled everything to deal with the panda crisis. The only person waiting was Juan Velasquez, the driver of the Panda Express. He was slumped in a chair, asleep, apparently worn out from the long drive.

His receptionist, Lynda Hayes, manned a desk nearby. Lynda was in her sixties and had worked for J.J. since he'd first started out. She had actually been a friend of J.J.'s mother, and she claimed to know J.J. better than he knew himself.

Lynda normally was calm as could be, but that morning, she seemed overwhelmed. She was frantically running through phone calls, switching quickly from one line to the other. "J.J. McCracken's office. No, I'm sorry, he's not available . . . J.J. McCracken's office. No, he isn't speaking to the press today, I'm sorry . . ." She gave us a quick wave as we entered, then pointed to the phone, signaling that she couldn't talk.

As we neared her desk, we could see that she was streaming a 24-hour news channel on her computer. The reason Lynda looked so harried instantly became clear: Word of Li Ping's disappearance had gotten out.

A banner on the screen proclaimed PANDA-MONIUM: CRISIS AT FUNJUNGLE! One of the big national news anchors, a woman named Heather Smith, was giving an update on the story. With her perfect hair and gleaming teeth, she looked like a female version of Pete Thwacker. "FunJungle has not issued any statement about the disappearance of Li Ping," she announced. "Although sources say the Chinese government is outraged and that the FBI is now involved in the investigation."

"Oh no," Summer gasped. She turned to Lynda and asked, "When did this happen?"

Lynda mouthed, "About an hour ago."

I checked my watch. It was 10:45. It surprised me that we'd missed word of this, but then, there were no TVs anywhere in the park.

"Daddy must be having a heart attack," Summer sighed.

On the computer monitor, Heather Smith said, "Now joining us to discuss the trials and tribulations of running a business like FunJungle is Walter Ogilvy, chairman of the Nautilus Corporation."

I instantly felt a chill go up my spine.

I had nearly died because of Walter Ogilvy.

He was J.J. McCracken's major business rival. The two men loathed each other. They were constantly trying to one-up each other, battling for control of the marketplace in several different arenas. The difference was, Ogilvy had no morals at all. J.J. wasn't exactly a saint, but next to Ogilvy, he seemed like one.

For example, Ogilvy had been behind sabotaging the shark tank at FunJungle. He had always claimed J.J. had stolen the idea for FunJungle from him; he'd planned to build a rival park called ZooTopia that had never gotten off the ground. Now he was determined to ruin FunJungle's success. He'd hired a thug named Hank Duntz to collapse the pedestrian tube that went through the shark tank and make it look like an accident. Unfortunately, I'd been inside the tube when it collapsed—along with Marge O'Malley and a police officer named Bubba Stackhouse.

Ogilvy had never admitted to the sabotage, of course. In the months since the shark tank incident, he and J.J. had been suing and counter-suing each other. Each had a huge stable of lawyers to sic on the other, and every time one got some traction, the other would bite back. Even though Hank Dunst had named Ogilvy as the man who'd hired him, that had been rejected by the courts because they felt Hank had been under duress when he confessed. (We had locked him in a room with an angry, poop-throwing chimpanzee to get him to admit the truth.) Since then, Hank hadn't said another word to implicate Ogilvy, which both my parents suspected meant Hank had been paid off by Ogilvy to take the fall for him.

And yet, here was the national news, inviting Ogilvy to talk about FunJungle. Ogilvy wasn't appearing on the program in person: He was simply phoning in while they displayed a photo of him. He didn't look particularly evil. He was in his seventies but looked much younger. (Summer claimed this was due to millions of dollars' worth of plastic surgery.) He had silver hair and wore the same kind of fancy suits that Pete Thwacker did. Even though Mom hated the man, she still admitted he was handsome.

"I can't believe they're letting that skunk on the air to talk about this!" Summer exclaimed. "He doesn't know anything about pandas! He's just going to bad-mouth my father."

I shushed her, wanting to hear what Ogilvy had to say.

"Mr. Ogilvy, you once considered opening a theme park very much like FunJungle," Heather Smith began, "but you ultimately chose not to, claiming the risks were too great. . . ."

"That's exactly right," Ogilvy said before Heather could even ask a question. "And sadly, J.J. McCracken is operating FunJungle in a way that amplifies those risks even more. He keeps trying to run that zoo like it's any other business. But it's not like any other business, because in a zoo, what you're selling is alive. When my food division sells a delicious cereal like Frootie Puffs, I don't have to worry that the Frootie Puffs are going to escape from the supermarket and maim some innocent shopper. But that's not the case with an animal."

"Are you implying that Li Ping escaped?" Heather Smith asked.

"I don't know what happened to Li Ping," Ogilvy replied. "Except that she's gone. And the blame for that should be placed squarely on J.J. McCracken. This is merely the latest in a string of serious mishaps at FunJungle, which is evidence that this business is a recipe for disaster. Frankly, I think it's only a matter of time before a *tourist* gets hurt at FunJungle, rather than a panda."

"Cram it, you big jerk!" Summer shouted, then spun toward us. "See? He's attacking Daddy, exactly like I said he would. And the anchor is just letting it happen. She doesn't care about Li Ping! She's only stirring up trouble to get better ratings."

Lynda took a break from answering calls and muted the program. "Maybe you shouldn't be watching this," she said, although she looked equally as angry at Ogilvy as Summer did.

Since Lynda actually had a moment to talk, I took advantage of it. I pointed to Juan and asked, "What's going on with him?"

"That woman from the FBI wants to interview him." The tone in Lynda's voice indicated she didn't like Molly O'Malley one bit. "She said he couldn't leave the premises until she'd taken his testimony. Only, she's been grilling the other driver for over an hour. And poor Juan here's plumb tuckered out after that drive. He drank three cups of coffee and still nodded off."

Sure enough, when I listened, I could hear the voices of Molly O'Malley and Greg Jefferson coming from the conference room. "Molly didn't question Marge?" I asked.

"She's going to," Lynda replied. "She told her not to leave the park until then. Lord have mercy, can you believe those two are sisters? They look as much alike as a pea and a poodle."

"They're both awfully stubborn," Summer said. She had calmed down and now turned her attention to why we'd come there in the first place: finding out what Molly O'Malley was up to. She pointed innocently to the room next to the conference room and asked Lynda, "Is anyone using that? Teddy and I have a school project we need to finish by tomorrow."

Lynda's eyes narrowed, betraying the tiniest bit of suspicion. "About what?"

"The Battle of the Bulge," Summer said without blinking an eye. "We're studying World War Two in American History."

She sold the lie so well, any doubts Lynda might have had vanished instantly. "Your father has some models of the amusement park set up in there, but I think if you're careful with them, he won't mind you using that room."

"Thanks," Summer said.

We were heading for the room when we heard voices coming from J.J.'s office. I could recognize J.J. easily, though the other voice was unfamiliar to me. Whoever was speaking was a woman with an extremely strong Southern accent.

Summer paused, so I did the same thing.

Lynda quickly closed the window on her computer screen

displaying the interview with Walter Ogilvy, as though she didn't want J.J. to catch her watching it.

A second later, J.J. exited his office. The woman with the Southern accent turned out to be Chinese. She was only about J.J.'s height, which was shorter than Summer, although she was wearing five-inch heels, so she towered above him. She had a lot of makeup pancaked on her face, and she wore a business suit that looked like it cost a few thousand dollars.

Four other Chinese people were with them, two men and two women. They were all older and wizened and wore traditional Chinese clothing: red jackets for the men and long red dresses for the women, all gaily embroidered with flowers and birds.

"I know it's a great deal of money," the woman was telling J.J. "But I also know you have insurance for exactly this sort of scenario. So you won't eat the cost anyhow."

"For the last time, Emily," J.J. replied. "This is out of my hands. The FBI is on the case, and they're telling me not to pay the ransom. That's federal policy for dealing with these things. If I pay it, it only encourages similar crimes down the line."

"This isn't a crime against an American citizen," Emily warned him. "Li Ping is Chinese. You have a lot of business interests in China, J.J. If you don't want any trouble with them, then I suggest you do whatever it takes to get that panda back."

J.J. looked extremely concerned by this statement, but then noticed Summer and me. He quickly broke into a big smile, putting on an act. "Hey kids, this is Emily Sun. She works for the Chinese Consulate in Houston. Emily, this is my daughter, Summer, and her good friend Theodore Fitzroy."

"It's a pleasure to meet both of you," Emily said sweetly, as though she hadn't been threatening J.J. a few seconds before.

"Nice to meet you, too," I said.

Summer said something along the same lines, though she didn't seem to mean it.

The other four Chinese people bowed to us politely. I got the impression that none of them spoke English.

"I'll bet you're wondering about my accent," Emily said. "Everyone does."

"I'm guessing you grew up around here," I said. "Your drawl is really similar to his."

Emily looked impressed. "That's exactly right. My parents immigrated here just before I was born. I was raised in San Antonio. In fact, I've never even lived in China."

"And China still lets you represent them?" Summer asked.

Emily laughed. "I still have Chinese citizenship. Although that's not even a requirement for my job."

"Speaking of your job, I know you have a very busy schedule today," J.J. said, nice and friendly, although it seemed like he was trying to get rid of Emily as fast as he could. "I greatly appreciate you making the time to stop by. . . ."

"Can the snake oil," Emily told him, dropping the friendly act. "And get Li Ping back." With that, she spun on her stiletto heels and marched to the elevator.

The other four Chinese people bowed to us once again, then followed her.

The moment Emily's back was turned, J.J. sagged. He looked as exhausted as Juan did. The events of the day seemed to have taken a lot out of him.

"She came all the way from Houston just to ride you about Li Ping?" Summer asked.

"No," J.J. said. "She was already here. For the sanctification ceremony for Panda Palace."

"Oh," Summer said, like she understood.

I didn't, though. "What sanctification ceremony?"

"The Chinese take their pandas very seriously," J.J. explained. "We're contractually bound to do all sorts of ceremonial things. Like, if we have a panda cub born, we have to wait a hundred days to name it in accordance with Chinese tradition. That whole gang is staying at the FunJungle Safari Lodge. They were going to sanctify the palace for Li Ping's arrival today . . ."

"Only, Li Ping didn't arrive," Summer finished.

"Exactly." J.J. sighed, then noticed Lynda signaling to him. She pointed to the phone, indicating he had many calls to make. J.J. turned back to Summer. "Sorry, sweetheart, but I don't have time to chat right now. Word of Li Ping's disappearance got out and I'm swamped up to my eyeballs. In fact, there's a good chance I'm gonna be working straight through dinner tonight."

"I figured as much," Summer said. "Teddy and I only came up here to get some schoolwork done. We were looking for a little quiet and some air-conditioning."

"I told them they could use the small office," Lynda said.

"Great," J.J. agreed, though he seemed distracted, like his mind was already a hundred other places. "Just be careful with all the stuff in there, okay?" He then asked Lynda, "What's going on with the feds?"

"I haven't heard a peep out of them in over an hour," Lynda reported. "They're still in there with the other driver."

J.J. looked at Juan, who had remained sound asleep on the couch despite everything that had happened. J.J. looked envious of the man. "Call Harry Boudreaux from my insurance company," he told Lynda. "I don't care where he is or who he's meeting with. I need to talk to him *now*." Then he went back into his office and shut the door.

Summer looked after him for a moment, then whispered

to me, "C'mon. Let's find that panda fast so Daddy doesn't have to deal with this anymore." She purposefully strode into the small office.

I tailed after her and shut the door behind us.

The small office wasn't really that small; it was merely dwarfed by J.J.'s enormous office next door. At the moment, it was being used to plan the newest section of FunJungle, the Wilds. While the rest of the park was designed as a zoo with a few somewhat educational thrill rides, the Wilds was going to be an unabashed amusement park. Blueprints and scale models were scattered about a table in the center. There was a river-rafting adventure that would send guests through manmade rapids; a terrifying-looking ride called Condor Strike that would simply lift guests twenty stories into the air and then drop them; and the Black Mamba, a big, elaborate roller coaster that looked like it was being eaten by a giant snake. (The first hill sent guests into the creature's mouth and then they'd careen through the darkness in its belly.)

Construction of the Wilds was already underway; J.J. wanted to have the rides open as soon as possible. Through the window, I could see all the way across the park to its location: a large brown scar on the earth where all the trees had been scraped off. (My family's trailer—as well as those of everyone else in FunJungle employee housing—had been removed from this area as well.) Bulldozers, cement trucks, and other construction vehicles trundled across it while two cranes maneuvered loads of stone and iron around. The steel frame of the Black Mamba jutted into the air, and there was a wide, snaking, cement-lined gouge for the Raging Raft Ride.

Summer signaled me to be quiet with a finger to her lips, then leaned against the office wall. I followed her lead, and her plan instantly became clear: We could hear Molly grilling Greg, the truck driver, in the conference room next door.

"So you drove the first shift from San Diego," Molly was saying, "then made a pit stop in Las Cruces around midnight, after which Juan took the second shift."

"That's correct," Greg replied. "He slept while I drove and I slept while he drove."

"And the only time you stopped on that entire drive was in Las Cruces?"

"Just like I've said a dozen times." Greg sounded extremely annoyed. "We were hungry and we all had to pee. So we pulled in at a truck stop to get some food and do our business. . . ."

"Doc Deakin included?"

"Yeah, he got out there too."

"So you all left the panda alone?"

"No. I kept an eye on the truck while everyone else went inside, and then when Juan came back from the john, I went in."

"So, if anyone had approached the truck during that time . . . ," Molly began.

"We would have seen them," Greg finished. "Nothing happened to the panda while we were there, I swear. She was still in the truck when we left."

"You know that for sure?"

"Absolutely. I locked her and Doc back inside myself."

"And after that, you all drove straight here?" Molly sounded skeptical.

"Why is that so hard to believe?" Greg asked.

"Because the idea of someone swiping a giant panda and a human being from a moving truck without anyone on that truck noticing sounds impossible."

"Well, it obviously isn't impossible, because it happened."

"How?" Molly demanded.

"They'd need to rig up another vehicle to make the attack, but it could be done," Greg explained. "One person would drive it while a team of other people would attack our truck from it."

"You mean, like some sort of Mad Max kind of thing?"

"Something like that. They'd need a platform built out onto the hood of the attack vehicle so that the kidnappers could stand on it. The driver of that vehicle would pull up close behind our truck. Then, someone on the platform would blow the lock on the rear doors. Once those were open, the attack team could enter the truck by leaping into it from the platform. They grab the vet and the panda and unload them back onto the attack vehicle, which then veers off and takes them away."

"And this is all done while both vehicles are traveling at seventy-five miles an hour?" Molly didn't sound convinced.

"I said it was possible," Greg replied. "I didn't say it would be easy."

There was a long pause. It seemed Molly was mulling all this over.

I stepped to the window and looked outside. The panda truck was parked almost directly below us. It had been moved from the veterinary hospital loading dock to the exterior fence of the park. From my angle, I couldn't see much of it except for the gray roof.

An FBI mobile crime unit was now parked next to it. I could tell this because it had "FBI Mobile Crime Unit" painted on the roof. Obviously, it wasn't designed to be a covert vehicle.

Summer waved me back to the wall. Molly had resumed her questioning.

"So, let's say this amazingly acrobatic high-speed assault actually happened," she said, not bothering to hide the disdain in her voice. "You really think it could all be done without alerting the people in the cab of the panda truck?"

"I *know* it could," Greg said. "Because none of us were alerted. I didn't wake up, and neither Juan nor your sister heard anything."

"My sister isn't exactly a top-notch law officer," Molly said.

"That's not what she told us," Greg countered. "She said she was some kind of elite zoo law-enforcement commando."

"Did she really?" Molly sounded amused.

"That's right. She said she was only pretending to be a security guard, but that she actually worked for the Federal Animal Protection Service or something like that. She said she was like James Bond and Jason Bourne rolled into one."

There was a noise I couldn't quite recognize in the conference room. It might have been Molly O'Malley laughing.

"My sister was blowing smoke," she said. "She is not an elite anything. She is a security guard, and not even a very good one. Meanwhile, your buddy Juan out there has been driving a truck for sixteen years. You'd think he'd have noticed if someone was making a full-scale assault on his truck while he was at the wheel."

"Not if whoever attacked it did it right."

"Or maybe Juan noticed and simply didn't say anything."

When Greg spoke again, he sounded even angrier than before. "Are you accusing Juan of being part of this?"

"It makes sense," Molly replied. "If he was in cahoots

with the perpetrators, he could let them know when you were asleep, maybe even slow the truck down to aid their attack. . . ."

"Juan would never do that. He's not a criminal."

"You don't know that for sure."

"Go get me a Bible and I'll swear on it. I've known him for ten years, and the guy's as honest as they come. He's never even run a stop sign."

"Everyone has their tipping point. A piece of ten million dollars is a big incentive."

"Not for Juan."

"You really expect me to believe a man with that much driving experience wouldn't notice an attack like this?"

"I don't know what you think driving a big rig is like," Greg growled, "but it's a whole different ballgame than driving a car. A truck is big and loud and it takes concentration. A lot of concentration. We're not just sitting in that cab, playing travel bingo and singing show tunes like this is some holiday road trip. We have to be focused at all times. And it's ten times worse at night, especially out on those highways where it's pitch-black and there's no light except for our headlamps. If some idiot cuts us off or a deer runs in front of us, we've got a split second to respond or else that truck ends up jackknifed across the freeway. Plus, there can be some nasty wind shear on that stretch of I-10. A big gust can come out of nowhere, and if you're not ready for it, the truck goes over and your precious panda ends up splattered all over the fast lane. So Juan would have had plenty on his mind during that drive. Your sister was the one who was supposed to be on the alert for any trouble. So if you want to start pointing fingers at people, maybe you ought to start with her."

There was another pause. When Molly spoke again, she didn't sound nearly as antagonistic as she had before. "Just so you know, I run a tight ship here. Marjorie hasn't escaped suspicion because she's my sister."

"I'll bet," Greg scoffed.

"I assure you, if I find that my sister is complicit in all this, I will treat her like any other criminal. I will arrest her and prosecute her to the full extent of the law."

A phone rang, interrupting the conversation. We heard Molly answer it. "Agent O'Malley speaking. . . . Where? . . . Okay, I'll be right there." She hung up, then said, "Mr. Jefferson, I need to go. Agent Chen here will continue your questioning."

"We're not done?" Greg groaned. "How many more questions could you possibly have? How much longer is this going to go on?"

Molly didn't answer him. Instead, we heard her gathering her things.

Summer bolted out the door of the small office. I followed her lead.

Summer quickly sat in the waiting area outside J.J.'s office, acting like she'd been there all along, and motioned for me to do the same.

I sat, and a second later, Molly exited the conference room. Behind her, I saw Agent Chen, one of the men who had been on the helicopter with her that morning, seated at the table across from Greg. I realized I had yet to hear Agent Chen say a single word.

Molly glanced at Summer and me suspiciously, then let it go and turned her attention to Lynda. "I need to see J.J. right now," she announced.

"Mr. McCracken is on a very important phone call," Lynda informed her.

"Interrupt it," Molly told her. "We found his veterinarian."

DOC

"**Where was he?**" J.J. asked, tailing Molly through the lobby of the administration building.

"Your own parking lot," Molly replied. "The Zoe Zebra section."

"Zelda," Summer corrected. We were following the adults.

Molly looked at Summer, confused. "What?"

"The character's name is Zelda Zebra," Summer explained. "All the sections of the parking lot are named in alphabetical order so the guests can remember where they parked. Zelda Zebra is the farthest from the front gates, because it's *Z*."

"I thought I made it clear I didn't want you kids hanging around this investigation," Molly said.

"This is no time to get territorial," J.J. told her. "Doc's a friend of theirs. They deserve to know what happened to him."

Molly looked like she wanted to argue this, then decided not to. "Right. It was the farthest section of the parking lot, away from the crowds. He was dumped on the edge of the asphalt with a sack over his head and his hands tied behind his back." She passed through the front doors of the building, and we followed her out into the heat.

"Where is he now?" J.J. asked.

"Hoenekker is bringing him in." Molly turned toward the veterinary hospital. "Some guests saw him and reported it to your security division. I've been told that he's in good physical condition. Hoenekker wanted to take him to your medical clinic, but Doc insisted upon coming to the veterinary hospital instead."

"Sounds like Doc, all right," I said. Doc didn't have much respect for the doctors who worked at the FunJungle health clinic, claiming both had barely graduated from medical school. My parents actually agreed with him. When my mother had fractured her leg a few months before, she'd gone to Doc to have it set, rather than the human doctor. "A bone's a bone," Mom had explained. "If Doc can fix a gorilla's leg, he can fix mine."

A souped-up golf cart swerved around a corner, racing toward the animal hospital. I could tell Marge was driving it even before I saw her at the wheel because Marge was the worst driver I'd ever met in my life. Instead of coming in a straight line, the cart was veering all over the place. As we watched, it clipped a trash can and scraped against a lamppost.

The front seat was built for two normal-size people, but Marge took up the whole thing. Therefore, Hoenekker and Doc both had to sit in the backseat. Both were clinging to the sides of the cart for dear life, desperately trying not to be pitched out onto the ground.

"They're letting my sister drive?" Molly gasped. "She'll kill Doc before I get a chance to question him."

An actor dressed as Larry the Lizard scrambled out of the golf cart's way, barely avoiding getting turned into roadkill.

"Watch where you're going!" Marge yelled, even though it had been her fault. She then completely forgot to watch where she was going herself. She was too busy giving Larry the stink-eye to realize she was bearing right down on us.

We all scattered like a herd of wildebeest facing a lion. Marge wove through us and plowed right into a large shrub outside the hospital.

Doc staggered out of the back of the golf cart, looking shaken. "I think I'd have been better off if I'd stayed with the kidnappers," he announced.

"It was my understanding that it was imperative to get you here as fast as possible," Marge said defensively.

Molly stepped forward. "Dr. Deakin, my name is Molly O'Malley. I'm the FBI agent in charge of this investigation . . ."

"O'Malley?" Doc repeated, then looked from Molly to Marge, scrutinizing them carefully. "You're related?"

"Marjorie is my younger sister," Molly said quickly, as if embarrassed by it. Doc's jaw dropped in surprise, but before he could say anything else, Molly told him, "I need to ask you some questions about your experiences with the kidnappers. If you'll accompany me, I have a room set up in the administration building."

"Sorry, but I have a kinkajou in dire need of bowel surgery at the moment." Doc sideslipped Molly and headed for the hospital doors. "And after that, I have a full day of other operations. Those kidnappers really mucked up my schedule."

Molly spun and followed him. "Dr. Deakin, I'm not asking you to come with me. I'm telling you."

"And I'm telling you I can't do it right now. There are animals in serious need of my help."

"This is a federal investigation," Molly said. "You are required to assist in it. If you disobey me, I can force you to comply."

Doc stopped and turned back to face her. "I already told your sister everything I know. Ask her."

"I'd prefer to hear it from you," Molly said.

"There's not much. I didn't hear or see anything."

"Nothing at all?" Molly asked, incredulous. "Come now, Doctor. They held you for at least twelve hours."

"I was asleep for all of it," Doc said. "First, they chloroformed me. Eventually, I woke up lying on a floor, with my arms tied and a burlap sack over my head. I yelled for someone, but no one came, so I went back to sleep."

"Why?" Molly demanded.

"Because I was tired, I was lying down, and frankly, there wasn't much else I could do. At some point, someone put me in a car, and the next thing I knew, I was lying in the parking lot here. No one ever spoke to me—or even spoke *near* me. My head was in the sack the whole time, so I didn't see a thing. They did pin a note to my clothes, but Hoenekker has it. That's everything I can tell you."

I looked at Hoenekker, as did Molly and everyone else. He held up a clear plastic evidence bag with a standard letter envelope in it. It was still sealed, and on the outside was typed: "For J.J. McCracken."

"This was on Doc when we found him," Hoenekker stated. "I haven't opened it yet."

Molly said, "Dr. Deakin, it would be in Li Ping's interests if you gave me a more formal interview."

"You mean, sit in a room for an hour telling you that I don't know anything else?" Doc asked. "Whoever these guys were, they were extremely careful. If you're looking for clues, I can't give you anything more than the one Hoenekker's holding." He started for the hospital again, but Molly stepped into his path.

"We're not finished here yet," she informed him.

Doc's eyes narrowed angrily. "Agent O'Malley, do you have the authorization to prevent a doctor from performing emergency surgery on a human being?"

"No, but . . ."

"Well, I'm about to perform emergency surgery myself. If you really think it's that urgent to talk to me at this very moment, feel free to sterilize yourself and come watch me resect this bowel. If not, then get out of my way. An animal's life is at stake."

Molly stepped aside, stunned. It appeared she wasn't used to people saying no to her. She helplessly watched Doc enter the hospital, then returned her attention to Hoenekker. "Do you have any information on the car that dumped Doc here?"

"No," Hoenekker replied. "As far as we know, no one saw it. Doc says he was lying there for a good five minutes before anyone noticed him. By that point, the car was long gone."

"Do you have security cameras in the parking lot?" Molly asked.

"Lots of them. I have my people combing through footage as we speak. Though this was out on the periphery, so I can't guarantee much."

Molly said, "If you find anything, I want to see it."

"Of course," Hoenekker agreed.

"How'd the guests handle finding a kidnapping victim in our parking lot?" J.J. asked. "Were they upset? Do I need to get Pete Thwacker on this?"

"The guests were quite calm and helpful," Hoenekker replied. "I don't know that they've connected this to Fun-Jungle at all, since it was on the outskirts of the lot. But bringing Pete on board to finesse the situation is probably still a good idea. I have their names and numbers."

"I'd like to talk to them myself," Molly said. Then she plucked the evidence bag with the letter out of Hoenekker's hand. "I assume you handled this carefully?"

"No," Hoenekker replied sarcastically. "I made sure I got my fingerprints all over it. Then I spit on it for good measure."

"There's no need for that tone," Molly told him.

"We're not amateurs here," Hoenekker shot back. "I could have opened that myself, but I chose to extend you professional courtesy. I'd appreciate it if you would do the same."

Molly backed down. "Point taken. I apologize."

"What do you think that is?" J.J. asked. "Another ransom note?"

"I assume so," Molly said. "But I want to make sure it's properly analyzed for evidence first. Once that's done, I'll contact you with my findings. Don't go too far in the meantime." She headed toward where the FBI's mobile crime unit was parked.

J.J. looked peeved at the way she'd spoken to him. He turned to Marge and snapped, "Get that golf cart out of my shrubberies."

"Yes sir, Mr. McCracken." Marge saluted respectfully.

J.J.'s phone rang. I caught a glimpse of the caller ID: Lynda from his office. J.J. answered, saying, "Tell me this is good news."

From his reaction, it obviously wasn't. The color drained from his tanned face so quickly, it looked as though he'd been bleached. Then he said a few words that would have gotten me detention at school.

"What is it?" Summer asked.

"The premier of China wants to talk," J.J. replied sourly. "And he's mad as a stirred-up hornet's nest." He returned his attention to his phone and hurried back into the administration building. "I'm coming back to the office right now," he told Lynda.

Hoenekker dropped in behind J.J., following him toward Administration. Summer and I did the same thing.

Only, before I could go two steps, Marge caught my arm. "Not so fast," she told me. "You and I have work to do."

THE SNEAK ATTACK

Marge's plan was simple. "I want to know what my sister's found out so far," she told me. "So while I distract her, you sneak into that mobile unit and get her evidence."

I looked to Summer, who was still hanging around. She stifled a giggle.

"Isn't sneaking into the FBI's truck and stealing their evidence against the law?" I asked.

"I didn't say *steal* it," Marge qualified. "I said 'get it.' Like take pictures of what they have or something like that."

"It's still illegal to enter their truck," I told her.

Marge frowned at me. "You know what else is illegal? Shoplifting." She tilted her head toward Summer, in case I didn't understand what she meant.

I got it, but Summer didn't. "What are you talking about?" she asked.

"Nothing," Marge said quickly. "Just a little code Teddy and I worked out. So, Teddy, are you going to help me or not?"

I looked to Summer again, hoping she would explain to Marge that this was a terrible idea. Instead, she grinned excitedly and said, "I'll help too!"

After that, I didn't really have much choice in the matter. Marge would use evidence against Summer to blackmail me if I didn't participate in her scheme—and Summer wanted to participate in it anyhow. Marge blackmailing Summer would be awful—but getting Summer annoyed at me wouldn't be great either. The best I could do was try to explain what was wrong with the plan in the first place. "I'm willing to help, but there's a big problem with breaking into the mobile unit, Marge: Your sister is inside it right now."

"So we'll get her out of there," Marge said confidently.

"What about all the other FBI guys?" I pointed out. "And even if you can lure them all out, don't you think they'll lock the unit?"

"Don't get your panties in a wad," Marge taunted. "I've got this all figured out." She started to slink down the alley toward the mobile unit, completely forgetting that J.J. had ordered her to get her golf cart out of the shrubs.

Marge's attempt to be stealthy was ridiculous. She wasn't exactly light on her feet. It was kind of like watching an elephant try to tiptoe. At one point, she actually flattened herself up against the wall behind a drainpipe, as if she could possibly hide herself behind something two inches wide.

Summer and I gamely slunk along behind her, doing our best not to laugh.

Eventually, we made it to the corner of the administration building and peeked around it.

I had a much better look at the mobile unit now than I'd had from seven stories above. The words "FBI Mobile Crime Unit" were painted on each side, along with several images of the FBI seal, some American flags, and one bald eagle. A set of doors was built into the rear with steps coming down.

Marge pointed to us, then to the truck, then made a series of complicated hand gestures I didn't understand. It looked like she was having an epileptic fit.

"What are you doing?" Summer asked.

"Don't you two know your commando hand signals?" Marge whispered.

"I don't think most people know those," I said, wondering if Marge even knew them herself.

Marge sighed, apparently annoyed by our lack of military training. "I want you to go over to the mobile unit and wait underneath it," she explained. "Then, when I lure my sister and the others out, you sneak inside and see what they've found so far."

I scrutinized the mobile unit warily. The body of it was a foot and a half off the ground, which would give Summer and me a decent amount of room beneath it, but that still didn't mean I wanted to go there. "What if they drive away? We could get flattened under there."

"Oh, relax," Marge chided, as though my concern for my own safety was somehow unreasonable. "You won't be there long. I'm gonna lure them out fast."

"What if you can't?" I pressed.

"Oh, I'll get them out," Marge said confidently. "I know my sister. She'll never pass up the chance to be a hero."

I started to ask her what this meant, but Summer grabbed my hand and yanked me toward the mobile unit. "C'mon," she whispered. "Let's do this." Either she wasn't as concerned for her safety as I was, or she actually trusted Marge on this.

We reached the mobile unit but paused before going underneath it, having the same idea at once. We pressed our ears against the rear doors to see if we could hear anything important happening inside.

We couldn't. Their voices were muffled through the thick walls.

Back by the administration building, Marge made some

more hand signals for us. I was pretty sure she wanted us to stop screwing around and get under the mobile unit, although it looked like she was doing some very bad disco dancing.

Summer and I slid under the mobile unit. It was awful. Heat radiated off the engine, and it reeked of gasoline. I gave Marge the thumbs-up to get going with her diversion quickly.

Marge pulled a gun out of her holster.

"Oh no," I gasped. "What's she doing?"

"Making sure her sister hears her." Summer clapped her hands over her ears. I did the same.

Thankfully, Marge thought to aim away from any buildings or people before firing her gun. Unfortunately, she was a terrible shot. Her first bullet blew the rearview mirror off the mobile unit. The second ricocheted off the panda truck. The third annihilated a streetlamp.

Each bang echoed loudly in the space between the buildings. In her haste to distract her sister, Marge hadn't considered what anyone else's reaction to hearing a gun discharge near a theme park might be. Or what the animals' reactions would be either. In the distance, I heard the startled trumpet of elephants and roar of big cats, along with many startled human screams.

But it certainly got the attention of the FBI as well. The agents all burst out of the truck above us with Molly in the lead. There were five of them now: three who had arrived on the helicopter, and two who must have come in the mobile unit. I could only see their feet from my position, but from their stances, I could tell they all had their guns out as well.

"What's the situation?" Molly yelled to her sister.

"Someone suspicious was poking around the panda truck!" Marge informed her.

"And you shot at them?" Molly snapped.

"They pulled a gun on me first!" Marge exclaimed. "They went that way!" She pointed along the side of the administration building.

"Fan out!" Molly ordered her agents. "Avila, follow me. Johnson, Ross, and McDonough, circle the admin building and try to head the perp off."

The agents sprang into action, racing off after the imaginary criminal.

Marge flashed a satisfied smirk at Summer and me.

"Marge!" Molly yelled. "Get your rear in gear! I need you to identify the suspect!"

Marge raced off after her sister.

Summer and I scrambled out from under the mobile unit. The rear doors were swinging shut, but Summer quickly lunged up the steps and caught them before they locked.

I heard more voices now. It sounded like people were coming our way, concerned about the gunshots.

Summer and I slipped inside the mobile unit and shut the doors behind us.

Thankfully, it was air-conditioned. The interior was spotless and sterile. There were several workstations with portable computers, microscopes, and plenty of technical equipment I didn't recognize.

"Don't touch anything," Summer warned me.

"No duh," I replied.

One computer was live-streaming a local newscast. The sound had been turned off, but it was obviously about Li Ping. A local TV reporter was positioned outside the front gates of FunJungle. The news crawl at the bottom of the screen declared: LI PING STILL MISSING. NO LEADS IN CASE YET. PREMIER OF CHINA REPORTED TO BE FURIOUS.

"How do you think the news even learned that Li Ping was missing?" I wondered. "Not that many people at Fun-Jungle knew, and all of us were supposed to keep it a secret."

"It wouldn't have been that hard for someone here to figure it out," Summer replied. "The FBI wasn't exactly subtle when they showed up. One of those people poking around the crime scene this morning probably put two and two together."

"And you think they went right to the news?"

"Definitely. News companies pay big money for tips like that."

"Isn't that illegal?"

"Probably, but it happens all the time. People are always trying to sell video of me to news services."

I sighed, well aware this was true. A few weeks before, Summer had accidentally dropped an ice-cream cone at Fun-Jungle and a day later, video of it was on a celebrity news site with the headline: BUMMER MCCRACKEN! SUMMER'S MASSIVE ICE CREAM FAIL. Even though it was the least interesting video ever, it still got several million hits.

We turned our attention to the rest of the mobile unit.

The envelope that had been pinned to Doc's chest was sitting on the desktop at the workstation farthest from the door. It had been removed from the plastic evidence bag. The envelope had been slit open, and the letter that had been inside was now unfolded next to it. It was a single sheet of white paper and had been printed off a computer:

Dear J.J. McCracken—

Deliver the ten million dollars to White Horse Road, exactly 1.3 miles west of Highway 281. There is a large oak tree on the south side of the road with a hollow in the back.

Place the money in a burlap sack. Unmarked twenty-dollar bills.

Bring the money at exactly twelve noon on Tuesday. We know you have it, so that should give you plenty of time to get it together.

Come alone. If you fail to deliver the money—or if you bring any law enforcement with you—bad things will happen to your panda.

There was a small brown object lying on the table with the letter. It was conically shaped, with a curve to it. Summer leaned in close. "What is that?"

"It's a claw," I told her. "Must be one of Li Ping's." I pointed to the smooth cut at the end of it. "Looks like they clipped it off her."

Summer's eyes lit up with understanding. "So we know they really have her. Of course! It's like when kidnappers send a lock of hair from their victims."

The letter sat next to a computer. The image on the screen was split in half. The left side displayed a fingerprint, enlarged to a hundred times its actual size, so big every ridge and whorl was evident. On the right side of the screen, hundreds of other enlarged fingerprints were quickly scrolling through, a dozen each second. At the bottom of the right side was the label "FBIFD."

"What do you think that means?" I asked.

"FBI Fingerprint Database?" Summer suggested. "I'll bet the one on the left came off the letter or the envelope, and on the right side, they're searching for a match!"

"How long do you think that will take?"

"Probably a while. I'll bet there's millions of fingerprints in the database."

I glanced back toward the mobile unit doors, wondering how long we had until the FBI realized they were on a wild-goose chase. "We should probably get out of here."

"Hey!" Summer exclaimed. "There's Xavier!"

She pointed to the computer that was live-streaming the news. Xavier was now talking to the reporter. He was still wearing his tuxedo and panda ears.

Despite the fact that she'd just warned me not to touch anything, Summer turned the sound up on the computer.

". . . so of course I'm disappointed," Xavier was saying. "I mean, I've been waiting months to see Li Ping. My whole life, I've wanted to see a panda. And now some jerk steals her? I hope that FunJungle and the police find her quickly and that she's okay."

The report cut to a grown man who was wearing a panda costume and had his face painted black and white. He was bawling. "Li Ping never did anything to anyone!" he sobbed. "Whoever stole her ought to go to jail for life!"

I clicked off the sound and checked my watch nervously. "We really ought to *leave now*."

As I said this, however, the fingerprint display on the other computer stopped running. A single enlarged print appeared on the right-hand side, along with the heading

"99.99% Match." A name appeared beneath it.

As much as I wanted to get out of there, even I couldn't resist seeing who the fingerprint belonged to. Summer and I both returned to the computer, seeking the identity of whoever had sent the ransom note.

The name on the screen was Carlos Edward Gomez.

"Ever heard of him?" Summer asked.

"No," I said.

"Me either." Summer started to type something on the computer.

I caught her arm. "Don't start messing with anything. We don't have time."

"Don't be such a spaz." Summer pulled away from me. "This won't take long. We'll be gone way before the FBI gets back."

A half second later, the FBI came back. The rear doors of the truck flew open. The sunlight from outside was blinding, casting the person who stood there in silhouette, but I could easily recognize the shape as that of Molly O'Malley. "I thought I made it clear that the two of you were to keep your distance from this investigation," she said coldly.

Summer was caught off-guard, but she recovered incredibly fast, spinning a lie with amazing skill. "We were looking for *you*!" she exclaimed. "Teddy and I had some ideas about this case and thought you should hear them. So we came down here, but no one was around . . ."

"Spare me the lies. I'm not an idiot." Molly grabbed both Summer and me by the collars and marched us out the door. "I know you two were in cahoots with my sister. She told me everything."

Outside, Marge stood between two of the FBI agents. Her arms were wrenched behind her back, handcuffed.

"She did?" Summer asked, looking betrayed.

"Actually, she claimed this was all *your* idea," Molly told me. "But I figure that's a lie as well."

"It is." I glared at Marge. "She's the one who made us do this."

"How?" Molly demanded.

Marge met my eyes. There was a threat in them. If I revealed her blackmail methods to Molly, Marge could still release the footage she had of Summer out of spite. And frankly, I was nervous about saying Summer had shoplifted right after Molly had just nabbed us for trespassing; I didn't want her to think Summer was a serial troublemaker. So, instead, I replied, "She just said she'd get us in trouble."

Molly stared at me for another few seconds. She seemed to suspect there was more to my story, but it was impossible to tell with her eyes hidden behind her sunglasses. Finally, she said, "It is a crime to tamper with evidence in a federal investigation. Since it appears you were coerced into this, I'm going to let you off with a final warning, but if I catch you anywhere near this crime scene again, I will have both of you arrested." She shifted her gaze to Summer and added, "I don't care who your daddy is. Is that understood?"

All of Summer's usual bravado vanished. "Yes," she said meekly.

Molly looked back at me.

"I understand," I said. "Is Marge under arrest?"

Molly said, "My sister not only participated in this bone-headed scheme, but she also discharged a firearm in a public area. I don't take behavior like that lightly."

I couldn't help but smile. I'd been handcuffed by Marge myself, so it was nice to see her getting a taste of her own medicine. Now that she'd been busted by her own sister, I figured she'd back off forcing me to investigate this crime. And maybe Summer would back off as well. Meaning I could go back to my normal life and stay out of trouble.

I couldn't have been more wrong. My troubles were just getting started.

THE RALLY

Molly O'Malley found an extremely effective way to guarantee that Summer and I couldn't do any more investigating: She called our parents.

They were all very upset with us. Even when we protested that Marge had coerced us.

"Since when have you ever done anything Marge wanted you to do?" Mom asked me. "You could have told us what she was doing, but you chose not to."

"It's not that simple," I said, but she and Dad were too annoyed to listen to any more.

J.J. had his driver take Summer home for the rest of the day. Mom brought me to her office at Monkey Mountain, then took my phone away so that I couldn't communicate with Summer—or do anything else online—and ordered me to read a book instead.

I tried. However, I couldn't focus. As much as I wanted to steer clear of the panda investigation, I couldn't stop thinking about it. Too many questions were tumbling around in my mind: Who was Carlos Edward Gomez? Had the bad guys really been able to kidnap Li Ping and Doc from a moving truck without anyone on board noticing? Despite Greg's insistence that it could be done, it still seemed like an insanely elaborate heist to me. Who had the skills, know-how, and funding to pull off something like that? Or was there another way it could have been done? Where was Li Ping? Did Doc know more than he was letting on? What would happen to the panda if J.J. didn't deliver the ransom money—or if he tried but things went wrong?

I also had questions about the incident at Dolphin Adventure: Had someone really been teaching the dolphins to steal people's bathing suits—and if so, why? Whose bathing suit had been left behind in the dolphin tank? And why was there tuna fish in the pockets?

It turned out, I wasn't the only one thinking about this. Around three in the afternoon, Olivia Putney called my mother. Mom spoke to her for a few minutes, growing more and more surprised.

Once she'd hung up, I asked, "What was that all about?"

"Olivia wants to know if you can help her figure out who's been getting into the tank at Dolphin Adventure."

"Can I? Even though it's investigating something?"

Mom thought about this for a bit, drumming her fingers on her desk. "I suppose. It doesn't sound as dangerous as dealing with kidnappers . . . and it seems like it's a bit of an emergency."

"Why?"

"Olivia said you had"—she paused to choose her words carefully—"an incident this morning with Snickers."

I could feel the blood rush to my face as I turned red. In all the excitement with Li Ping, I had forgotten to tell Mom about the mishap at Dolphin Adventure. "Yes."

"Well, they just had a similar incident with another dolphin. And a paying guest."

"Uh-oh. What happened?"

"Twix tried to pull his bathing suit off during a session. But she wasn't quite as good at it as Snickers. She only got the bathing suit down to the man's knees. The man didn't like it, though, so he punched Twix. And then, Twix bit him. On the bottom."

I laughed, despite myself.

"It's not funny," Mom said.

"Actually, it kind of is."

She was watching the rally instead. The whole scene appeared to make her angry.

A keeper was standing nearby, keeping a wary eye on the proceedings. Her name was Chloé Dolkart, and she'd originally worked at Monkey Mountain but had recently transferred to take care of the panda. Chloé was an extremely intelligent and enthusiastic keeper, though today she was obviously nervous. It should have been an extremely busy day for her, but now, since the panda was missing, she didn't seem to have anything to do. She noticed me and came over. "Hey, Teddy."

"Hi, Chloé. When did all this start?"

"About fifteen minutes ago. I think they all felt like they needed to do something. They were all very upset when Li Ping didn't come on exhibit. And then word of the panda-napping got out."

"Panda-napping?"

"That's what they're calling it. Instead of your standard kidnapping. So finally, Crazy Panda Guy there got up on the table and started shouting."

While the crowd continued to chant "Bring Li Ping back!" Crazy Panda Guy started imploring them like a Sunday preacher. "Lift up your voices, my friends! Let the world hear us! Let those horrible people know we will not sit quietly while our panda has been taken from us!"

The rally was growing bigger. People began to wander over from other exhibits. The actors dressed as Eleanor Elephant, Kazoo the Koala, and Li Ping began to clap along—although their job descriptions prevented them from making any vocalizations.

I wondered if the person in the official Li Ping costume should even be there, since the actual Li Ping was missing. It seemed like a bad idea to me, but maybe whoever was in charge of the actors hadn't felt the same way. They were still letting someone dress up as Kazoo the Koala, even though the real Kazoo had returned to Australia months before; apparently, the guests enjoyed seeing someone dressed like a koala, even if there wasn't a real koala around.

"Have you heard anything about Li Ping?" Chloé asked hopefully.

"Not really," I said. I figured anything I'd learned from poking around the FBI investigation ought to be kept a secret.

"Oh," Chloé said. "I was hoping that since, you know, you've been involved in so many other cases here . . ."

"Not this time. The FBI is handling it."

"Well, I hope they know what they're doing. Pandas aren't easy to take care of."

"I'm sure we'll get her back," I said, even though I wasn't really sure at all.

"We better," Chloé said. "I mean, if the panda-nappers think all they have to do is give Li Ping a bunch of bamboo and she'll be fine, they're sorely mistaken. Pandas don't eat just any bamboo—and Li Ping is pickier than most. There's only one kind she likes. If the panda-nappers don't have it, she might not eat. Or she might get really stressed out. Neither one would be good."

"I guess not," I agreed.

"Plus, pandas eat more than most people realize. At least twenty-five pounds a day. But sometimes up to forty. Do you think the panda-nappers will have that much around?"

"I doubt it." I was surprised to learn how much pandas ate. They had never seemed big enough to put that much food away.

"We will not rest until Li Ping is returned!" Crazy Panda Guy proclaimed. "We will not give up our vigil until she is safe and sound once again!"

By Panda Palace, the Chinese women began their own dance while the men plucked old-fashioned string instruments. The dance was very methodical and deliberate. The women moved as though they were in slow motion.

Emily Sun stood close by, observing everything with a big frown.

"Have you told the FBI about this?" I asked Chloé.

"I haven't had a chance. I keep thinking someone will

come along to talk to me, but no one has. And I don't even know how to get ahold of them myself." Chloé brushed the hair from her eyes and looked to me expectantly. "Could you tell someone to talk to me?"

"I don't think so. The FBI doesn't really want anything to do with me."

"How about J.J.? He listens to you, right?"

"Sometimes. I guess I could talk to Summer."

"Anything you could do would help."

I quickly wrote a text to Summer, urging her father to ask the FBI to talk to Chloé, wondering if it would ever happen.

"In addition," Crazy Panda Guy was saying, "we will not let FunJungle lie to us about the state of Li Ping anymore! If they know anything about our panda—good or bad—then we deserve to know it too!"

The crowd cheered about this as well, although the actors playing the FunJungle characters seemed to grow worried and started to sidle away.

As I sent the text, an elderly woman approached. If there hadn't been so much else going on, I probably would have noticed her sooner: She was dressed very differently from the usual FunJungle tourist. Most visitors to the park wore T-shirts and shorts, while this woman was wearing a nice white pantsuit and long lace gloves more suited to a cocktail party. She also had an enormous sun hat, with an entire bouquet of flowers in the band and a brim so wide it was hard to see her face. "Excuse me," she said in a honeyed Southern drawl. "I couldn't help overhear you talking about Li Ping."

Chloé and I both turned to her, worried. We probably weren't supposed to be talking about the FBI investigation in front of guests.

"Are you involved with the care of the pandas here at FunJungle?" the woman asked Chloé, then leaned in to examine the name tag on her uniform. "Chloé, is it?"

"Uh, yes," Chloé said.

"It's a pleasure to meet you," the woman said. "My name is Flora. Flora Hancock."

"You're the animal lady!" I exclaimed before I could think better of it. Her name had come up during the Kazoo investigation. She supposedly owned a great number of wild animals, including things like panthers and tigers, on a large ranch somewhere north of FunJungle.

Flora appeared pleasantly surprised, putting a gloved hand to her chest. "And you are . . . ?"

"Teddy. Teddy Fitzroy."

"Both his parents work here," Chloé explained.

"And how is it that you know of me?" Flora drawled.

"I've just heard your name a couple times," I said. "People say you have your own private zoo."

"I wouldn't say *that*." Flora opened a lace fan and flapped it in front of her face. "I merely own a few exotics. I truly love animals, you see. And I was *so* excited about Li Ping. I had Arthur drive me all the way down here to see her today." She pointed her fan toward a man I hadn't noticed before.

The man stood a respectful distance behind her. He was about the same age as Flora, dressed in a nice suit that looked extremely uncomfortable, given the heat. He nodded graciously to us.

"Is that your husband?" Chloé asked.

Flora laughed. "Goodness, no! Arthur is my man-servant!"

Chloé turned beet red in embarrassment. "Oh. I'm sorry . . . uh . . ."

Flora waved this off, indicating it didn't bother her. "Anyhow, we were absolutely *devastated* to hear that Li Ping had been stolen. Do you have any idea who did it?"

"No," I said.

"But we'll find them," Chloé added quickly. "And we'll get her back."

"I certainly hope so." Flora clucked her tongue sadly. "I can't believe those scoundrels would actually steal a panda. And you say they probably don't even have the right bamboo for her?"

"That's right." Chloé was speaking nervously, as if still

embarrassed about mistaking Flora's servant for her husband. "There are over fourteen hundred different types of bamboo in the world, but wild pandas only eat about forty of those. And Li Ping only eats *one*."

"Only one?" Flora repeated, surprised. "What kind?"

"It's called Wolong bamboo. I don't know why she likes that and not any other, but that's the case. Maybe she got spoiled, growing up in captivity. But it's not a common bamboo. If whoever took her doesn't have it . . ."

"Oh dear," Flora gasped, fanning herself as though she might faint. "Oh dear, that wouldn't be good at all."

Next to Panda Palace, the crowd was still growing around Crazy Panda Guy. "If FunJungle can't get Li Ping back, then we deserve another panda!" he exclaimed. "And free annual passes!"

The crowd cheered louder at this than anything he'd said so far.

Several FunJungle security guards had gathered around the perimeter of the crowd. They looked to one another uneasily, apparently thinking this protest should be broken up, but in no hurry to upset the crowd.

To the side of it all, the Chinese men and women appeared to have finished their ceremony. They were no longer dancing or playing instruments. Instead, they were all drinking sodas out of souvenir FunJungle cups.

I realized Emily Sun was staring at me. She was looking straight through the crowd, her mouth a thin, angry line. She didn't seem happy to see me there.

I realized I had dallied way too long. If Mom was really going to check up on me, then I needed to get to Dolphin Adventure quickly.

Chloé and Flora were really hitting it off, bonding over intriguing panda facts. "Did you know that pandas are pigeon-toed?" Chloé was saying. "They walk with their front paws angled inward."

"My goodness," Flora said. "I had no idea."

"I have to go," I told them. "It was nice to meet you, Miss Hancock."

"A pleasure," Flora drawled.

"If you hear anything about Li Ping, let me know," Chloé said.

"Will do." I hurried toward Dolphin Adventure. As I ran along, I realized that now that I had my phone back, I could find out one more important thing about the panda investigation: the background of the man whose fingerprint had been on the ransom note. Using the voice system on my phone, I asked, "Who is Carlos Edward Gomez?"

The phone didn't answer right away. There were many spots at FunJungle where cell coverage wasn't great—we were pretty far from civilization, after all—and I was in one of them. By the time I reached Dolphin Adventure, I still didn't have a reply.

The entrance was cordoned off with ropes and signs informing guests that the exhibit was closed due to "maintenance issues." Kristi Sullivan, who worked in Public Relations, was standing nearby, stuck with the thankless job of handling the angry guests whose dolphin encounters had been cancelled. "We here at FunJungle sincerely regret any inconvenience this has caused," she was telling a cluster of annoyed Italians. "The money you paid has already been refunded to your credit card, and we'd like you to accept this voucher for a free souvenir soda at any FunJungle vendor as our apology."

"We don't want souvenir soda!" a tourist exclaimed. "We want dolphins!"

Kristi caught sight of me and signaled that she was too busy to even say hi. So I slipped under the ropes and entered the dolphin area. It was eerily silent, compared to the chaos around the panda exhibit. Normally, the tanks would have been full of excited guests. Now there was no noise except for the occasional splash of a swimming dolphin.

I was heading to the check-in area, looking for Olivia, when my phone finally announced, "Okay, I found this on the Web about Carlos Edward Gomez."

I glanced at the screen, and what I saw made me stop in my tracks.

Carlos Edward Gomez was the president of the Nature Freedom Force.

THE TANK

The top hit for Carlos Edward Gomez was his Wikipedia page. According to it, Gomez was one of the founders of the NFF, although he'd been involved with several other animal rights groups before, including the Animal Liberation Front. The first photo of him was a police mug shot. He was young, with long hair and a mustache, and he was smiling despite having been arrested, as though he was pleased it had happened. The article claimed he'd actually been arrested several times—for something called monkey-wrenching. I had no idea what monkey-wrenching was, but before I could look it up, Olivia ran over.

"Teddy! Thanks for coming!" She was back in her usual bathing suit, although her hair was dry and frizzy again, indicating it had been a while since she'd been in the water.

"I really appreciate this. We're in kind of a pickle here."

I slipped my phone back into my pocket, figuring the panda case could wait. After all, I was supposed to be keeping my distance from it. "I'm happy to help, but . . . have you called park security about this?"

"Of course. But they're really busy with this whole stolen-panda thing."

"I thought the FBI was handling that."

"They still need help from security gathering information, I guess."

"Oh," I said. I figured they were still looking for the car that had dumped Doc in the parking lot.

"So it looks like it's just you and me. C'mon, I'll show you where we found the second bathing suit." Olivia led me past the check-in area for the dolphin swims. This was a small building with a registration counter and, this being FunJungle, a tiny gift shop where people could buy dolphin-themed merchandise. It was empty except for the wife of the guy who'd been bitten on the bottom, and an unlucky Dolphin Adventure employee named Nick who was stuck dealing with her.

"No one here ever informed us that there was a danger of being bitten by one of your stupid dolphins!" the woman was screaming.

"Actually," Nick said, "you signed a waiver that did inform you of potential risks . . ."

"Potential risks? My husband is now missing a piece of his rear end! The doctor says it probably won't grow back! He'll have to go through the rest of his life with a divot in his buttocks! Because your dolphin attacked him!"

"In self-defense. Your husband punched her."

"It was trying to steal his bathing suit! That dolphin was a pervert! I didn't see anything about perverted dolphins on my waiver! I ought to sue this park for a million dollars."

Olivia hurried me past before the woman spotted us. "She's been in there for half an hour," she explained, "instead of with her 'poor' husband. Who isn't in that bad shape at all. I saw the aftermath. He's not missing a chunk of his butt. It's only a little scrape. Twix barely nipped him."

"Then why's she flipping out?" I asked.

"She's probably trying to shake us down. To see if J.J. McCracken will cough up some cash rather than go to court. The sad thing is, it'll probably work."

"Really?"

"Oh yeah. It won't be a million dollars, but it could definitely be a couple thousand. J.J. doesn't want the public to hear that one of his dolphins bit someone's butt. It'll hurt business. So it's cheaper to pay off someone like this. And that woman knows it. She's probably thrilled that her husband got bitten. Gives her a chance to get her whole vacation here paid for—and then some."

We reached the edge of the tank and began to circle around it, heading toward the employees-only area at the far end.

Several dolphins immediately raced over to us. Olivia's presence usually meant playtime and fresh fish.

"Sorry, guys," Olivia told them. "No fish right now. We're just passing through."

The dolphins continued to vie for our attention anyhow, clicking and whistling at us. A five-year-old named Pop Rocks even leaped into the air and did a flip.

I paused, considering the layout of Dolphin Adventure. Most exhibits at FunJungle had big fences or large moats to prevent people from going in with the animals, or they were located inside buildings where the doors could be locked. Dolphin Adventure wasn't like that. The only barriers to the exhibit were a short fence around the beach, and a four-foot wall that surrounded the rest of the tank. A small child could have easily climbed over either one of them.

"If someone was in the park after hours," I observed, "they could easily get into this tank."

"Yes," Olivia admitted, "but FunJungle is locked up at night. No one's supposed to be in here unless they work here."

"So whoever got in with the dolphins must work at FunJungle," I said, then thought to add, "Or they snuck in somehow."

"People have snuck into the park before," Olivia reminded me.

"Yes, but since then, J.J. has really beefed up security around the perimeter. Plus, the only place anyone ever got in was the fence around SafariLand. That's an awful long way from here, and you'd have to come through a huge exhibit full of wild animals. It seems like a huge amount of work to get into the dolphin tank. Plus, it's dangerous." I knew this from experience. I'd faced down wild animals at night in the Asia Plains. There were some very big and scary animals out there, like Cape buffalo, and even the medium-size antelope could still trample you or gore you with their horns.

"So?" Olivia countered. "I'm sure there are people out there who *really* want to swim with dolphins. Or maybe someone found a place besides SafariLand to sneak into the park."

"It'd still be much easier to already be inside FunJungle," I insisted. "And a lot of people work here at night: janitorial staff and nighttime keepers and security guards and stuff."

"You think a security guard actually broke the rules and went swimming with the dolphins?"

"Maybe." I looked into the tank. I was broiling in the heat. It was extremely tempting to leap over the wall into the cool water. And there were dolphins as a bonus. However, the dolphin swim cost hundreds of dollars. Lots of people couldn't afford it—or it was a once-in-a-lifetime experience.

"What if one of the other employees got jealous of you guys over here? They're out there in the sun, doing their jobs all day, and you're here in a giant pool playing with dolphins."

"That's not exactly all we do." Olivia sounded a bit insulted. "Taking care of all these dolphins is a lot of work."

"Yeah," I admitted, "but it probably still looks like paradise compared to a lot of other jobs at FunJungle. Some employees have to unclog toilets all day. Or shovel elephant poop. Or walk around in a big, hot animal costume when it's a hundred and ten degrees."

Olivia considered that, then nodded acceptance. "I suppose that's possible." She started walking around the tank again. The dolphins followed her.

I followed her too, realizing I had to bring up one other idea. I'd been hesitant to mention it, though. "Maybe one of the other trainers taught the dolphins to steal people's suits."

"No way." Olivia seemed offended by the idea, which was exactly why I hadn't brought it up before.

"Why not?" I pressed. "I know you said the dolphins could pick up behaviors from people by accident, but yanking off someone's bathing suit kind of seems like something that would be taught. And only a trainer would know how to do that."

Olivia frowned. I got the sense that this had occurred to her already, but she hadn't wanted to mention it either. Finally, she said, "All the trainers here are very committed to these animals. We all know we have plum jobs here, and we've worked really hard to get them. I can't imagine anyone would jeopardize that by teaching the dolphins an aggressive behavior for no good reason."

"Well, maybe they had a reason."

"Like what?"

Now that I thought about it, I really couldn't come up with a good answer. The best I could manage was, "Maybe they thought it'd be funny?"

"Funny enough to get the whole exhibit shut down and lose a bunch of business? It doesn't make sense. And I can't come up with any other reason that does."

We reached the farthest end of the tank from the beach. This was where most of the maintenance equipment was. It took a great deal of machinery to keep a fake ocean going without letting the water get stagnant and start breeding fungus. Most of it was hidden behind a blue wall with a huge photo mural of a Caribbean beach on it, though there was also some equipment at the bottom of the tank.

Olivia pointed down to a pipe that ran just above the floor of the tank. "That's where we found the bathing suit, tucked under there."

The pipe was painted blue to make it blend in with the floor, and it was so far down, I couldn't see it very well.

"Olivia!" A voice carried across the water. It was Nick,

the poor guy we'd left with the angry wife of the dolphin-bite victim. "Can you come here? This woman really wants to talk to someone higher up than I am!"

Olivia sighed, obviously not thrilled by the prospect. "Guess she wants to yell at someone else for a while. Will you be all right out here by yourself?"

"Sure," I said. "Can I walk around the tank?"

"Yeah. Just stay clear of the machinery, okay? I'll be back as soon as I can." Olivia ran around the tank toward the offices. The dolphins all followed her, abandoning me. After all, she was the one who usually brought them the fish.

It suddenly occurred to me why someone would have tuna fish in the pockets of their bathing suit. Olivia and the other dolphin staff used fish to train the dolphins. If the dolphins did something good, they were rewarded with food. But the fish was delivered early every morning. By the end of the day, it was probably gone. Or if anything was left, it was most likely locked up.

So if someone was looking to train the dolphins themselves, they would probably have to bring their own fish. I had no idea if dolphins would eat canned tuna or not, but it would probably be easier to smuggle a tuna sandwich into the park than an entire dead mackerel.

The dolphins finally realized Olivia wasn't going to feed them, so they abandoned her and started racing around the bottom of the tank. I tried to watch them, but it was hard to see. The sun was reflecting off the water so brightly it was blinding. However, there was an underwater viewing area for guests on the far side of the tank from the check-in area. I figured I could get a better view of the dolphins—and the tank itself—from there, so I circled around that way.

The underwater viewing area was really well designed. The ground around the tank had been excavated so that the walkway sloped below the surface of the water, leading to a twenty-foot-long, eight-foot-high wall of thick glass. Since the water went right to the top of the glass, signs warned guests that they were in an official "Splash Zone" and could possibly get wet. As I'd suspected, my view of the park's eight dolphins was much better from here. Four had formed a small pod and were racing each other, while three others were doing lazy laps. The last one was down near the pipe Olivia had pointed out before, lying motionless on the floor.

I figured it was sleeping. Since dolphins breathe air, they can't sleep the same way humans do, because then they'd sink and drown. (Also, being asleep out in the ocean would leave them vulnerable to shark attacks.) So they actually shut down half of their brains at a time, letting one side sleep while the other monitors their surroundings and controls their breathing. In the wild, dolphins would sleep motion-less at the surface of the water or swim very slowly, but in captivity, they were known to occasionally snooze at the bottom of their tanks as well. (Possibly because they knew there were no predators in captivity.) At times like this, the dolphins would use their oxygen very slowly, surfacing every once in a while for a breath before drifting back down again.

The tank was so big, I could barely see the far side of it. The dolphins over there looked as small as minnows.

But I had a great view of Twix, who came right up to the glass to greet me. I recognized her from a small scar on her nose, as well as her cheerful attitude. I wondered if she might recognize me, since I'd spent so much time in the tanks with her lately.

Normally, the viewing areas were exceptionally crowded, but today I had Twix all to myself. Olivia, Nick, and the angry woman were all the way on the far side of the tank, in the check-in area.

I made a circle in the air with my finger, giving Twix a signal I'd seen Olivia do a hundred times.

Twix twirled in the water like a ballerina doing a pirouette.

"Awesome!" I exclaimed. "Now try this." I flapped my hand.

Twix flapped her pectoral fins in response.

I'd never had a dolphin respond to my commands before. It was almost as amazing as getting to be in the water with them.

I gave Twix another command. And another. And

another. She performed them all, apparently having just as much fun as I was. I forgot about everything else for a while. The stolen panda. The intruder who'd left their bathing suit behind. Marge, Molly, and the entire FBI.

I was so focused on the dolphin, I didn't notice I was no longer alone until it was too late.

A reflection in the glass suddenly caught my eye. Something big and black and white was directly behind me.

A panda bear.

I whirled around, fearing that maybe Li Ping hadn't been stolen at all but had simply escaped and was now loose in the zoo. Lots of people think of pandas as being docile, like they're giant teddy bears. But they can actually be dangerous, seeing as they're big and strong and have sharp teeth and claws.

Now that I was looking directly at the panda, rather than a reflection, I realized it wasn't Li Ping at all. It was only someone wearing the zoo's Li Ping mascot costume.

I heaved a huge sigh of relief. "You shouldn't sneak up on people like that," I gasped. "You scared the daylights out of me."

"You ought to be scared, you little brat," the person in the costume growled. The voice was deep and ominous.

It was only then that I noticed the costume wasn't complete. Instead of wearing the oversize paws on his hands, the man was wearing black gloves.

And one of those hands was pointing a gun at me.

ANGRY PANDA

I raised my hands and backed up against the
glass of the dolphin tank. There was no place for me to
run; I was right out in the open. I was terrified—and yet,
at the same time, I was still having trouble believing that I
was being threatened by a man in a panda costume. A lot of
strange things had happened to me at FunJungle, but this
was definitely near the top of the list.

"What were you doing snooping around the exhibit?" he
demanded.

"I was just looking at the dolphins," I replied, trying to
remain calm. "That's all!"

"Not *this* exhibit!" the man snapped, like I was an idiot.
"The Li Ping one! Panda Pagoda."

"Panda Palace?"

"Who cares what it's called? What were you looking for over there?"

"I wasn't looking for anything!"

"Don't lie to me! I saw you!"

I flashed back to my time at the rally, recalling the panda I'd seen clapping along with the crowd over there. It must have been the same person who'd spotted me and then followed me to the dolphin tank.

If someone wanted to keep tabs on what was happening at FunJungle, wearing a mascot costume was a great way to do it. You could go almost anywhere in the park without anyone questioning why you were there—or who you actually were inside the costume. I had even worn a costume myself before, while investigating Kazoo the Koala's disappearance. It was amazing how quickly people stopped thinking of you as a fellow human and started regarding you as a piece of scenery.

But there were disadvantages to the costumes as well. They were hot and bulky and hard to move in. Plus, the heads made them top-heavy and were difficult to see out of. In most, the only way to see was through the character's mouth, which was often angled downward. This made it very hard to look people in the eye. Even children. This seemed to be the case with the Li Ping costume as well. At the moment, my attacker had his head tilted back at an awkward angle so he could look at me.

I figured if I was going to get out of this, I had to use the costume to my advantage.

Out of the corner of my eye, I could see Twix was still at the glass behind me. She seemed fascinated by the giant panda. There was an extremely good chance she'd never seen a panda before—or a human dressed as one. I had no idea if she knew what the gun was.

"I wasn't snooping," I repeated. "I swear. I was coming over here and I stopped to see what was going on with the rally."

"You were talking to a keeper."

"Only about the rally! That's all! And she came over to *me*. I wasn't looking for her."

"Do not lie to me, kid. I know all about you—and your habit of getting involved in things that shouldn't concern you."

"I'm telling you the truth!" I pleaded.

"That's it." The panda waddled toward me menacingly. "Now I'm gonna have to get mean."

I clenched my upraised hands into fists, giving Twix the signal Olivia had taught me that morning. In response, Twix rocketed to the surface and spit a mouthful of water over the top of the wall. Her aim was perfect. She nailed the approaching panda right in his face.

If my attacker hadn't been wearing a giant panda head, he might have been temporarily blinded by the sudden blast of salt water and dolphin spit, allowing me to escape. But the head now worked to my advantage a different way. My attacker didn't see the water coming at all. All he knew was that something had struck him. He craned his head upward, startled, trying to see what it was, and in doing so, temporarily lost his balance. He tilted backward, wheeling his arms to steady himself, which meant that, for a few seconds, the gun was no longer pointed at me.

I charged, driving my shoulder into his chest.

The stomach was well padded to give "Li Ping" an adorable pot belly, but I still hit it hard enough to make my attacker grunt in pain. He toppled over backward, landing spread-eagled on the cement.

He didn't let go of the gun, though. I was hoping he would, so I could grab it and toss it into the dolphin tank, but he held on tight. I didn't want to get into a fight over it with him still holding the trigger end, so I ran for my life instead, praying he wouldn't be able to get back up anytime soon in that suit.

As I took off, I gave Twix the signal for one more spit take.

She happily complied, blasting the panda once again.

This time, some salt water got into the gaping mouth of the suit. I heard my attacker splutter angrily. He was writhing around on his back like a turtle flipped on its shell, trying to figure out how to get on his feet again with the giant panda head weighing him down.

I raced around the tank as fast as I could. Because it was circular, I didn't have to go too far before the upended panda had disappeared from sight around the curve of the glass wall. That meant I was out of bullet range, in case he wanted to take a shot at me, but I didn't relax for a second. I kept running, screaming for help at the top of my lungs.

Twix zipped along the opposite side of the glass, keeping pace with me, like this was all a game.

The walkway rose back to the same level as the surface of the water, and I came to the fake beach where the guests entered the tanks. I clambered over the picket fence and charged across the sand toward the offices. I'd never thought the beach was that big, but now that my life was at stake, it seemed endless. The sand was much harder to run on than the pavement had been, giving me the nightmarish feeling of spinning my legs but not going anywhere at all.

Olivia burst out of the check-in building, alerted by my yelling. Nick and the angry woman followed her.

"What's happening?" Olivia called out. "Is something wrong with the dolphins?"

"Someone's trying to shoot me!" I told her.

Nick, in an amazing display of cowardice, ran right back inside and slammed the door.

The angry woman didn't budge. She seemed to think I was a gibbering idiot.

Olivia bravely ran toward me, coming to my aid. She leaped over the fence from the other side, dashed across the sand, grabbed my hand, and dragged me toward the safety of the check-in building.

Twix skimmed through the shallows by the beach, chattering happily. A few more dolphins raced over, not wanting to miss out on the fun.

I chanced a look back behind me, but didn't see any sign of the giant panda.

"Where'd this happen?" Olivia asked as we ran.

"In the underwater viewing area," I gasped.

"What'd he look like?"

I paused before answering, knowing what I was about to say was going to get me a strange look. "He was dressed as Li Ping."

Sure enough, Olivia gave me the look. She almost stopped running, thinking this was a joke.

"I'm not kidding!" I told her, so she'd pick up the pace again. "He's wearing the park's panda mascot costume!"

We reached the fence at the other end of the beach, vaulted over it, and dashed past the angry woman into the check-in building. Thankfully, Nick had failed to lock the door behind him. We scrambled behind the safety of the check-in counter, only to find Nick huddled there.

He shrieked in fear. "Get away from me! Someone's trying to kill you!"

"Get a grip, you weenie," Olivia snapped. She then pulled out her phone and dialed park security.

They promptly put her on hold.

The angry woman stormed back inside, even more annoyed now. "If you think you can weasel out of your obligations by pretending there's a crisis, you're all dumber than I thought," she informed us.

"This isn't pretend," I told her. "There's really someone dangerous out there!"

"In a giant panda costume," the woman repeated disdainfully. "Sure there is."

"If I was really going to make something up," I told her, "do you think I'd make up something so ridiculous?"

"If this panda's so dangerous, how'd you get away from him?" the woman asked.

"I got a dolphin to spit in his face," I said.

This did not help make my story any more believable. The woman glared at me sternly. "Are you on drugs, young man?"

Meanwhile, Nick was scrambling around the small gift shop on his hands and knees. "We're sitting ducks in here!" he wailed. "We need something to defend ourselves. . . . Aha!" He grabbed a large plastic toy dolphin and tried to wield it like a baseball bat, but when he cocked it back over his shoulder, it slipped out of his sweaty hands and sailed through a window.

Park security must have picked up, because Olivia started speaking into her phone. "This is Olivia Putney at Dolphin Adventure. There's a man with a gun over here dressed as a panda. We need all available security here right away. . . . Yes, that's right. Dressed as a panda . . . Yes, I'm sure it's not a real panda with a gun. How would a panda get a gun? . . . Can you just send everyone you can? Our lives are in danger!"

Nick now approached a small aquarium full of sea anemones. "Wait a minute!" he exclaimed. "These are poisonous! If the panda comes in here, we could throw these at him!"

The angry woman glared out the window, still refusing to believe there was any real danger. "I don't see any panda out there."

"Get down!" I warned her. "I'm serious about all this!"

"If there was really a crazy person dressed as a panda stalking you, then there ought to be a crazy person dressed as a panda out there," the woman said. "But there's not. I know what a panda looks like. Trust me, there isn't one."

Olivia, Nick, and I crawled over to the wall, got on our knees, and peeked out the window. The woman stared at us like we were morons the entire time.

She was right, though. There was no sign of the angry panda.

We stayed in the check-in building, just to be safe. We waited there until park security showed up. The woman berated us for various things the entire time: We were fools for hiding from an imaginary panda assassin, we ought to get our dolphins checked for rabies, J.J. McCracken ought to cough up a few million dollars for her husband's pain and suffering, and all the snacks in the park were overpriced.

Chief Hoenekker led the security brigade. Either the FBI didn't need his services anymore, or this was a big enough emergency to require his attention. Thankfully, he took me seriously when I explained what had happened. Then he told us to remain in the safety of the office while he and his team searched Dolphin Adventure. When they came up empty there, they swept the entire park for the man dressed as a panda.

They didn't find him, though. Or the costume.

Any sign of my attacker had completely vanished.

QUESTIONING

I had come face-to-face with a lot of dangerous animals in my life, both at FunJungle and in Africa, but I'd never been as shaken as I was after confronting the man in the panda suit. Because the animals were never being malicious; they were simply animals. Their behavior, no matter how menacing, was purely instinct. Sometimes, if they were carnivores, they might have viewed me as a potential meal, but many times, the animals were probably feeling just as threatened by me as I was by them.

However, the man in the Li Ping costume hadn't been acting on instinct. He hadn't come after me because I was food. He had done it because he was a bad person, pure and simple.

After my run-in with him, I just wanted to go home. I wanted to be with my parents, where I'd feel safe.

Unfortunately, Molly O'Malley wouldn't let me. She wanted to interrogate me first. Now that I'd been targeted, I was part of her investigation and had to be questioned while the events were still fresh in my mind.

So, at Molly's behest, Chief Hoenekker brought me back to the top floor of the administration building. This time, I got to sit in the conference room and be grilled myself. Because I was a minor and obviously rattled, Molly allowed my parents to join me. We sat on one side of the big conference table while Molly and Agent Chen sat on the other. Agent Chen took notes on a legal pad and recorded everything with his phone as well. I still hadn't heard him say a single word. I was beginning to wonder if he was mute.

Hoenekker and all the other FunJungle security people were dismissed.

Juan and Greg, the drivers of the panda truck, were no longer around. I figured they'd finally been allowed to leave, though when I asked Molly about it, she told me that wasn't any of my business.

Then she said, "My team has reviewed the footage from Dolphin Adventure and determined that you were telling the truth about being attacked by a man in a panda suit."

"Of course he was telling the truth!" Mom exclaimed. "Teddy wouldn't lie about something like that."

"Mrs. Fitzroy, I'm questioning your son, not you," Molly

said sternly. "If you can't allow me to do that without interruptions, then I'll have to ask you to leave. Do you understand?"

"Yes," Mom agreed sullenly.

"You must admit that Teddy's story sounded bizarre?" Molly asked her.

"Teddy isn't a liar, Agent O'Malley," Mom replied.

Molly returned her attention to me. "After you knocked over the panda and ran away, he didn't follow you. Instead, he fled via a separate exit from the dolphin area. We're still trying to track his movements through the park after that, although it's not easy."

"Why not?" I asked.

"It involves sifting through the feeds of thousands of separate cameras. And while it normally ought to be easy to track someone in a panda suit, on this particular day, there are a staggering number of other people dressed like pandas at the park."

"But the Li Ping costume is still different from what those people are wearing," I pointed out.

"True," Molly conceded, "and yet, there are enough people wearing black and white and face paint and those ridiculous panda ears to make the job of tracking your assailant quite difficult. Therefore, any information you can give us would be greatly appreciated. First of all, what can you tell me about your attacker?"

"Not much," I answered. "I couldn't see him at all in the costume. I only heard him."

"What was his voice like?" Molly pressed.

"Very deep."

"Was there anything else notable about it? Was it raspy or gravelly? Did he have a lisp or some other speech impediment?"

"No speech impediments. But it was kind of gravelly, I guess."

"And you're one hundred percent sure it was a man?"

"Yes."

"Was he tall or short?"

There were quite a few FunJungle characters that were so short, only little people could play them: Larry the Lizard and Kazoo the Koala, for example. But the person dressed as Li Ping had loomed over me. "Tall."

"How tall?"

"Six feet, maybe?"

"And why did this person threaten you?"

"I don't know."

Molly leaned forward across the table and said, "You don't? Think about it."

I did. I tried to replay the events at the dolphin tank over in my mind, though to my surprise, they were already fading. It all had happened quickly, and I'd been very frightened.

Mom put her hand on mine. Even though it was a small gesture, it calmed me down and helped me think. The events came into focus. "He thought I'd been snooping around the panda exhibit."

Molly arched an eyebrow. "You weren't?"

"No."

"Tell me the truth, Teddy."

"I am."

"This is a federal investigation," Molly warned. "If you don't stop playing games, I'll ship you off to juvenile hall."

Now it was my father who couldn't keep his silence anymore. "He told you he wasn't snooping! What point is there in badgering him about it?"

Molly turned on him angrily. "The point, Mr. Fitzroy, is that despite repeated warnings to steer clear of this investigation, your son has continued to meddle in it. And, from what I understand, he has meddled in several previous mysteries at this zoo as well."

"Teddy didn't meddle in those mysteries," Dad corrected. "He *solved* them."

"Well, it's *my* job to solve this one, not his," Molly said curtly. "Every time Teddy interferes, it makes my job harder. Now he's been threatened by a hostile element for snooping around, and I'm supposed to believe that person only *thought* he was snooping?"

"That's the truth," I protested. "I haven't been investigating at all. I was in Mom's office right up until I was asked to go to the dolphin tanks. All I did was walk by Panda Palace on the way there, and there was a rally about Li Ping, so I stopped to watch it. Then Chloé Dolkart, one of the panda keepers, came over, and I talked to her about the rally. That's when the guy in the panda costume saw me."

"You're sure about that?" Molly asked, still sounding skeptical.

"Pretty sure," I replied, then remembered something. "I also saw someone dressed as Li Ping near the panda truck this morning! Right before you got here. Maybe it was the same person! I'll bet no one was really supposed to be dressed as Li Ping today, since Li Ping wasn't even here. . . ."

"That makes sense," Mom put in. "The park wouldn't want mascots out representing an animal that had been stolen."

"The guy must have seen me this morning," I said. "Then he recognized me at Panda Palace and followed me to Dolphin Adventure."

"So your idea is what, exactly?" Molly inquired. "That this guy was hanging out in a stolen Li Ping costume, just in case someone came snooping around?"

"Yes. If you want to keep an eye on things here, a mascot costume is a great way to do it. People forget there's a human inside and say things right in front of you. I know because I wore one once."

Molly looked to my parents, apparently unsure if she should believe this.

"It's true," Mom said.

Molly tapped her fingers on the table thoughtfully, then told Agent Chen, "Text Hoenekker. See if all the Li Ping costumes are accounted for."

Agent Chen nodded and dutifully sent the text.

"By the way," I said, "when I was at Panda Palace, Chloé Dolkart said no one from the FBI had come to talk to her yet."

"Why would we talk to a panda keeper?" Molly asked.

"Because she knows a whole lot about pandas. Maybe she knows something that might be helpful to the case."

Molly thought so little of this suggestion, she didn't even bother to respond to it. Instead, she opened her laptop computer and brought up a video file. "Teddy, I want you to listen to this and then tell me if it's the voice you heard."

"Agent O'Malley," Mom said, "I apologize for interrupting, but Teddy has a point. Chloé might know some information that could be important to recovering Li Ping."

Molly made no attempt to hide her annoyance. "*I* will decide what is important in this case, not you. And what is important right now is identifying Teddy's attacker. If we can do that, it might give us a lead to who is behind Li Ping's kidnapping. So Teddy, listen."

She played the file. A deep voice spoke. It sounded like someone making a speech to a group of people. "The Nature Freedom Force is committed to the abolition of all zoos, everywhere, no exceptions."

"That's not the voice I heard," I said.

"You're sure?" Molly asked. "Listen to some more."

She played another clip: "We must be willing to do whatever it takes to accomplish this goal!"

The cheers of the people listening followed.

I shook my head. "That definitely wasn't the same person. Was that Carlos Gomez?"

Molly looked up at me in surprise. Then her gaze hardened. "You saw that in the mobile unit, didn't you?"

I shrank under her glare, which gave me away.

Molly grew even more annoyed.

"Wait," Dad said. "Was the NFF behind Li Ping's kidnapping?"

"That's classified," Molly replied sharply.

"I don't think they did it," I said.

Molly's gaze grew even harder. "I'm not asking for your opinion."

"It just doesn't make sense," I continued. I knew she didn't want me to say it, but I needed to. I'd had the idea all day, and I probably wouldn't get another chance to share it. "The whole reason the NFF wants to shut down zoos is to keep animals from being in captivity. So why would they steal one and hold it hostage?"

"For money," Molly said, like it was obvious.

"And then they'll give the panda right back to the zoo?" I asked. "Gomez just said they wanted zoos abolished."

"I can't explain what they're thinking," Molly told me. "But I do know all my evidence points to the NFF."

"All you have is a fingerprint from the ransom note," I pointed out.

"We have *two dozen* fingerprints from the ransom note," Molly said, and then seemed annoyed that I'd gotten her to even admit that much. "And as I said, this isn't open for discussion."

"You have two dozen fingerprints on one piece of paper?" I asked. "That's weird, isn't it?"

Molly ignored me and returned her attention to her laptop. "I want to play another sound file for you . . ."

I didn't back down, though. "Gomez didn't leave one fingerprint in the entire panda truck, and then he leaves two dozen on the ransom note? That seems idiotic."

"Just because someone is a terrorist doesn't mean they're a genius," Molly snapped. "And even geniuses make mistakes."

"It just sounds like someone's trying to frame the NFF," I

told her. "Like maybe they stole a piece of paper from Carlos Gomez and used it for the ransom note to throw you off."

"Teddy has a point," Mom piped up, unable to hold her tongue anymore. "It wouldn't be the first time a criminal has tried to frame an animal rights group for something here."

Molly didn't bring up the next sound file. Instead, she stared at all of us. Her finger slowly tapped on the conference table like a metronome, filling the uncomfortable silence in the room. It seemed as though Molly had realized I might be right, but didn't want to admit it.

Eventually she asked me, "And who, pray tell, do you think concocted this elaborate setup?" There was a mocking tone to her voice, like she was toying with me.

"Well," I said carefully, "you suggested some other of possibilities yourself. Animal traffickers. Or someone with a grudge against the Chinese—"

"I know what I said," Molly interrupted. "I'm asking you who *you* think did it, smart guy."

I swallowed hard, unsettled under Molly's harsh gaze. But then both my parents looked at me supportively, bolstering my confidence. "Walter Ogilvy," I said.

"The billionaire?" Molly laughed derisively. "Why would he steal a panda?"

"To hurt J.J. McCracken," I told her. "They hate each other. Ogilvy claims J.J. stole the idea for FunJungle from him, even though J.J. didn't. Ogilvy even tried to sabotage FunJungle once already."

"That still hasn't been proven," Molly countered.

"Only because Ogilvy has the clout to slow down the justice system," Dad said, no longer able to hold his tongue either. "A man who worked for one of his shell corporations tried to destroy Shark Encounter—and Teddy almost died as a result!"

"Stealing Li Ping is even worse for FunJungle than sabotaging the shark tank," I explained. "First, it makes the park look terrible. Then millions of dollars that J.J. spent to bring Li Ping here and build a panda exhibit and advertise it go to waste. And it'll cost FunJungle millions more when everyone who was coming to see the panda here cancels their trips. Plus, J.J. has a ton of business interests in China that could all be jeopardized because of this."

Mom reacted to this last one in surprise. "How do you know that?"

"Some woman from the Chinese Consulate was here earlier today," I said. "She told J.J. he'd be in a lot of trouble if he didn't get Li Ping back."

"That's exactly where your argument falls apart," Molly told me. "The panda is being held for ransom. Which means whoever took it expects to give it back. Which won't damage J.J.'s business dealings at all."

"Unless they don't really intend to give it back," I argued. "If the whole ransom thing is just a scam to make it look like the NFF is responsible, then Ogilvy wouldn't really care about returning Li Ping to us."

"Which would be even worse for J.J. McCracken and FunJungle," Dad concluded.

Molly stared at us all once more, her finger tapping on the conference table. "It would," she said finally. "Although there's one more flaw in your accusation. So far, there hasn't been one shred of evidence against Walter Ogilvy—while there is plenty against Carlos Edward Gomez and the NFF."

"You mean the fingerprints?" I asked.

"Those—and the car that dumped Doc in the parking lot," Molly replied. "We found footage of it and got the license plate. It was registered to Gomez as well."

This was news to me, but I rallied on. "You really think Gomez would use his own car to do something like that? Maybe someone stole it. . . ."

"Or maybe all the evidence is correct, and there's not some crazy conspiracy," Molly said dismissively. "Your standard criminal isn't that smart. They make dumb mistakes all the time. And it appears Gomez has made plenty."

I noticed that even my parents seemed daunted by this last piece of evidence. Or at least, they weren't arguing my side anymore. I made one last attempt to protest, but Molly cut me off. "You've had your say, Teddy. Now it's time to get back to business. Listen to this clip."

She played it. It, too, sounded like someone was making a speech at a rally: "So what if the government has a problem with our methods? We need to fight for the animals!"

It was a deep and gravelly voice. The exact same as the man dressed as the panda.

Molly could tell I recognized it just by watching my face. "That's him, isn't it?"

"I'm pretty sure," I admitted. "Who is it?"

"His name is James Van Amburg. And he's also one of the founders of the NFF."

Molly turned her computer around so I could see the screen. The clip she'd played was a video. It was now paused on the face of James Van Amburg. He was a tall, muscular guy with a bald head and shoulders as wide as a Cape buffalo's horns. He didn't look that mean in the picture, but knowing that he'd threatened my life earlier that day made him seem very scary.

"Yet another piece of concrete evidence against the NFF," Molly said proudly. "And not a piece of paper or a car that could have been stolen, but an actual human being from that organization."

There was a knock at the conference room door.

"We're in the middle of something important," Molly said.

"It's Chief Hoenekker," came the reply. "I have some information about that panda costume."

"Come in," Molly said, and Hoenekker did. He nodded brusquely to my parents and me. It seemed like he was embarrassed to be seen reporting to Molly in front of us.

"That was fast," Molly told him.

"I was already looking into it when I got your text," Hoenekker explained. "I figured it might be a lead. According to Pete Thwacker, no one has been authorized to pose as Li Ping in the park yet. J.J. felt it would be in poor taste to have anyone acting like Li Ping before Li Ping was actually here. So the Li Ping costumes are supposed to still be in storage. Five were ordered. We like to have multiples in case any of them are compromised."

"Compromised?" Molly repeated.

"They get damaged a lot," Hoenekker explained. "The actors fall down and dent the heads. Or a guest spills food on one and stains it. And, apparently, the actors have been known to vomit inside them."

Molly and Agent Chen both made faces of disgust.

"It gets very hot inside them," Mom said. "The heat can make the actors sick."

Molly returned her attention to Hoenekker. "Let me guess: All five suits are no longer accounted for."

Hoenekker turned pink around the ears in embarrassment. "That's correct. At some point after the costumes were delivered, an employee at the storeroom discovered one was missing."

"And you didn't know about this?" Molly asked accusingly.

"This is a very big park, and incidents occur here every day," Hoenekker said defensively. "I can't be informed of every single thing that goes wrong. There wasn't even any proof that the costume was stolen; merely that it was missing. It might have been misplaced. So, it was reported to security, and an officer was dispatched to deal with it . . . but the investigation failed to turn up anything."

"Who was the officer?" Molly asked.

Hoenekker frowned, as though he knew the answer wasn't going to be appreciated by anyone. "Marjorie O'Malley," he said.

SABOTAGE

"What is monkey-wrenching?" I asked.

My parents both looked at me, intrigued.

"Where'd you hear about that?" Dad asked.

"Carlos Gomez went to jail for it," I explained.

We were walking back home through FunJungle. Since the days were getting longer, the park was staying open much later than in the winter. It was five o'clock and the park was still packed with tourists; in fact, more were showing up, mostly locals coming by for the evening. For me, though, it had been a very long day, and my parents and I were all beat.

Two FunJungle security guards followed us. Their names were Marcus and Jethro. They were big, imposing guys, and J.J. had ordered them to keep an eye on me. "Someone's got it in for you," he'd told me. "Maybe they were just trying to scare you off, but I'd rather not take any chances." He had ordered the guards to stay posted around our house all night, on the alert for any sign of trouble.

Normally, I would have expected Mom to protest something like this; she didn't like accepting favors from J.J. But today she hadn't. That meant she thought the extra protection was a good idea, which made me nervous.

"Monkey-wrenching is sabotage for environmental reasons," Mom told me. "Sometimes, when groups have seen no other option to protect wildlife or endangered habitats, they have resorted to it."

"Like what?" I asked.

"It could be anything," Mom said. "Like putting iron spikes in trees so that lumberjacks can't saw them down. Or pouring sugar in the gas tanks of bulldozers. But it got its name from the act of throwing monkey wrenches into heavy machinery. If you destroy someone's construction equipment, then they can't tear down a forest."

"Or you at least delay them from tearing down the forest for a while," Dad put in.

"Do you know what Carlos Gomez got busted for?" I asked.

"He attacked a zoo in Wyoming," Dad answered. "They were holding some wolves there and he set them free. In his defense, it was a small, poorly run zoo and they apparently weren't taking very good care of the animals."

"There is never any defense for sabotage," Mom said coolly, then turned to me. "It's against the law."

"Those wolves would have died if it wasn't for Carlos," Dad told her.

"We don't know that for sure," Mom argued. "And what Carlos did was still a crime. Such behavior might have short-term gains, but it ultimately makes the whole animal rights movement look like a bunch of radicals and troublemakers. Which doesn't do any of us any good."

"It does the animals some good, though," Dad said pointedly.

There was something in their conversation that struck me as odd. "Dad, have *you* ever done any monkey-wrenching?"

"Of course not," he said, but he had a guilty smile. "Like your mother said, it's against the law."

"Looks like the rally's over," Mom said, obviously trying to change the subject.

We were passing Panda Palace. It was much quieter than it had been earlier in the day. The crowds had dispersed. The PandaManiacs had either gone home, or grown tired of moping around the empty exhibit and left to do something more interesting.

"Hoenekker sent some of his guys over here to break the rally up," Dad explained. "Said they were disturbing the peace."

He looked to me. "Is this where you saw James Van Amburg?"

"Yes." I pointed to the entrance of Panda Palace. "The rally was over there, and James was by those trees with some other mascots."

"Boy," Mom said, "Marge is really in hot water for not finding that costume."

"Good," I said, a little more harshly than I intended. "She deserves it."

"Hold on now," Mom cautioned. "I know we've all had our issues with Marge before, but locating that costume wouldn't have been easy."

"Although . . . ," Dad began, but then seemed to reconsider and stopped.

"Although what?" Mom asked.

Dad glanced back toward Marcus and Jethro to see if they were close enough to overhear us. They were giving us our space, though, so he said, "There's always the possibility that Marge didn't even *try* to find the costume."

"You mean, she just didn't bother?" I asked.

"Er . . . no," Dad said. "I mean, maybe she was involved with its disappearance in the first place."

Mom gaped at him. "Jack! You're actually suggesting Marge was connected to the panda-napping?"

"I am."

"There's no way," Mom said. "Marge is way too committed to her job to break the law."

"That's right," I agreed. After all, why would Marge ask me to help her find the panda thief if she was the thief herself?

"Think about it," Dad said. "Marge holds a grudge longer than anyone I've ever met—and I'll bet she has a big one against J.J. And maybe Hoenekker, too. After all, J.J. demoted her from her job running security—and then gave it to Hoenekker."

"So you think she decided to help steal the panda to make them all look bad?" Mom asked doubtfully.

"Or maybe she did it for a cut of the ransom money," Dad suggested. "She was supposed to find the panda costume, but she never did. And she was supposed to guard the actual panda, but somehow, it was stolen on her watch. That's awfully suspicious."

"Yes," Mom owned, "but you're forgetting something important: Marge is completely incompetent. If she was really going to be involved with stealing Li Ping, it never would have worked out this well."

"I'm not saying she was the brains of the operation," Dad insisted. "Only that she might have been involved. Suppose someone from the NFF asked her to help kidnap the panda. Her part isn't very difficult: Don't find whoever stole the panda costume. And pretend not to notice when the kidnappers attack the truck during the drive. Basically, all she had to do was perform poorly at her job, which is what she does here on a regular basis."

I considered arguing that my father was wrong, but I didn't. For starters, I couldn't reveal that Marge was blackmailing me into investigating; my parents would immediately tell J.J., and Marge would release the footage of Summer. But something else held me back: My father had a good point. The whole time I'd known Marge, she'd been awfully vindictive toward me, and all I'd done to deserve it was play a few pranks on her. Meanwhile, J.J. and Hoenekker had cost her a job and greatly embarrassed her. It now occurred to me that there was another reason Marge might have wanted me to snoop around the case: to find out if her sister was onto her. After all, her only plan so far had been for me to infiltrate the FBI mobile unit and see what information they'd learned.

Marge hadn't come to me until *after* her sister had arrived at FunJungle. Perhaps she had thought she was going to get away with the panda-napping, then freaked out when Molly showed up, knowing Molly would do anything to track down the criminal—even if it was her own sister.

Mom had fallen silent herself, giving Dad's theory some consideration. We were nearing the employee exit at the rear of FunJungle. Until recently, our home had been close by, but now the place where our trailer—and the rest of employee housing—had been was the future site of the Wilds. J.J. wasn't even trying to hide the construction: He *wanted* guests to see that rides were being built, so they'd get all excited and return when the new area opened. A wooden wall ran across the path that would serve as the future entrance to the Wilds; it was gaily painted with representations of the rides-to-be, along with holes where you could peek through and watch the construction underway.

Mom glared at the construction site, the way she did every time we passed it.

I said, "If Marge is really involved, do you think Molly would actually arrest her?"

"Molly already *did* arrest her," Mom pointed out. "Today after Marge forced you to sneak into the mobile unit for her."

"That wasn't a real arrest," Dad told us. "I think Molly only cuffed Marge to show she meant business. Hoenekker worked out some deal to get Marge off. She has to keep clear of the investigation—and she's barred from carrying a weapon anymore. Not even a Taser."

"Hoenekker should have done that months ago," Mom put in.

"However, if Marge truly turned out to be involved in a

serious crime like this," Dad went on, "I'm sure Molly would make sure she was prosecuted for it. There doesn't seem to be much affection between those two. And Molly seems very committed to her job."

"But like you said, Marge wouldn't be the brains behind the operation," I said.

"Marge isn't the brains of anything," Dad replied.

"So who is?" I asked. "Do *you* think the NFF is behind the panda-napping?"

Mom and Dad shared a look, as though they were trying to figure out how much to say to me. Then Dad said, "I share the same concerns about the NFF that you do. This doesn't seem like their style. And they're a small, cash-strapped operation. I don't think they have the funds or the skill to hit a truck while it's moving down the highway."

"But James Van Amburg threatened Teddy today," Mom said.

"Teddy didn't actually *see* James," Dad countered. "He only says the voices sounded the same. There are plenty of other people with deep voices like that."

"I don't know," I said. "It was awfully gravelly. . . ."

"Then maybe someone imitated James, wanting you to *think* he was attacking you," Dad said. "Maybe this whole thing was just another part of a frame job for the NFF."

Mom still seemed skeptical. "You think someone actually pretended to be James Van Amburg and threatened Teddy with a gun solely to point the finger at the NFF?"

"Why not?" Dad asked. "It seems to have worked. Notice that they threatened Teddy, not an FBI agent or any adult. He's only a boy—and more susceptible to coercion like that." He glanced at me. "No offense."

"None taken," I said.

Dad continued on. "By his own admission, Teddy wasn't snooping around. So why come after *him*? Unless it was part of a setup."

Mom grew thoughtful once more. So did I. My father's argument made sense, and it made me angry. I had been scared to death by the panda with the gun. To think that it was all simply done to make me a pawn was infuriating.

We passed out of the park through the rear employee exit. Marcus and Jethro dutifully followed us. The employee parking lot sat to our left, heat shimmering off the asphalt, turning all the cars parked there into mirages. A path led through the woods—or at least, what woods remained now that the Wilds was being built—toward employee housing. As we headed into the trees, the noise of FunJungle was replaced by the clamor of the construction site: the rumbling of bulldozers, the clang of hammers, the beeping of trucks backing up.

"So, if it's not the NFF, who *did* steal the panda?" I asked.

"I think you made a pretty good argument for Walter Ogilvy," Dad replied. "And I wouldn't rule out exotic animal traffickers, either. I can guarantee you there are plenty of people willing to pay big bucks for a giant panda."

"And you think these traffickers might have faked the ransom, too?" Mom asked.

"Why not?" Dad replied. "It's definitely thrown the FBI off the track."

"There's also the crazy idea that the FBI is actually right," Mom suggested. "And that this all really *is* a kidnapping by the NFF."

"But if it's not," I pressed, "then the FBI is getting distracted from the *real* criminals. And every minute they're distracted, Li Ping is in more danger!"

Mom held up an open hand, signaling me to calm down. "I think we can trust the FBI to handle this, Teddy. They don't need you getting involved."

"But—" I began.

Mom cut me off. "We've talked enough about Li Ping today, don't you think, Jack?" She gave Dad a meaningful look. I'd seen it before. It meant that if Dad didn't want to end up in the doghouse, he had better not disagree with her.

"Your mother's right," Dad told me. It didn't seem like he was only saying it to humor her. It seemed like he really believed it.

A cloud of mosquitoes suddenly swarmed us, which meant we were almost home.

Our new employee housing was called Lakeside Estates, but the "lake" was really only a muddy sinkhole. After the spring rains, it had filled with water to a depth of six feet and been fun to swim in for two days. Then the water had grown stagnant and started breeding mosquitoes by the ton.

Mosquitoes were a fact of life in much of Texas, though for some reason, they avoided FunJungle. My parents presumed that J.J. was covertly fumigating the place with powerful pesticides—tourists didn't want to be mauled by mosquitoes at a theme park—but J.J. never copped to it. Sometimes it seemed as though every mosquito in the area was being diverted to Lakeside Estates. Each night, they hovered outside an invisible barrier near our home, waiting to attack us and siphon us dry.

We dashed through them, swatting left and right, racing for our trailer.

Except for the sinkhole, Lakeside Estates was prettier than the old employee housing area, but that was mostly because it was hard to imagine a place being *uglier* than the old employee housing area. Back there, a bunch of cheap mobile homes had been scattered randomly in the woods without any thought to appearance or community.

Now J.J. had sprung for nicer trailers for everyone (thanks to a little arm-twisting by my parents), and they had been arranged in two concentric circles around a central patch of dirt. J.J. had promised that, at some point, he would replace the dirt with a swimming pool, but for the time being, he'd sprung for a spindly volleyball net and a game of horseshoes. Mom, Dad, and I were pretty much the only people who ever used any of them—most of the other residents were workaholics with no kids—but we had managed to organize a volleyball tournament twice. (The mammalogists had beaten the herpetologists and ornithologists both times.) There was also a bit of landscaping that was coming into spring bloom. It might have all been a decent place to hang out if it weren't for the mosquitoes.

We slipped through the door of our house, squashing any last bloodsuckers.

Marcus and Jethro posted themselves outside, in the shade of a cedar tree, where they could keep an eye on our house.

I felt kind of bad for them. With the heat and the mosquitoes, standing guard over us wasn't going to be much fun. But I was still relieved they were there.

Of course, it wasn't that nice *inside* our house either. My parents didn't like wasting electricity, so they always turned the air-conditioning off when we left. The trailer was as hot and humid as a sauna.

Mom flipped on the a/c. "I'm making chicken for dinner tonight," she informed us, then told me, "Hit the showers, kid."

"Right now?" I asked.

Dad sniffed the air around me and teasingly wrinkled his nose. "Yes, now. Before that stink makes the paint peel off the walls."

"You should talk," Mom told him. "You're next. Both you guys reek, and that's coming from someone who works with gorillas."

Dad held up his hands in mock surrender. "All right. We get the picture." He grabbed a beer from the fridge and hustled me down the short hall toward my room.

While Mom went to work in the kitchen, I lowered my voice and said, "Dad, be honest. Did you ever do any monkey-wrenching?"

A brief flash of guilt flickered across his face before he thought to correct it. "Why do you ask?"

I realized he hadn't said no. "I just got a feeling."

Dad ushered me into my room and lowered his voice, not wanting Mom to hear him through our paper-thin walls. "On occasion, when I've been on assignment in other countries, I've found that the government wasn't enforcing their wildlife laws as well as they should have. So I took matters into my own hands."

I probably shouldn't have found this impressive, but I did. "Like what?"

"A few years ago, I was in a national park in India where a corporation was building a hotel without a permit. It was right in the middle of critical tiger habitat. So . . . I might have set some of their construction equipment on fire."

I grinned. "And that stopped them from building the hotel?"

"No," Dad replied sadly. "The developer's insurance bought him brand-new equipment. My actions didn't make a difference for the tigers—and I came awfully close to getting thrown in a rural Indian jail, which would have really screwed up my life."

"Was that the only time you ever did anything like that?" I asked.

"The point I'm trying to make is, monkey-wrenching probably causes more problems for the people who do it than the people they're trying to stop. Especially in this country, we can usually trust the law to do the right thing. So don't even think about it. And get cleaned up." Dad ducked out of the room.

I realized that, once again, he hadn't answered my question. And he'd said we could *usually* trust the law.

I peeled off my clothes and headed for the shower, wondering if we could trust the law this time.

Because if the FBI was wrong about the NFF, then Li Ping was in serious trouble.

TRAFFICKERS AND GOAT SUCKERS

"I know who took Li Ping!" Ethan Sokol announced.

He set his lunch tray on our table in the school cafeteria and slid into a seat across from me. Xavier and Summer were already there, along with our friends Violet Grace and Dashiell Alexander. Ethan, Dash, Summer, and Violet were all eighth graders, a year older than me. The boys were two of the best athletes at school, while Violet was the head cheerleader.

Violet excitedly responded to Ethan before I could. "Really? Who took her?"

"The chupacabra!" Ethan replied.

Everyone groaned.

"The Mexican goat sucker?" Xavier asked disdainfully, taking a bite of his sandwich. Now that we were in school, he'd traded his tuxedo for his standard outfit: jeans and a FunJungle T-shirt. "That's an urban myth."

"It is not," Ethan argued, dead serious. He was a smart kid, but he had a weakness for science fiction. Two weeks earlier, he'd claimed he'd heard a werewolf baying near his house one night; it had turned out to be the neighbor's cat in heat. "My grandfather saw one out on his ranch."

"No kidding?" Summer asked. "When?" She said it like she was interested, but I knew she was only leading Ethan on.

"A couple years ago." Ethan dug into his enchiladas, then spoke with his mouth full. "It was sucking all his goats dry. Draining all the blood right out of them. Every couple days, he'd come outside and find one of them all shriveled up, like a goat raisin."

I snickered at this. I couldn't help it. No one else at the table could keep a straight face either, except Summer.

"A goat raisin?" Dash echoed.

"Yeah," Ethan went on. "You know, like all the blood was gone from it, so it was nothing but skin and bones. My grandfather started staying up, sitting on the porch with a shotgun. A couple nights later, he hears this horrible scream from the goat pen, and this insane shriek, so he aims his flashlight that way, and there's a chupacabra, attacking his goats. It took off the moment it saw him, but he fired a few shots at it and scared it off. It never came back again."

"What did it look like?" Summer asked.

"He said it was like part coyote, part lizard. Black as night, except for its eyes, which were blood red."

I was trying so hard to keep from laughing, I couldn't eat my lunch. "And you think one attacked the truck with Li Ping?"

"Absolutely." Ethan jammed half an enchilada into his mouth. "The truck was attacked out in West Texas, right? That's where chupacabras live. And you said the panda disappeared without a trace? Well, chupacabras don't leave anything behind."

"I thought they left goat raisins," Dash teased.

"This isn't funny!" Ethan snapped.

It was, though. Violet was giggling so much that her soda came out her nose.

And yet, Ethan's suggestion wasn't even the most ridiculous one I'd heard that day. Since the moment I'd arrived at middle school, my fellow students had been approaching me with ideas about who had stolen Li Ping. Erin Eanes had accused her uncle, who she said had serious post-traumatic stress disorder after leaving the army and had always wanted a panda. Dina Zywica claimed that space aliens had captured Li Ping for an extraterrestrial zoo. Lane Hagino suggested our PE teacher, Coach Redmond, most likely because Coach Redmond had made Lane run laps after school on Friday and Lane was still annoyed about it. And a dozen kids had accused the Barksdale twins, because the Barksdales were jerks and nobody liked them.

"Chupacabras don't exist," Xavier said. "Trust me. I'm an expert on cryptozoology."

"What's that?" Violet asked.

"The study of mythological animals," Xavier said proudly. "Like dragons and yetis and sasquatches. The chupacabra is a modern-day invention. The entire myth can be traced back to a comedy routine by this guy in Puerto Rico back in the 1990s. . . ."

"That's not true," Ethan protested.

"Then why is there no mention of chupacabras *any-where*—in any newspaper or magazine or news report—until after 1995?" Xavier crammed a handful of Doritos into his mouth. "How had no one ever seen a half coyote, half lizard running around Texas before that?"

"Because they didn't exist before that," Ethan declared. "They were created in a government lab. But something went wrong and they escaped and the government has been trying to cover it up ever since."

Everyone laughed at this, too. Xavier threw up his arms in exasperation. "I can't reason with this guy."

"Fine," Ethan sneered. "Laugh now. But you won't be laughing when chupacabras breed enough and we run out of goats. Then we'll be next. Everyone's so worried about zombies—"

"Actually, I don't think anyone's worried about zombies," Dash interrupted.

"Well, wait till the chupacabras come for us," Ethan finished. "I'll be ready, but you won't. And it'll be your funeral."

"Sadly, Ethan, I can prove that a chupacabra didn't take Li Ping," Summer said, polishing off the last of her lunch. Her family's personal chef had made her yellowtail sashimi with sides of snap bean salad and Mediterranean couscous.

I, on the other hand, had a turkey sandwich and celery sticks. "Summer," I warned. "We're not supposed to reveal anything about the case."

Summer completely ignored me and blurted out, "There was a ransom note left behind."

Violet and Dashiell were thrilled to be let in on this. "No way!" Violet gasped. "The panda was kidnapped?"

"*Panda*-napped," Summer corrected.

Xavier wheeled on me, annoyed. "I texted you last night to ask if there was a ransom note and you said no."

It was one of about two hundred texts he'd sent me, all asking questions about the case that I wasn't allowed to answer. I'd had to feign ignorance in response to each one.

"Because that's not supposed to be public knowledge," I said, fixing Summer with a hard stare.

Summer waved this off, unimpressed. "The FBI only told us that because they're being all territorial."

"The FBI is investigating?" Violet asked, even more intrigued.

"Aha!" Ethan cried. "That *proves* the chupacabra was involved!"

"Calm down, psycho," Dash teased. "How did some kind of goat-sucking coyote lizard leave a ransom note?"

"It's all part of the government cover-up to hide the fact that chupacabras exist," Ethan said flatly. "First, they plant the note to make it seem like humans stole the panda. Then they send the FBI in to take over the whole investigation so that no one learns the truth."

Xavier collapsed on the lunch table, pretending to be exhausted from this discussion. "Talking to you," he said, "is like trying to reason with a brick."

"Ha ha," Ethan sniffed. "If you're such a genius, then *you* explain how the panda disappeared."

"Maybe the Loch Ness Monster ate it!" Dash suggested.

Everyone laughed except Ethan, who slugged Dash in the shoulder. Then he looked to Xavier again. "C'mon, Einstein. I'm waiting."

"How should I know?" Xavier said. "Ask Teddy. He's the one who's working with the FBI."

"No I'm not," I told them. "The feds don't want me

involved. I'm completely in the dark on this one."

"I'll bet," Xavier said sarcastically. "Summer's dad wouldn't let them do that to you."

"He can't tell the FBI what to do," I pointed out.

Xavier turned to Summer, knowing that she was more likely to tell him the truth about the investigation.

"It's true," she said. "Sorry, but Teddy's off the case. He and I tried to poke around yesterday and got run off. All he's investigating now is why the dolphins have started pantsing people."

Violet snorted soda out her nose again.

Dash burst into laughter. Ethan did too, having already forgotten about being annoyed at the rest of us.

"Pantsing people?" Xavier repeated.

"That's right," Summer replied. "They've been yanking down the bathing suits of people in the tank with them."

"Men or women?" Ethan asked.

"All men so far," Summer said.

Dash seemed disappointed by this. "How many times has it happened?"

"A couple," Summer told him. "Thankfully, it's only happened to one guest, though."

"So who else got pantsed?" asked Ethan. "One of the trainers?"

Summer didn't answer, but her eyes flicked to me,

which was enough answer for everyone else. They all turned my way.

"A dolphin yanked down your bathing suit?" Dash asked me.

By this point, my face had flushed so red, I couldn't possibly deny it. "Yes," I admitted.

Dash and Ethan howled with laughter. Summer joined in as well. Violet tried to contain herself, like it was bad manners to laugh at me, but she couldn't rein it in.

Only Xavier stood up for me. "It's not that funny," he said.

"Actually, it was," Summer corrected.

"What happened?" Dash asked Summer. "Give us all the gory details. How many other people were around?"

I winced, hoping Summer wouldn't tell the whole embarrassing story. To my relief, she noticed my discomfort and altered the facts. "No one else was there," she said. "Only me, and I didn't really see it. It was before the park opened. The dolphin pulled down Teddy's suit, and Teddy pulled it right back up again before I even knew what was going on."

Either the others didn't believe this, or they didn't *want* to believe it. "That's it?" Ethan asked. "That's the whole story?"

"That's the whole story," I repeated. "And then another dolphin did it to a guest yesterday."

"Now, *that* was funny," Summer said, trying to get the

story off me. "A dolphin pulled the guy's suit down and he freaked. He hit the dolphin, and then the dolphin bit him on the butt."

The guys all laughed at this, though Violet looked concerned. "Was the dolphin hurt?"

"I don't think so," I said. "And the guy wasn't either. But his family was really upset. So one of the trainers asked me to help figure out who taught the dolphins to yank down people's suits in the first place."

"They don't think the dolphins could have just figured out how to do it on their own?" Violet asked.

"They're pretty sure someone got into the tank and taught them how to do it," I said.

"And they asked you to look into it?" Xavier said. "Instead of Li Ping's disappearance? 'Cause it seems like Li Ping is a lot more important than dolphins stealing a few bathing suits."

"She is," I agreed. "But the FBI doesn't want my help."

"So who do they suspect?" Xavier asked.

"I don't know," I lied, then gave Summer a glance. I hoped she'd follow my lead and not spill the beans about what we'd learned from the FBI. I was quite sure the FBI wouldn't appreciate our doing that.

Summer got the message. "They won't share anything with us."

"Whatever," Dash said. "Who stole her?"

"Animal traffickers," Xavier told him. "People who bring exotic species into this country to sell as pets."

Ethan snickered at this. "And you thought my chupacabra idea was stupid?"

"Animal trafficking is a huge business," Xavier said defensively. "Like, billions of dollars a year, easy."

"But not in *this* country," Dash said. "That happens other places, right?"

"No, it happens right here," Xavier said gravely. "All the time. I know people like to point the finger at China and other countries, but according to the World Wildlife Fund, Americans buy just as many illegal animal species as China every year. Maybe even more."

"What kind of animals?" Violet asked.

Xavier grinned at her, seeming pleased to have her attention. "All kinds. Mostly, it's smaller things like birds, monkeys, and reptiles, but they even move bigger animals. Not long ago, I heard US customs busted someone trying to sneak a drugged tiger cub into the country inside a suitcase."

"Ugh," Summer groaned. "What kind of sick jerk would do something like that?"

"It's even worse for the smaller animals," I said. "Sadly, traffickers usually aren't very careful with them. They just go out into the wild and steal them, and for every one that gets to a buyer safe, a bunch die in transit."

Violet gasped. "That's horrible!"

"I know," Xavier agreed. "But the people who buy these exotic animals don't care. There wouldn't be a trafficking business at all if people weren't willing to pay thousands of dollars for something that ought to be in a zoo or the wild instead."

"And you think these people actually stole a panda from a moving truck?" Ethan asked doubtfully.

"You think a *chupacabra* stole a panda from a moving truck!" Xavier retorted.

"Chupacabras are far faster and more powerful than any-one realizes," Ethan told him. "The government bred them to be living weapons. Only, they turned on their creators."

Xavier rolled his eyes, then returned his attention to the rest of us. "A panda is probably the gold standard of exotic pets. There are less than three thousand of them on Earth, and no matter how much money you have, there's no way to get one legally. The Chinese government won't let it happen. So they're probably worth hundreds of thousands of dollars on the black market. If not millions. Li Ping was already inside our country. It was a once-in-a-lifetime opportunity for the traffickers to snatch her. If they had a buyer willing to pay serious cash for Li Ping, it would have been worth the risk."

Summer sat upright, remembering something. "Teddy! Isn't there some rich lady who lives up by Waco with a whole zoo full of exotic animals? Dora Peacock?"

"Flora Hancock," I corrected. "I actually met her at Fun-Jungle yesterday."

"What?" Summer said accusingly. "Why didn't you tell me that?"

"It didn't seem that important," I replied. "And a lot of other stuff was going on." I gave her a pointed look. Summer was aware I'd been threatened by James Van Amburg, but that was also information that the FBI didn't want us sharing with the public.

"Right," Summer said, backing down. "So what happened with her?"

"Not much. I was watching that crazy rally outside Panda Palace with one of the keepers, and she came over to us. She'd come to FunJungle to see Li Ping and wanted to know if we could tell her anything about the crime."

"Do you think she might have been connected to it?" Violet asked excitedly.

"If she had stolen the panda, why would she then come all the way to FunJungle to see it?" Dash asked condescendingly.

"To make everyone *think* she hadn't stolen the panda," Violet replied sharply, annoyed by Dash's tone.

"I don't think she was involved," I said. "I think Dash

is right. She seemed genuinely upset that Li Ping wasn't there . . ."

"She could just be a good actress," Summer pointed out.

"And from what I know about her, she's bought all her animals legally," I continued. "I don't think she deals in the black market."

"How can you be so sure?" Xavier asked. "For all we know, she could be the animal trafficking queen of Texas."

"There are plenty of other people who own exotic animals," I said. "I've heard that there are more than four thousand pet tigers in Texas *alone*. That's more than there are left in the wild. Anyone who owns a tiger might have wanted a panda, too."

"Why would someone like that even have to bring traffickers into it?" Dash asked. "If they wanted a panda badly enough, and they had the cash to get one, couldn't they just put together a team to steal it themselves?"

Everyone considered that, then conceded Dash had a point. "I don't see why not," Summer said.

Dash pressed on. "So imagine one of these collectors is already a criminal. Like a drug lord or something. There was this guy named Pablo Escobar down in Colombia who had a private zoo. With zebras and hippos and everything."

"Oh yeah!" Xavier chimed in. "I heard about him! After the feds raided his compound and captured him, most of the animals escaped into the rain forest. A lot of them got eaten, but the hippos are still running wild down there."

"Yeah, right." Ethan laughed.

"It's true," I told him. "My dad went down there to take photos of them for *National Geographic* a few years back."

"No way." Ethan stared at me, jaw agape. "That's insane." It seemed odd that he was having a harder time believing this than the idea of a covert government-designed coyote lizard that was sucking goats dry all over Texas.

"Well, what if there's some new guy like Pablo Escobar?" Dash asked. "And he wants a panda. Maybe it's one of these new big-time drug dealers down in Mexico. They all have their own private armies. It's probably not too hard to move a panda over the Rio Grande without getting noticed. Drugs and guns get moved across it all the time. So this drug dealer sends a team of his guys to West Texas, and they hit the truck and run the panda south of the border."

"But what about the ransom notes?" Violet asked.

"A diversion," Dash declared. "To throw the FBI off."

Everyone seemed to buy that as well. It all made a surprising amount of sense to me. I hadn't thought about a major criminal wanting to steal the panda for himself, rather than hiring a middleman to do the job, but it seemed completely plausible. Far more plausible than the Nature Freedom Force ransoming the panda.

Only, the FBI had made it clear that they had no interest in hearing from me.

On the other hand, they might listen to J.J. McCracken, who would always listen to his daughter. I turned to Summer. "Could you . . ."

"Tell Daddy about this?" she finished, holding up her phone. "Already on it." She set about texting him.

"You should tell him about the chupacabra, too," Ethan suggested.

Dash and Violet both pelted him with crumpled napkins.

The bell rang, signaling the end of lunch. The entire cafeteria echoed with a collective groan as all the students realized it was time to return to class. Everyone at our table stood slowly, milking our remaining free time for as long as we could.

I grabbed the trash from my sack lunch and looked to Summer, who was still texting her father. "Want me to toss your stuff too?"

"My hero," she teased, but she flashed a smile that said she really did appreciate it.

Xavier looked to Violet. "I'd be happy to take your trash."

"Aw, thanks," she said, sliding it over to him.

Xavier beamed as though a princess had knighted him, which confirmed my suspicions that he had a huge crush on her. This wasn't exactly incredible detective work, though.

Most boys in my class had a huge crush on Violet. Xavier eagerly grabbed her garbage and headed to the closest trash can with me.

"You really don't know *anything* else about the Li Ping case?" he asked me.

"I don't," I lied. "The FBI doesn't want me involved."

In truth, I would have loved to tell him what was really going on, from my infiltrating the mobile unit with Summer to being threatened by the man in a panda costume. I hated keeping secrets from friends. But the FBI had warned me to keep my mouth shut, and I knew that if I told Xavier only one thing, he wouldn't be satisfied. He'd hound me until I'd shared everything, and then he'd probably tell Violet, who'd tell someone else, and word would eventually get back to the FBI that I was shooting my mouth off. It was easier to simply pretend that I knew nothing at all, no matter how much Xavier grumped about it.

"I'll bet you know more than you're letting on," he said accusingly. "You always do."

"Not this time," I replied.

Before Xavier could argue this any more, TimJim Barksdale came along. The Barksdale twins were bullies and idiots. A lot of kids joked (behind their backs) that they'd been born with only one brain to share between them—and that it was defective. Since they were always together and no one could tell them apart, we all referred to them as TimJim.

"You're actually throwing food away?" either Tim or Jim taunted Xavier cruelly. "I thought you ate everything you saw, Fatso."

Xavier did his best to ignore them, knowing that any response he gave would only get him in more trouble.

As he went to dump his trash, though, TimJim swatted it out of his hands, scattering it all over the floor.

"Hey!" Xavier shouted before he could think about it.

"What?" Tim or Jim challenged, looming over him. "You got a problem with us?"

"TimJim!" Dash yelled. "Back off!"

TimJim turned, startled, to see Dash and Ethan glaring at them. My friends were much tougher and stronger than they were, and TimJim knew it. They quickly raised their hands, showing they meant no harm. "We weren't causing any trouble," one of them said.

"Pick that trash up," Ethan told them, and they instantly scrambled to do it.

Xavier and I laughed at this.

"Laugh now, while you can," Tim or Jim threatened us. "You won't be smiling next year, when your boyfriends graduate and won't be here to protect you from us."

"Aren't you graduating too?" I pointed out.

"Nope," the other brother said, like it was something to

be proud of. "We flunked. They're holding us back next year. So watch out."

They plunked the trash in the can and then, since Dash and Ethan were still keeping an eye on them, slunk out of the cafeteria.

I felt my stomach sink into my shoes. I'd already been upset about the fact that Dash, Ethan, Violet, and—most importantly—Summer were moving on to high school next year. But I'd at least expected to be free of TimJim as well. The news that the good kids were leaving and the bad kids were staying really rattled me.

Xavier looked shaken as well. Being a short, hefty kid made him a much bigger target for thugs like TimJim than I was—although I'd had my share of run-ins with them.

"Why do they have to be such jerks?" I muttered as we filed out of the cafeteria. "There's just no reason for it."

"Oh, bullying always happens for a reason," Xavier told me.

I turned to him, struck by the thought. "What?"

"Tim and Jim don't feel good about themselves," Xavier explained. "So they try to make themselves feel better by demeaning other people. That's what the research on bullying claims, at least."

"Right," I agreed, although I wasn't really thinking about TimJim anymore. I was thinking about the other person who'd threatened me recently: the man in the panda costume.

I'd been working under the assumption that James Van Amburg—or whoever it might have been—had threatened me to keep me away from the case. But now that I thought about it, that logic was flawed. After all, the FBI was running the investigation, not me. If anything, all the man in the panda costume had done was reveal his presence in the park—and possibly his identity—which was a huge mistake. So why had he come after me?

As Xavier had said, bullying always happened for a reason.

The man hadn't threatened me until after he'd seen me talking to Chloé Dolkart outside Panda Palace. He'd even expressed concern about it, asking why I was snooping around.

Which indicated he was worried I'd learned something important from Chloé.

Was Chloé involved with the crime, then? Or did she simply have some crucial knowledge about pandas that James Van Amburg didn't want me to know? If she did, Molly O'Malley hadn't shown much interest in talking to her.

"What's wrong?" Xavier asked.

I snapped out of my thoughts and realized he was still beside me, weaving through the crowded halls on our way to class.

"What do you mean?" I asked, trying my best to sound normal.

"You've been on a whole different planet for the last minute," Xavier informed me. "You walked right past your locker. Don't you need books for your next class?"

"Shoot. I do." I spun around and headed back the way I'd come.

Xavier followed me. "You've had an idea about the case, haven't you?" he asked. "I know that look. You get it when you're putting things together."

"I wasn't thinking about the case," I told him, but it was a lie.

Someone had to talk to Chloé Dolkart, and they had to do it fast.

16

PANDA PALACE

My original plan was to convince someone else to talk to Chloé, rather than me. After all, the last time I'd talked to Chloé, I'd been assaulted by a panda with a gun.

Unfortunately, I couldn't find anyone from the FBI to do the job. By the time the school bus dropped me off at FunJungle, the feds had cleared out. The panda truck was still roped off as a crime scene, but there was no one around it and the mobile crime unit was gone. If Molly O'Malley or any other agent was still up in the administration building, I had no way of finding out. I couldn't pass through security without an appointment, and no one was going to schedule one for me.

If Summer had been there, she could have gotten me up. Maybe she could have even encouraged her father to pressure the FBI to talk to Chloé. But Summer had a horseback-riding lesson scheduled after school, and her mother refused to let her skip it. Summer swore she would come by FunJungle as quickly as possible after her lesson, but I was on my own until then.

I briefly considered going to Hoenekker, but I was sure that would be a waste of time. After all, the FBI had dismissed *him* from their investigation, and he'd never been a big fan of having to work with me; he'd only done it because J.J. had ordered him to. If I asked him to talk to Chloé for me, he'd probably tell me to stick to my own business.

So I went myself. Yes, it was a little reckless, but it seemed far less dangerous than many things I'd done while investigating before. I was merely heading to an empty exhibit to talk to a keeper, not swimming in the hippo tank or climbing onto the roof of World of Reptiles.

Even so, I was cautious about it, keeping alert for anyone else suspicious as I headed over. My guess was that James Van Amburg—or whoever had threatened me—wouldn't be lurking around Panda Palace in a Li Ping costume anymore. But there was a good chance he, or someone else who worked for the bad guys, was still keeping an eye on the place. I yanked a baseball cap down over my eyes and fell in with large groups of people so I wouldn't look like I was a kid on my own.

There were no crowds around Panda Palace. Everyone seemed to be avoiding the place, like it had bad karma.

I slipped inside the exhibit. The interior continued the Chinese theme of the exterior, centered around some large bamboo gardens where Li Ping—and eventually the male panda—would be on display. It was beautiful, but without tourists or pandas, it was also echoey and sad, like an abandoned house.

Chloé Dolkart was sitting inside the exhibit, in one of the gardens, reading a book. She had propped a folding chair by a little man-made creek and was sitting in the shade of a Chinese elm tree. It looked like a really lovely place to read, although I was quite sure she wasn't supposed to be sitting there at all, much less reading on company time. But then, she didn't have an actual panda to take care of.

There was a large sheet of glass between me and Chloé. Despite the multiple DO NOT KNOCK ON GLASS signs, I knocked on the glass.

Startled, Chloé promptly toppled out of her chair and dropped her book in the creek.

When she saw it was only me, she relaxed, then grabbed the book out of the water and pointed toward an employee access door to the right of the glass. I went over there and waited. The door, like every other employee access door at FunJungle, had a coded entry system with an electronic keypad.

After a few seconds, Chloé opened it from the other side, glanced around to see if I was alone, then ushered me inside. "Cripes, Teddy. You nearly gave me a heart attack."

"Sorry. I was only trying to get your attention."

Chloé led me down a concrete hallway with windows that looked out onto the exhibit, trying to shake the water off her book the whole way. "I know I'm not supposed to be in the exhibit like that," she said guiltily. "But I'm required to stay here while I'm on duty, and it's a lot nicer out there than it is in here."

She led me into her office. I could immediately see her point. The room was large, but dark and cramped, as it seemed to be designed more for storing panda supplies than getting any work done. Save for a small desk, the room was mostly shelves. They were filled with plastic toys for Li Ping, as well as lots of canisters of food and sheaves of bamboo that were turning brown, now that there was no panda to feed it to.

On the plus side, though, the room smelled fantastic. Much better than any other office at FunJungle, most of which reeked of musk and animal pee.

I sniffed the air. "Is that cinnamon?"

"Yup." Chloé pointed to a shelf where several restaurant-size tubs of it were lined up. "Li Ping loves it. Turns out, different pandas are into different smells. Some like honeysuckle, some like wintergreen oil. There's one in San Diego who's into rubbing alcohol. The idea is, once Li Ping gets here, whenever we want to lure her out on display for the tourists, we can just sprinkle some cinnamon around the exhibit and she'll run right out."

The mention of cinnamon jogged my memory a bit. I couldn't quite remember the whole conversation I'd had with Chloé the day before, but it seemed to me that she'd said something about food that was important. "So pandas eat stuff besides bamboo?" I asked.

Chloé answered my question with a question. "Is this about Li Ping?"

"Kind of."

"Did you ever tell the FBI to talk to me?"

The question instantly confirmed that Molly hadn't bothered to send anyone by. I felt a flash of annoyance. Before I could really think about what I was doing, I lied and said, "Yes. And they sent me."

"Instead of an agent?"

"They're really busy . . . and they figured I knew you anyhow. . . ."

"And you've solved all those other crimes here," Chloé added, coming around to the idea. "Plus, I'll bet you know more about animals than any of them do."

"Right," I said. "So . . . about the food?"

"Oh. Right!" Chloé beamed, excited to be a part of the investigation. "In the wild, pandas eat *mostly* bamboo. It's about ninety-nine percent of their diet. But they occasionally also eat things like small rodents or musk deer fawns."

"Whoa," I said. "Pandas eat meat?"

"Well, they're *bears*. Although here, we weren't really planning on feeding them meat. Most zoos don't. But we did intend to supplement their bamboo with other things." Chloé pointed to more large canisters on the shelves. "Sugar cane, rice, high-fiber biscuits. Plus some more perishable stuff like yams and apples."

"Can pandas get by without any bamboo at all, then?"

"I suppose they could, but behaviorally, that probably wouldn't be the best idea. The concept behind all panda conservation is to eventually release pandas back into the wild. Probably not Li Ping herself, but maybe her offspring. So the pandas need to know how to forage in their natural habitat, and that means learning to eat bamboo. Lots of it. Most of a panda's waking life is spent eating. In the wild, they'll spend about sixteen hours a day doing it. In captivity, we try to simulate that."

"And I guess their digestive tracts are designed for bamboo too?" I asked.

"Actually," Chloé replied, "they're not."

"Really?"

"Really. Like I said, the panda is a bear, so it has the digestive tract of a carnivore. Meanwhile, bamboo is a grass."

"It is?"

"The fastest-growing grass on earth. Some varieties can grow a few inches a day. Now, grass is hard enough to digest when an animal is designed for it, like a cow. They have really long digestive tracts with four stomachs to handle the job. And they regurgitate their cud to chew it repeatedly. But a panda doesn't have anything like that. Its digestive tract is short, like ours. So it barely gets any nutrients at all from the bamboo. That's why they have to eat so much of it."

Our conversation from the day before came back to me. "Right. Yesterday you said they have to eat twenty-five pounds a day."

"*More* than twenty-five," Chloé corrected. "A big male can eat up to forty pounds of bamboo a day. But the average is around thirty."

Something clicked in my mind. I suddenly realized what the important thing I needed to know about pandas was. "So if they eat that much bamboo and they can't digest it well, how much do they go to the bathroom?"

"Constantly," Chloé said. "They'll poop forty times a day. Food goes straight through them. Feed one an apple, and it'll be out the other end in fifteen minutes. The bamboo takes a bit longer, though. It's not unusual for them to produce fifty pounds of poop in a day."

"But that's even more weight than they take in," I pointed out.

"Exactly. The water they drink combines with the food in their digestive tracts. It comes out in these big old nuggets about the size and shape of an avocado."

"Holy cow."

"You mean holy something else," Chloé said. "Everyone else at FunJungle thinks this is going to be a big glamour job. Like, I'm just going to sit here and pet the pandas all day. But they're a lot of work. They're tough to feed, they're nearly impossible to breed, and man, that's a lot of poop to clean up every day."

It's still a lot less than the elephants, I thought. But I didn't say it. As it was, my mind was racing with other ideas. I'd found out what I needed to know from Chloé. And it changed everything about the investigation. I needed to get in touch with the FBI right away.

"Well, thanks for your time," I said, edging toward the door.

Unfortunately, Chloé seemed desperate to talk. She'd been forgotten in all the chaos about the panda. A large part of her job was supposed to be talking to guests about the pandas, but she hadn't had a chance to do it yet. So I was her test audience. "Want to know something else amazing about pandas?" she asked. "Their jaw muscles are massive! It comes from all that bamboo chewing. That's why their faces look so round. Which is part of the reason they look so cute to us. Human baby faces are round too."

"Fascinating," I said. "Sorry, but I really have to go. . . ."

"Or did you know that a panda is only the size of a stick of butter when it's born? And it only weighs three to five ounces. That's 1/900th the weight of its mother."

Normally, I would have loved to hear more panda facts, but time was of the essence and I was desperate. I pulled out my phone, pretending a text had come in, and faked reading it. "Oh man!" I gasped. "This is from the FBI! I have to report back to them right away!"

"Ooh!" Chloé exclaimed. "Has there been a break in the case?"

"I think so. Thanks for all your help!"

"Happy to give it. And if you want to come back to hear some more, feel free. I'm here all day. By myself. With nothing else to do." She looked so sad, I almost stuck around for a few additional panda facts. But I couldn't. Because if I was right about what I was thinking, then the FBI was making a huge mistake in their investigation.

"I'll come back soon," I told her, then ducked out of the office, wound my way back through Panda Palace, and hurried across FunJungle.

As I did, I quickly dialed Summer on my phone.

She picked up on the second ring. "Hey. What's up?"

"I learned something important about the panda case. I need to talk to the FBI right away."

"It might be too late for that. They're arresting Carlos Gomez right now."

"What?"

"It's all over the news. Where have you been?"

"Investigating! And the FBI is wrong! I don't think the NFF had anything to do with this!"

Summer said something else, but I couldn't make it out. I was crossing the dead zone for cell service at FunJungle.

"Hold on, I can't hear you," I said.

There was a lot of static on the line, and then I caught a faint bit of Summer's voice. "I can barely hear you either. You're . . ."

I stopped and backed up a few feet, where the reception had been merely lousy, rather than horrible. "Summer? Hello?"

". . . getting to FunJungle right now . . ." she said. "Meet . . . Polar Pavi . . ."

"Meet you at Polar Pavilion?" I repeated.

There was something that sounded vaguely like "yes" followed by one last snippet of conversation: ". . . too hot outside . . ." After that, the call dropped.

I took off for Polar Pavilion.

Summer was right; it was way too hot outside. Even hotter than the day before. I hadn't run far before I'd sweated right through my shirt.

I was almost at Polar Pavilion when I heard someone shout my name. "Teddy!" There was a screech of tires to my left, followed by the scream of some tourists and a thump.

I turned to see Marge O'Malley at the wheel of her golf cart. She was back on the job—and causing trouble as usual. She appeared to have slammed into a tourist and knocked the poor fellow into the landscaping. His pale legs waved in the air while the rest of him was buried headfirst in a shrubbery.

"Why don't you watch where you're going?" Marge snapped at him, then returned her attention to me. "Teddy! Wait right there! I need to talk to you!"

I kept on running. The last thing I needed at the moment was Marge trying to horn in on my investigation. She wouldn't be any help at all—and she was probably the only person at FunJungle who Molly O'Malley wanted to hear from less than me.

Luckily, Marge couldn't follow me right away. She still had to help the tourist she'd bowled over. So she kept bellowing at me, as though that might work. "Teddy! Teddy!!! Teddddddddyyyyyyyy!!!!"

I pretended like I didn't hear her, which Marge must have known was an act. She was so loud, people in the parking lot had probably heard her. The next time she saw me, she'd definitely be angry with me, but at the moment, that was a relatively minor problem.

I shoved through the doors into the Polar Pavilion. The Arctic air hit me like a slap in the face. Now that I was so sweaty, it was actually a bit *too* cold in the exhibit. It felt as though all the water on my body had instantly turned to ice, much of it in very uncomfortable places, like my armpits and my underwear.

I glanced around for Summer but didn't see her. It was feeding time for the penguins, so almost all the guests were crowded around that tank, rather than the polar bears. In fact, the polar bear viewing was about as empty as I'd ever seen it. The bears themselves weren't putting on much of a show. They were merely lying on the ice, half-asleep. So even the few tourists in the area were migrating toward the penguins.

If Summer wanted to meet me, I figured she wouldn't be in the crowds; she'd be out where I could see her. Only, given that I hadn't heard much of her call, I had no idea what she even thought her ETA at Polar Pavilion would be.

I fished my phone out to see if she'd texted me more information.

As I did, I suddenly became aware of one other person in the pavilion. Someone was coming up behind me very quickly. The thud of his feet on the floor gave me the uneasy sense of trouble approaching.

I spun around to face him.

Or, at least, I tried.

Before I could, whoever it was grabbed me from behind and hoisted me into the air.

Then he threw me over the railing into the polar bear exhibit.

POLAR BEARS

Even though I was only in the air for a second, if that, it felt as though time was stretched out. Each fraction of that second seemed considerably longer, as so much was happening at once.

As I flew through the air, I torqued my body around, grasping for my attacker, figuring that my only recourse was to grab on to him and thus, keep from going over the rail. I didn't spin quickly enough, though. He'd moved too fast and was much stronger than I was, flinging me surprisingly far out over the water. I didn't have a chance to grab him—although I did catch a glimpse of his face.

James Van Amburg.

Even though this glimpse was incredibly brief, I still recognized the big, burly body and bald head from the photo

Molly had shown me. The look on his face was eerily stoic, given what he'd just done to me. He showed the same amount of emotion most people showed for a fly they'd swatted.

No one else in the exhibit seemed to have noticed me. James had chosen the perfect time to attack. Everyone else was watching the penguins.

The polar bears noticed me, however. I heard both of them huff with what might have been excitement or hunger.

I tried to yell for help.

By then it was too late. Before I could make a sound, I hit the water.

It was freezing. The shock of it instantly made my muscles seize and my lungs collapse, catching any noise I was about to make in my throat.

I quickly sank below the surface. James had thrown me so hard that I plunged several feet down before stopping. I got a mouthful of water, which tasted disgustingly of salt and raw fish and chilled my insides as well.

The moat was painted black so that the polar bears would stand out when viewed from above. Inside, it was dark as a cave, with only weak blue light filtering down through the ice chunks floating on the surface. The cold surrounded me and crushed me. It was like when you get a brain freeze from eating ice cream, only throughout your entire body.

The cold clouded my brain, too. I knew there were polar

bears in the exhibit with me. And I knew that, if the bears didn't get me, the icy water could make me hypothermic and kill me as well. I had to move quickly if I wanted to live. But I couldn't get my limbs to start moving the right way. I struggled to orient myself and paddle upward.

I hadn't had the time to take a good breath before being thrown into the water. My muscles and my brain were screaming for oxygen as I fought my way upward. The darkness of the moat seemed to close in.

And then, miraculously, I burst through the surface. I clonked my head on a chunk of ice and sucked in air, thrilled that I was somehow still alive.

For a few more seconds, at least.

There was a loud grunt from behind me. I swiveled around to discover that one of the polar bears had dove into the moat and was coming for me. A huge blur of white sliced through the water.

"Help!" I yelled, as loud as I could, then swam like heck.

A few months before, during a different investigation, I had ended up in the shark tank. And while that had been scary, I had known that sharks generally don't attack humans. Especially sharks in zoos, which are well fed and content.

Polar bears were something else entirely.

Polar bears in the wild occasionally stalked humans. And they had been known to maul people who'd ended up in their zoo exhibits. I was significantly smaller than the bears, and the smells that FunJungle pumped into the exhibit kept them stimulated and ready to hunt; to them, I was potential prey. Even if they weren't hungry, they were still territorial, and I had invaded their space.

I had found myself in some dangerous situations before, but I'd never felt that I was actively being hunted before. It was the most terrifying thing I'd ever experienced.

I swam away as fast as I could, but weighed down by my wet clothes and shoes, I was no match for the bear. It quickly bore down on me.

I reached the wall of the moat where I'd been flung over the railing, but there was no way to climb out. The surface was slick, and safety was seven feet above my head.

There was a terrifying growl behind me. The polar bear lifted its head from the water and came in for the kill, so close I could smell the stink of its breath from its gaping mouth.

Right before it reached me, something landed on it.

It was big and it dropped right onto the bear's head, making an enormous splash like a depth charge detonating. I was doused with water once again. The salt stung my eyes and clouded my vision, so I couldn't quite see what was going on in front of me. I could only make out blurry shapes. The big white one, which I figured was the polar bear, had been driven underwater by a big tan one.

I wiped my eyes with my hands, and my vision cleared. What I saw was so astonishing, I thought maybe I still wasn't seeing things quite right.

Marge O'Malley was in the tank with me.

Jumping in like she'd done had been insane, but she seemed amazingly serene in the face of death. "Hold on, Teddy," she told me. "I'll get you out of here."

The bear recovered quickly, resurfacing beside us with a roar. It raised a paw the size of a baseball mitt out of the water, claws extended, intending to swat Marge's head right off her neck.

Marge calmly sprayed it in the eyes with pepper spray.

Now that she'd been barred from using guns or Tasers, it was the only weapon she was still allowed to carry. It caught the bear completely by surprise. It yelped in pain, then reeled away from us and thrashed in the water as its eyes burned.

"Ha!" Marge laughed triumphantly. "Not so tough now, are you?"

Unfortunately, there was still one more polar bear in the exhibit. The second one, which was even bigger than the first, had now joined the hunt. It stalked toward the edge of its ice floe, growling ominously.

"How much more spray do you have?" I asked.

"Uh, that's it," Marge said, not so confident anymore.

"Teddy!" a voice above me yelled. My favorite voice in the entire world. Summer. "Catch!"

An emergency life ring plunked into the water next to me, attached to a rope that snaked up over the railing. I quickly wrapped it around my torso.

Maybe I should have offered Marge the chance to go first. After all, she'd saved my life. And it would have been the chivalrous thing to do.

But I was well past chivalry. I was cold and wet and scared—and I was relatively sure that Summer couldn't pull Marge out by herself. Which meant neither of us would get out alive.

The rope went taut as Summer hauled on the other end.

My adrenaline was kicking in with a vengeance. Even though the wall was slick and wet, I somehow managed to find hand- and footholds on it. I couldn't have scrambled out on my own, but it was enough to give Summer a bit of help as she struggled to reel me in. In only a few seconds, I was up the wall, over the railing, and back to safety.

Marge was still in serious trouble, though.

I shrugged off the safety ring so we could use it again. There wasn't even time for a hug from Summer. She took the ring from me and threw it back into the water.

"Marge, grab on!" she yelled.

In the exhibit, the second polar bear leaped from the ice floe, belly flopping into the water.

Marge clung to the ring. She didn't even bother to try putting it over her torso; there was no way it was going to fit around her body. It would have been like trying to get a Life Savers candy around a potato. The best she could do was stick an arm through it and cling on tight.

Summer and I hauled as hard as we could on the rope, but it was no use. We couldn't budge Marge an inch.

Luckily, help was on the way. People were racing over from the penguin tank. I realized, to my astonishment, that I had barely been in the polar bear exhibit any time at all. Though it felt as if I had first cried for help hours earlier, it had only been a minute, if that. The tourists were coming to the rescue.

Behind them, I caught a glimpse of James Van Amburg, his bald head gleaming in the blue light of the penguin tank. Now that his attempt to kill me had failed, he was fleeing the scene.

He was heading the opposite direction of the crowd, shoving people aside left and right.

"Stop that man!" I yelled. "He's the one who threw me in!"

It only came out as a hoarse croak, though. My throat was fried from yelling and swallowing salt water. Most people either didn't hear me, or they didn't believe me, or they knew there was something much more important at stake: saving Marge. Only one person made an attempt to stop James, but the big bald man swatted him aside like a mosquito.

Everyone else grabbed the rope and yanked on it as hard as they could, straining to haul in Marge. I did too. In my wet clothes, I was freezing, but I couldn't just sit by while Marge was in trouble. Not after what she'd done for me.

In the exhibit, the first polar bear was still wailing in pain from the pepper spray. The second one had almost reached Marge.

Marge aimed her pepper spray canister at it and hoped for the best. But only a tiny trickle came out. So she threw the spray bottle at the bear, clonking it on the head.

This didn't repel the bear at all. Instead, it got angrier.

There were now over a dozen people on the rope, though. With a mighty heave, we hoisted Marge out of the water. Or, at least, part of the way out of it. In addition to her usual bulk, her uniform was soaked, increasing her considerable weight. Water cascaded out of every pocket and crease. All of us working together only managed to pull her up a few feet.

Which meant her legs were still dangling in the water. The bear lunged for her. Marge swung her feet away, but the bear snagged the leg of her pants with the claws of one paw and pulled down.

Now we were in a tug-of-war, us versus a polar bear, with

Marge serving as the rope. She clung to the life preserver as tightly as she could, but she was slipping.

So she dealt with the bear the only way she knew how: She got angry at it.

"Let go of me, you stupid bear!" she yelled, kicking at it with her other foot. "Back off, or I'll make a rug out of you!"

The bear was putting up a heck of a fight. All of us on the rope were yanked toward the railing as the bear struggled to drag Marge down. The rope started to slide through our hands, burning our palms.

The second bear shook off the pain in its eyes and rejoined the action, swimming back toward Marge.

More people scrambled to help, grabbing what was left of the rope and clinging on tight.

As the second bear bore down on her, Marge managed to finally land a good kick on the first. She drove her foot right into its nose.

The bear reared back and sneezed, losing its grip on Marge's pants.

All of us on the rope suddenly found ourselves in a tug-of-war with no one on the other end. We sailed backward, crashing to the floor, while Marge rocketed up and slammed into the railing.

"Ouch!" she yelped, then turned her anger on the people

who had just saved her life. "Watch what you're doing, you idiots!"

For a moment, it appeared that everyone was considering letting her drop back into the polar bear exhibit.

But we didn't. Instead, we held on tight while Marge clambered over the railing to safety.

In the exhibit, the polar bears gave up the hunt and calmly swam back to their island, as though this sort of thing happened every day.

Now Summer finally had the opportunity to rush to my side. She threw her arms around me and asked, "Are you all right?"

"Yes," I said. "Thanks to you—and Marge."

It seemed like I should be exhausted after the ordeal, but it hadn't taken all that long, and my body was humming with adrenaline.

Marge appeared to be having the same experience. She didn't collapse with exhaustion—or bother to thank anyone for their help. Instead, she looked around the room, then frowned and asked me, "Teddy, where's the jerk who threw you in there?"

Much of the crowd gasped, stunned to hear someone had done this on purpose.

"It was James Van Amburg," I said, pointing toward the door. "He ran that way."

"How much of a head start does he have?" Marge asked.

"At least a minute," I replied. "We'll never catch him."

"Maybe not on foot," Marge told me. "Luckily, I have a vehicle."

HOT PURSUIT

Marge's golf cart was parked right outside the
Polar Pavilion, next to an overturned trash can that she had
apparently run into while parking it. A disgruntled janitor
was scooping all the scattered trash into a plastic bag.

Marge slid into the driver's seat. Since she took up the
whole thing, Summer and I had to jump into the backseat.
It was probably better that way, though; neither of us wanted
to be pressed up against Marge, who now stank of fish guts
in addition to her usual funk.

Not that I smelled much better myself. Plus, my clothes
were still partially frozen, while my shoes squelched wetly on
my feet.

Normally, I might have left Marge to take up the chase
herself, not wanting to end up in more danger. But Marge

needed the extra eyes to keep a lookout for James Van Amburg in the crowds—and frankly, I wanted to make sure the guy paid the price for pitching me into the polar bear moat.

"There he is!" I shouted, pointing.

In the distance, James Van Amburg was racing through the crowded concourse, heading toward the park exit.

Marge punched the accelerator. The golf cart took off with surprising speed, nearly flattening the janitor, who had to leap out of the way. He dropped the bag of trash he'd collected, and Marge promptly ran right over it, scattering all the garbage once again.

The janitor shouted something at us that the FunJungle Employee Handbook expressly forbade employees to say in front of the guests.

To pursue James, we had to cut directly across Adventure Road, the main route around the park. It was wall-to-wall tourists, but that didn't slow Marge for an instant. She just plowed straight ahead and let everyone else fend for themselves.

Tourists scattered, screaming, as the cart bore down on them. They scrambled onto benches, dove into the landscaping, and shimmied up trees. And Marge yelled at all of them like somehow *they* were at fault. "Watch out!" she bellowed. "This is an emergency! FunJungle Security coming through!"

Luckily, James Van Amburg was easy to keep an eye on.

His big size now worked against him. He stuck out above the crowds, and his bald head shone brightly in the hot sun. Plus, as a big man, he wasn't that fast. We were gaining ground on him, thanks in part to Marge's staunch refusal to go around any obstacles. Instead, she made a beeline for our target, not caring what was in the way.

We clipped two more garbage cans, toppling them and scattering their contents. We plowed through a decorative flower bed, steamrolling the tulips. And we caromed off a popcorn cart, which promptly rolled down a hill, upended over a railing, and tumbled into the camel exhibit. As if there wasn't enough commotion already, every wild bird in the area immediately sensed there was free popcorn around and homed in on it. Clouds of pigeons made a beeline for the camels, along with a few stray seagulls and peacocks. Any unfortunate guests caught in their path were strafed with bird poop.

Through all of this, Summer and I clung on to the golf cart for dear life. Several times, we were almost pitched out of our seats.

In the oppressive heat, my frozen clothes were defrosting quickly, creating rivulets of water that trickled down my body. It occurred to me that there was something I still needed to say to Marge: "Thanks for saving me."

"I was just doing my job," Marge replied gruffly, then yelled at a Japanese family, "Get out of the way, morons!"

The family bolted so quickly, their Li Ping ears fell off. Marge drove right over the souvenirs, crushing them into pulp.

"It was still dangerous," I said, hanging on as we jumped a curb into a topiary garden.

"When you're in security, it's your sworn duty to serve and protect." Marge smashed through the plants, reducing a few topiary warthogs to twigs.

Summer and I shared a concerned look. Marge seemed surprisingly blasé about the whole rescue. Either she was in shock, or despite working at FunJungle, she'd never bothered to learn anything about polar bears. I figured it was probably the latter—but I wasn't quite sure.

We hurtled onward through the garden, guillotining a topiary rhino, then roared back out onto the concourse, leaving a trail of shredded bushes in our wake.

Marge snapped her radio out of her holster and sent out a broadcast. "This is Officer O'Malley. I am in hot pursuit of a suspect in the Li Ping kidnapping, currently heading toward the front gates by way of Hippo River. Requesting backup immediately."

"Marge?" Hoenekker asked over the radio, sounding worried. "Did you say 'hot pursuit'?"

"Yes sir. I have spotted James Van Amburg and am running him down."

"That golf cart is not intended for high-speed chases!" Hoenekker warned. "Especially inside the park!"

"I won't have to chase him much longer if I get my backup," Marge replied. "Now, I need a barricade erected across the front gates with a whole mess of armed guards to prevent the suspect from leaving the property . . . Whoa!"

As the crowds scattered in front of us, a small child had been left behind. Marge veered wildly to avoid him, losing her grip on her radio, which flew from her hand and sailed into a lemur exhibit. "Crud!" Marge exclaimed, then yelled back at the toddler, "You owe me a radio, you lousy rugrat!"

Ahead of us, James Van Amburg raced past Mulumbo Point and disappeared behind the waterfalls of Hippo River.

Over the sound of all the angry tourists screaming at Marge for driving like a maniac, I heard music. Festive dance music. I looked through the trees in the direction of the front gates and saw something very large moving behind them.

"Uh, Marge . . . ," I said.

"Not now!" Marge snapped, swerving through a horde of guests. "I need to concentrate!"

"But Marge . . ."

"Shut your trap, Teddy!"

"Marge! There's a parade ahead!"

For the spring, J.J. McCracken had decided to institute a parade at FunJungle every afternoon. "Everyone loves parades," he'd claimed. "Disney World must have seventeen a day." This was a massive exaggeration, but when J.J. wanted something done, it got done.

And so, the FunJungle Friends Dance 'n' Sing Parade was born.

The annual San Antonio Battle of Flowers Parade had recently taken place, and afterward, J.J. had snapped up several used floats for a bargain. They had originally been covered with live flowers, but the Special Events and Entertainment department had swapped those out for plastic ones, then slightly modified the themes to be more relevant to a zoo. (The local Elks Club's "Remember the Alamo" float had become, with a slight bit of modification, "Remember the Armadillo.") Then some attractive girls and guys were hired to wear skimpy clothes and dance on the floats, while all the FunJungle mascots were ordered to abandon their usual posts and join the festivities. The route began near the front gates, where it would draw the most attention, then looped the park on Adventure Road. It wasn't a very impressive parade, but the tourists seemed to appreciate it, and on occasion, FunJungle would spice it up a bit by inviting a local high school marching band to play. (According to J.J., the great thing about high school bands was that you didn't have to pay them; they would happily perform in return for free FunJungle tickets.)

A marching band was playing that day. I heard them

before I saw them. Being a typical bunch of high school musicians, they were butchering whatever song they were performing so that it was completely unrecognizable. But they had drawn a good-size crowd nonetheless. It was probably mostly their families, but since a standard school band had over a hundred kids in it, that was still a lot of parents and siblings.

We zoomed around Hippo River to find our path blocked by a sea of people. They were lined up three deep on both sides of Adventure Road while the parade passed between them.

Ahead of us, James Van Amburg was rudely shoving his way through the crowd. He knocked two little kids on their butts, then ducked between the marching band and the "Hooray for Hippos!" float.

Marge yelped and stomped on the brakes. We skidded wildly, but there wasn't room to stop. Rather than mow down some innocent parade-goers, Marge swerved into the landscaping. Unfortunately, the particular spot she chose had a small hill in it, which was perfectly sloped to form a ramp.

"Bail out!" I yelled to Summer, although she had already realized this was the smart thing to do. Marge didn't. As the cart crashed through the small barrier hedge, Summer and I both leaped off. We landed on the grassy hill and tumbled down it, while Marge and the cart rocketed off the top.

"Look out!!!" Marge howled to the crowd ahead. Thankfully, her voice was loud enough to overwhelm even the marching band. The tourists scrambled out of her path just in time. The cart crashed to earth and skidded into the middle of the parade.

The band's song ended abruptly in a blare of frightened trumpet blasts as the musicians scattered. Marge sluiced through them and slammed into the "Salute to Marsupials" float head-on. The float stopped so abruptly that all the dancers and mascots were thrown off their feet. While most collapsed into a pile on the float itself, the poor actor playing Kazoo the Koala sailed through the air and landed atop the roof of Marge's golf cart with such force that the head came off his costume. Dozens of children shrieked in horror as their favorite koala was decapitated right in front of them. The enormous disembodied head then rolled through the marching band like a bowling ball, knocking over the trombone section like tenpins.

I scrambled to the top of the hill, spitting out grass, to see that James Van Amburg had made it through the parade route and was well on his way to the front gates. Some Fun-Jungle security guards were racing into the entry plaza and probably could have stopped him—but they were too distracted by the chaos Marge had caused. They ran toward us, rather than James, allowing him to slip right past them.

Summer and I both shouted to the guards that they needed to turn around because a major criminal was getting away, but they couldn't hear us over the cacophony of startled guests and screaming children.

Marge did her best to take up the chase, throwing the golf cart into reverse despite the fact that there was a beheaded koala clinging to the roof. I recognized the unfortunate soul as Charlie Connor, an actor who'd had his share of mishaps at FunJungle before. Charlie held on tightly to the roof, white-knuckled in fear, screaming various curses in front of the crowd as Marge raced backward through the madness. Sadly, Marge was even worse at driving in reverse than she was at going forward. She swerved to avoid a toppled saxophonist, slewed off Adventure Road, and smashed through the fence into the flamingo pond. The cart stopped abruptly, axle-deep in flamingo muck, while poor Charlie went flying.

If it hadn't been traumatic enough to see Kazoo lose his head, the children now all got to see him splat into some of the most foul, bird-poop-laden water in the park. The flamingos promptly fled through the hole in the fence, amping up the chaos along the parade route even more. They'd all had their wings clipped, so they couldn't fly away, but that didn't stop them from flapping their limbs wildly in the hopes that they might suddenly take off.

Summer and I raced across the parade route, pursuing

James, but he was already on his way out the gates. He paused and looked back for a moment, flashing us a cruel grin, then slipped out into the parking lot.

Most of the FunJungle security guards who had arrived were tending to the crowd, making sure that no one was hurt—thankfully, no one appeared to be, save for a few scrapes and bruises—although a few were trying to round up renegade flamingos. I spotted Hoenekker as he arrived on the scene. He planted himself in front of Marge's golf cart before she could drive out of the flamingo pond and do any more damage.

I ran over to Hoenekker, intending to alert him about James Van Amburg's escape. "Teddy!" he growled. "I should have known you'd be involved in this!"

"I'm sorry," I said, "but it's an emergency. . . ."

"No emergency is worth causing *this*!" Hoenekker waved to the crowd of angry tourists, upended performers, and escaped flamingos. He was livid, his face as red as a scarlet macaw. "Do you realize how much trouble you've caused here?"

I glanced back toward the front gates, but James Van Amburg had vanished from sight.

I started to make one last plea to go after the man who'd nearly killed me, but before I could, Marge laid on her horn. "Move it, Chief!" she yelled. "I have a criminal to catch!" She stomped on the accelerator, but instead of moving forward, her wheels just spun idly in the pond, showering poor Charlie Connor with more flamingo muck.

Hoenekker didn't budge. Instead, he stared bullets at Marge and replied, "Your days of pursuing criminals here are through, O'Malley. You're fired."

BIG TROUBLE

FunJungle Security hauled Marge, Summer, and
me to J.J. McCracken's office. The three of us ended up seated
before J.J.'s desk, while Hoenekker stood to the side. Marge
and I hadn't even been allowed to change clothes. We were
still damp and had to sit on FunJungle beach towels from the
Emporium so we wouldn't leave wet spots on J.J.'s fancy couch.

An enormous television was tuned to CNN. It was cov-
ering the panda story, a BREAKING NEWS banner across the
screen. The FBI had announced that they'd made an arrest in
the case. There was footage of Molly O'Malley and the other
agents leading a man I recognized as Carlos Edward Gomez
from his home in handcuffs.

The sound on the TV was muted, but even if it had been
on, we probably couldn't have heard it over J.J.'s voice. If

we'd thought Hoenekker was angry, it was nothing compared to how enraged J.J. was.

"Look at that mess!" he roared, pointing down to Fun-Jungle's entry plaza through his office windows. "A trail of destruction from the Polar Pavilion all the way to the front gates! Reckless driving inside a family theme park! Parade floats ruined! Escaped animals! Kazoo the Koala decapitated in front of children! God only knows how many lawsuits we'll end up with!"

"We were in pursuit of a known criminal . . . ," Marge began weakly.

"That's no excuse for destroying my park!" J.J. roared. "There are ways to deal with a criminal that do not involve causing chaos and mayhem on a mass scale! If you needed help, why didn't you alert Hoenekker?"

"I *did* alert Hoenekker," Marge replied sullenly. "But he turned out to be more interested in stopping *me* than the criminal."

J.J. shifted his gaze toward Hoenekker, who stood at military attention. "I mobilized my men immediately," Hoenekker reported. "However, by the time we arrived on the scene, the troubles along the parade route distracted them. They prioritized ensuring the safety of the visitors over apprehending Van Amburg, which unfortunately allowed Van Amburg to escape."

"How'd he even get into the park at all?" J.J. demanded. "Weren't your men warned to keep an eye out for him at the gates?"

"They were," Hoenekker admitted sheepishly. "But—"

"The security force here is completely incompetent," Marge finished. "I would've had him if you hadn't interfered."

"For all we know, you might have destroyed half this park if I hadn't interfered!" Hoenekker raged. He turned to J.J. "I can't have a loose cannon on my force like this any longer. I know you've always respected her determination, but between her colossal failures on the panda case and this, we have to let her go."

J.J. didn't argue. He simply nodded and said, "I understand."

Marge gave a strangled gasp and fixed J.J. with a look of betrayal. "You can't fire me!" she yelled. "Not after all I've done for this park!"

"It's done," J.J. told her. "Go clean out your locker."

For the past year, I had been hoping to hear those words. I had always imagined the day Marge got fired would be one of the happiest of my life. It should have been thrilling to see my biggest antagonist finally get her comeuppance. But now that the moment was here, I was surprised to find I wasn't that happy at all.

Marge was devastated. She seemed like a shell of herself as she slowly rose from the couch. It occurred to me that Marge didn't have much besides this job, and now . . . it was gone. Plus, for all her faults—and there were about ten thousand of them—she *had* risked her life to save me from the polar bears.

Meanwhile, I also needed Marge around a bit longer. With James Van Amburg's attempt on my life and the ensuing chaos, there hadn't been a chance for me to tell anyone my new thoughts on the Li Ping case. I still had some questions that only Marge could answer.

"Wait," I said.

Marge paused on her way out. Everyone turned toward me, surprised I'd spoken up.

"Teddy," J.J. said ominously, "don't start with me."

"I'm not trying to . . . ," I said.

"Why is it," J.J. went on, "that whenever a crisis occurs at this park, you're always there? The shark tank implodes; my daughter's dangling in the air above the crocodile pit; a dead hippo falls out of the sky and sullies a hundred distinguished guests. And no matter what, you're involved."

"Daddy," Summer said sternly. "That's not fair. Teddy wasn't responsible for any of that!"

"Maybe not entirely," J.J. conceded, "but he's not completely without blame either. Some people are simply magnets for trouble. And Teddy, in all my life, I have never met anyone who attracts trouble more than you. I don't know if it's that you're reckless or unlucky, or that you keep getting involved in things you're not supposed to. . . ."

"Last time he got involved in a case, it was because *you* forced him to," Summer said petulantly.

"I'm not saying I haven't had a hand in all this at times," J.J. replied. "Although today's catastrophe had nothing to do with me. And yet . . ." He turned to me. "There you were, smack in the middle of it."

"I was only trying to help find Li Ping," I said.

"Well, this time, no one asked you to," J.J. snapped. "In fact, the FBI specifically ordered you to keep away from this case. And yet, you wouldn't, despite ample proof that they have things under control. In fact, they have already made an arrest in connection with the crime. . . ."

"But they're wrong," I said.

"Oh come now!" J.J. cried. "I know you have a great track record solving crimes, kid. But the feds had a ton of evidence against the NFF."

"It was planted," I told him. I did my best to sound confident, although in truth, I didn't have proof that I was right about my hunch. Not yet, at least.

On the television, Molly O'Malley appeared, making a statement to the press. Marge tensed angrily at the sight of her sister. J.J. flipped the sound on so we could all hear her.

We picked up Molly midsentence. ". . . need to share the credit with my entire team, who worked tirelessly to root out these criminals. I'm aware that Carlos Gomez and the NFF have issued statements professing their innocence, but I can assure you those are lies. I will stake my reputation on proving they are guilty of this heinous crime."

J.J. muted the TV again and turned back to me. "Sure looks to me like the FBI knows what they're doing."

"But they haven't found the panda yet, have they?" I asked.

J.J.'s swagger faded. I'd caught him by surprise. When he spoke again, he didn't sound quite so sure of himself. "Not as far as I know. But you honestly expect me to believe that an entire team of FBI agents is barking up the wrong tree? You were just pursuing James Van Amburg yourselves. Isn't he one of the founders of the NFF?"

"He *was*," I acknowledged. "But I don't think he's working for them anymore. He's working for the bad guys instead."

"Who *are* . . . ?" J.J. demanded.

I grimaced. "I don't know yet."

J.J. gave a short bark of derisive laughter. "Ha! That's all you've got? A hunch?"

Summer rushed to my defense. "Daddy, you know how

smart Teddy is. You've said it yourself a dozen times. So if he thinks something stinks about all this, then something stinks. James Van Amburg just tried to kill him, for Pete's sake! Because he realized Teddy had evidence that proved the NFF wasn't involved."

"And how would he know that?" J.J. asked.

"Because Teddy told me so," Summer declared. "He said it on our phone call."

"I had just left Panda Palace," I explained. "I guess Van Amburg was keeping an eye on me again. He must have overheard me, then followed me to Polar Pavilion and thrown me in with the bears to make sure I didn't tell anyone what I knew."

"J.J.," Hoenekker interrupted, "at this point, it is still conjecture that Van Amburg threw Teddy into the polar bear pit at all. My men are examining the security footage from the Polar Pavilion to confirm if that's what actually occurred."

"To confirm it?" I repeated, annoyed. "Why? You think I might have just jumped in with the polar bears for fun?"

"I think it's possible that you have misconstrued the situation," Hoenekker replied. "There were dozens of people in that exhibit and no one else saw him throw you in. . . ."

"*I* did," Marge said. "I was coming through the doors

when it happened. That's how I knew Teddy was even in the water."

"As we have established, your skills at deduction are questionable," Hoenekker said.

"You know what's not questionable?" Marge snapped. "That you're a pinhead."

She and Hoenekker started shouting at each other, all their rage bubbling out. J.J. had to rush between them. "Both of you, can it!" he roared.

Marge and Hoenekker fell silent but kept glowering at each other.

J.J. looked to me. "All right, Teddy. I'll bite. What evidence did you find that was worth him killing you over?"

"Pandas make fifty pounds of poop a day," I reported.

"Fifty pounds?" J.J. asked. "That can't be healthy. No wonder they're going extinct."

"They don't digest bamboo very well," I explained.

"So?" Hoenekker asked.

"Li Ping was on the truck for a long time before she got kidnapped," I went on. "They made a pit stop halfway through the trip in Las Cruces and the panda was still on board. That had to have been at least eight hours, right, Marge?"

"That's correct," she confirmed.

"But when the truck got here," I said, "there wasn't any poop in it."

Everyone fell silent as that sank in.

Hoenekker's jaw swung open. "Son of a gun, you're right."

"He is?" J.J. asked.

"Of course he is!" Summer declared. "Teddy's never wrong!"

"There was a bunch of bamboo," Hoenekker said, "but no poop."

"It's not like we could have missed it," I added. "According to Chloé Dolkart, it's big, like the size of avocados. And pandas do it forty times a day."

"Hold on," Marge said, trying to make sense of what was going on. "Are you saying that whoever stole Li Ping also swiped a whole bunch of panda poo?"

Summer smacked her forehead, stunned by how dense Marge was.

"No," I said. "I'm saying the panda poo was never there. Because the *panda* was never there. Someone switched the trailers on the trucks."

"What?" Marge asked, still trying to understand.

"They didn't hit the truck while it was in motion," I said. "Instead, they took a trailer that looked exactly like ours, made it up to *look* like a crime scene, with the blown locks and the chloroform and everything, and then swapped it with ours at some point on the trip. They got the panda cage and all the furniture for Doc right, but they forgot about the poop. Or maybe they just didn't know how much pandas go to the bathroom."

"I sure didn't," J.J. muttered. "Fifty pounds. Wow. That's more than a good dog weighs."

"Now, hold on," Hoenekker argued. "You can't swap trailers while the truck is moving."

"Well, no," I agreed. "However, if you had a team of people on the side of the road, you could do it pretty quickly, I think. Much faster than you could break into the trailer, steal Li Ping, and kidnap Doc."

"But then the drivers would have to be in on it," Hoenekker pointed out.

"Only *one* would," I corrected. "Juan Velasquez was driving at the time. For this to work, he would have had to park on the side of the road to uncouple the first trailer, then move the cab to hitch up the second trailer. If he did it quickly enough, Greg Jefferson could have slept through the whole thing."

"And what about Marge?" Hoenekker asked. "She was right there in the cab next to Juan. How could she have missed all this?"

"Because she was asleep too," I said.

Everyone looked to Marge.

"I wasn't!" she said defensively. "I was awake the whole time!"

"Are you sure?" I asked.

"Of course I'm sure!" Marge exclaimed, though she didn't sound quite so confident this time.

"If you fell asleep on the job, it's best to be honest about it," J.J. informed her. "Li Ping's life is at stake."

Marge shrank toward the wall. "I . . . I might have nodded off for a tiny bit. I mean, I didn't think I did, but it was such a long drive. And I did get a little drowsy around Fort Stockton, even though I got a big old tub of coffee in Las Cruces."

"Did *you* buy the coffee?" I asked.

Marge thought about it, then frowned. "No. Juan did. He claimed it was regular, but it sure didn't work for me."

"You wouldn't have needed to be asleep very long for this to work," I told her. "Maybe you didn't even realize you'd done it. It happens to me sometimes, when I'm really tired."

"Me too!" Summer chimed in. "Like when you and I were watching that boring movie at my house the other night, Teddy. I wouldn't have even known I was falling asleep except that the movie seemed to keep jumping ahead."

"Wait one blasted second," J.J. said. "This still seems

highly speculative to me. What's the point of stealing the whole trailer rather than just stealing the panda?"

"For one thing, it's faster," I explained. "And it's probably easier. Instead of having to wrestle the panda and Doc out of the trailer on the side of the highway and put them in a different vehicle, the thieves could just attach the entire trailer to a different truck, drive it off wherever they wanted, and deal with Doc and Li Ping when they got there."

"And you don't think Doc would have realized something was going on?" Hoenekker asked.

"Not if he slept through it," Summer pointed out. "He said he was asleep right up to the point where they chloroformed him. Or maybe they chloroformed him while they were switching the trailers. Either way would have worked."

J.J. glowered. "I suppose. But it still wouldn't be so easy to pull this off. You'd need an exact replica of the panda trailer we designed."

"I don't think it *was* an exact replica," I said. "That's where they messed up. I mean, they could fake the outside and the cage and the furniture, but they couldn't fake what Li Ping and Doc would do inside. They didn't think about the panda poop. And they made it look like Doc watched a nature documentary on his DVD player. One about lions. You could always call him and ask if he actually watched it. I'll bet he didn't."

J.J. considered that, then grabbed his phone and said, "Lynda. Get Doc for me, right now. He's probably gonna say no, but tell him it concerns the fate of Li Ping."

While we waited for Doc, J.J. flipped the phone to speaker so we could all hear.

I shifted nervously on the couch. As far as I knew, Doc hated television and never watched it—but I wasn't completely sure.

Summer put her hand on my knee. "Relax," she whispered. "I know you're right."

"I have Doc for you," Lynda announced over the phone.

Then Doc came on, sounding annoyed. "I'm about to go into surgery, J.J. I don't have much time. . . ."

"This will only take a few seconds. When you were in the trailer with Li Ping, did you watch any of those nature documentaries we provided for you? The one about lions?"

"Why would I do that?" Doc snorted. "I see enough lions at work. And I know more about them than any documentary crew."

"So you didn't watch any of the movies?" Hoenekker pressed.

"I didn't even turn on the TV," Doc replied. "I read a book the whole time, up until I fell asleep."

"That's all we needed to know," J.J. said. "Thanks for the info." He hung up.

"There was no book left behind in the trailer," Hoenek-ker reported.

"I'll be darned, Teddy," J.J. said, sounding kind of impressed. "Looks like you're right once again. They cloned the trailer."

"Which is why I don't think the NFF could have done it," I said. "A trailer like that must be awfully expensive, right?"

"They're not cheap," J.J. concurred.

"From what I understand," I went on, "the NFF doesn't have much money. But whoever pulled off this heist must be loaded. They bought a trailer—and possibly paid off Juan and James Van Amburg as well."

"Then who was it?" Summer asked. "Animal traffickers?"

"I'm not sure," I admitted. "But the trailer itself is the big clue to figuring that out. Whoever made it had to know exactly what the *real* trailer was going to look like. So who built the real trailer?"

"I don't know," J.J. said.

"You don't?" Summer gasped.

"A million decisions get made at my companies every day," J.J. informed her. "I can't be in on every single one of them." He grabbed the phone again. "Lynda, call Carter Hanauer in Transportation. Find out from him who built that panda trailer for us."

"Right away, J.J." Lynda said.

J.J. hung up, then looked to the TV again. Molly O'Malley was still confidently talking to the press, completely sure she was right about the Nature Freedom Force's guilt. J.J. turned back to me. "The FBI sends a whole crack division out here to handle this, and they didn't see what you did. Not a single one of them thought to go talk to the panda keepers."

"Actually," I said, "that was Marge's idea."

Summer gaped at me in surprise. So did Marge for a moment. Then she caught on to my lie and acted like she'd known this all along.

I was as shocked as either one of them that I'd said it. The idea had simply popped into my head, and before I even knew what I was doing, I'd spoken up.

J.J. didn't buy it for a second. "Really?" he asked skeptically.

"Really," I said, trying my best to sell it.

"And why didn't you go to the keepers yourself, Marge?" Hoenekker asked, equally as suspicious as J.J.

"I didn't think you'd approve," Marge replied. "You had made it very clear that I was not to interfere with the panda case."

"But Marge just had this sense that the FBI was making a mistake with the NFF," I said. "So she asked me to talk to Chloé, and then we all agreed to meet up at the Polar Pavilion to discuss what I'd learned. But James Van Amburg got the jump on me. Thankfully, Marge was there to save my life."

Summer joined in now, coming to Marge's aid as well. "Maybe Marge got a little crazy going after James Van Amburg, but the guy had just tried to kill Teddy. Marge didn't want to let him get away."

"And he wouldn't have, if I'd had a little more help from security," Marge said pointedly, glaring at Hoenekker.

Hoenekker shrank under her gaze. "I promise you, we'll find him."

J.J. looked from Marge to me to Summer, then back to Marge again. It didn't seem like he really believed us, but he seemed intrigued that I—and more importantly, Summer—had gone to bat for Marge. "Chief, maybe we were a little hasty in our dismissal of Officer O'Malley."

"Perhaps," Hoenekker said. He didn't really seem to agree with J.J. He simply didn't want to contradict his boss.

Before he could say anything else, my parents burst into the office. They ran right to me and hugged me tightly. "Are you all right?" Dad asked.

"I'm fine," I told him.

"How does this keep happening to you?" Mom asked. She continued holding on to me, despite the fact that I was damp and soaking through her shirt.

"I don't know," I said. "I was being careful this time! All I did was talk to a keeper!"

"We're not upset with you," Dad assured me. "We were just so scared when we got the news."

Mom looked at Marge. "We hear we have you to thank for saving Teddy."

Marge waved this off. "It was no big deal. They were only bears. It's not as if they're dangerous, like lions."

"Uh . . . Marge," Dad said. "Polar bears are easily as dangerous as lions. Probably even *more* dangerous. They've been known to hunt humans."

Marge paled. "You mean I could have been killed in there?"

"Not just killed," Summer said gleefully. "You could have been mauled, eviscerated, and then eaten."

Marge wobbled on her feet as the realization of what she'd done sank in. And then, she passed out. She pitched forward onto J.J. McCracken's coffee table, which promptly collapsed underneath her.

Hoenekker rushed to her side to see if she was all right.

Lynda buzzed through on J.J.'s phone. "J.J., I spoke to Carter Hanauer. He says the panda trailer was custom built by SponCo Trucks."

"And who owns SponCo Trucks?" J.J. inquired.

"It's a subsidiary of the Nautilus Corporation," Lynda replied.

J.J. stiffened at the name. So did I. We both knew who ran the Nautilus Corporation.

"Walter Ogilvy," J.J. growled.

"The man who busted the shark tank with Teddy in it?" Mom asked.

"One and the same." J.J. angrily pounded his desk with a fist. "He built a fake trailer, stole my panda, and framed the NFF. And the FBI bought it hook, line, and sinker like a bunch of blasted fools. We better get ahold of them fast so they can track down Van Amburg and get him to turn evidence on Ogilvy."

Hoenekker's phone buzzed urgently. He read the text and smiled. Then he said, "J.J., I'm not sure bringing in the feds gets us anything. For all we know, they won't even listen to us." He nodded toward the TV, where Molly O'Malley was still conducting her press conference. "They seem awfully convinced that they've got the right guys."

"Look, Chief," J.J. said, "I know you've got your tail in a twist because of how the feds treated you, but I have to get that panda back and, frankly, I need the A-team for this. I know you're a good man, but as for our security here, well . . . they're a little out of their league on this case."

"Maybe not," Hoenekker replied, hanging up the phone. "It just so happens, we've arrested James Van Amburg."

THE CONFESSION

FunJungle had a small jail in the basement level of the administration building. There were only two cells, and they weren't designed to hold people long-term, like in a real prison. They were merely to keep anyone FunJungle Security arrested—for shoplifting, say—until someone from another law enforcement agency could collect them.

To everyone's surprise, Kevin Wilks, the bumbling idiot from security, had caught James Van Amburg. Kevin was quite pleased with himself and happily related the story to Summer, my parents, Marge, J.J., and me as we followed Hoenekker through the basement to the jail.

"I was stationed outside the front gates," he explained, "working bag check for the incoming guests. Then I heard all the commotion with Marge crashing into the parade. So

I ran to the gates to see what was going on, and I saw Teddy and Summer up on that little hill by Hippo River, pointing at this big bald guy all excitedly."

"Wow," Summer said. "Someone actually noticed us."

"Yeah, *me*," Kevin said proudly. "But I couldn't hear you over all the chaos. I didn't realize the guy had tried to kill you, Teddy. I figured he'd swiped Summer's purse or something. So as he came out the gate, I pulled my Taser and ordered him to stop."

"And he listened?" I asked.

"Oh no," Kevin said. "Not at all. He shoved me out of his way and tried to make a run for it."

"So what'd you do, chase him down and tackle him?" Summer asked.

"Er . . . no," Kevin replied. "When he pushed me, I tripped over a little kid and, uh, sort of accidentally fired my Taser."

"So you tasered James Van Amburg by accident?" Mom gasped.

"No." Kevin said. "I tasered a *different* guest by accident. But then she fell down and Van Amburg tripped over her and knocked himself unconscious on the curb."

Hoenekker cringed, looking mortified by this story.

"Wow," J.J. muttered. "This is a real crack staff we have here."

"Thanks!" Kevin said, failing to grasp J.J.'s sarcasm.

"Any idea what this accidental tasing's gonna cost me?" J.J. asked.

"Well, the woman *was* pretty upset," Kevin admitted. "Especially because it happened in front of her grandkids."

"You tased a grandmother?!" J.J. exclaimed, horrified.

"She was a very young and healthy grandmother," Kevin said in his defense. "Not one of those old, wrinkly grandmothers. And once Pete Thwacker offered her and her whole family free annual passes for the next few years, they agreed not to sue us. Anyhow, by the time we took care of all that and got Van Amburg cuffed and made sure he was only unconscious and not dead or anything, all of you guys were gone. So some of the other guards and I brought Van Amburg over here, and that's when I finally tracked Chief Hoenekker down."

We stopped by a door with a plaque marked JAIL. FUN-JUNGLE SECURITY ONLY. Hoenekker told Kevin, "You're dismissed, Officer. Thanks for your work."

"Just doing my job, sir!" Kevin saluted and marched back toward the elevator.

Marge glared after him. "It's guards like that who make the rest of us look bad."

"Yes," Hoenekker grumbled. "I'd hate to have his arrest of Van Amburg cast a bad light on your destruction of the parade today." He unlocked a door next to the jail.

This led into a small, narrow observation room. There was nothing in it except six chairs, which faced a large window. The window looked into the jail, which wasn't that big either: It only had the two holding cells and a small desk for the guard on duty. James Van Amburg paced back and forth nervously in one cell. The other was empty. The guard at the desk was a young woman I didn't recognize. Neither she nor James seemed to notice us through the window.

"This is one-way glass," Hoenekker explained. "We can see in, but they can't see out. To them, it merely looks like a mirror. Everyone but Officer O'Malley will remain in here while I extract the confession from Van Amburg." He shifted his attention to Marge. "And you will not speak unless I ask you to. This is my show, not yours, is that understood?"

"Yes sir," Marge agreed.

Hoenekker turned to me. "Before I begin, I need you to tell me for certain: Is that the man who threw you into the polar bear exhibit?"

"Yes," I said.

"That's him, all right," Summer echoed.

Hoenekker didn't seem convinced. "Don't be cavalier about this. Take your time. I need you to be one hundred percent sure we have the right person."

I was already a hundred percent sure. With his big size, his bald head, and his mean, beady little eyes, James Van

Amburg was hard to confuse with anyone else. However, I pretended to take my time scrutinizing him to assure Hoenekker we had the right man. "That's definitely him."

"Yes," Summer agreed. "He's the one who attacked Teddy."

"Very good," Hoenekker said. "Now, Teddy and Summer, as witnesses to Van Amburg's actions, I'll need you to stay here the entire time to verify or counter his statements." He inserted a small transmitter into his ear, then pointed to a microphone with a red button by the window. "If I look to the glass, I'm asking you for confirmation. You can let me know through that mic. Now, exacting a confession can take quite some time. Hours, maybe. A seasoned criminal won't be in any rush to admit his guilt, let alone turn evidence on someone as powerful as Walter Ogilvy." He looked to my parents and J.J. "None of you are required to stay the whole time. . . ."

"We know," Mom said. "But it's important for us to see that this man gets what's coming to him."

"No one throws my son into a polar bear exhibit and gets away with it," Dad added.

J.J. said, "If that ape can tie Walter Ogilvy to all this, I want to be here for every last moment of it."

"Very well. Then we'll begin." Hoenekker led Marge next door.

The rest of us took seats in the observation room. The

six chairs were in two rows, so Summer and I sat in the front while our parents sat behind us.

Through the one-way glass, we watched Hoenekker and Marge enter the jail.

James Van Amburg looked at them expectantly through the bars of his cell.

"Are you the guy in charge?" he asked. I hadn't heard him speak yet that day; it was the same deep, gravelly voice that had threatened me at Dolphin Adventure. "How long are you gonna keep me here?"

Hoenekker didn't answer him. Instead, he told the guard on duty, "You're relieved, Private. I need to be here with only Officer O'Malley and Mr. Van Amburg."

"Yes sir," the woman said, and quickly left the room.

"I said how long are you going to keep me here?" James asked again, sounding more upset this time.

Once again, Hoenekker ignored the question. Instead, he took the chair from the desk, dragged it closer to the holding cell, and sat down. "Mr. Van Amburg, you're in a great deal of trouble. You threw a young boy into the polar bear exhibit. I have corroboration from the boy himself, as well as another witness *and* Officer O'Malley here." He pointed to Marge, signaling this was her time to talk.

"That's right," Marge agreed, staring bullets at the prisoner. "I saw the whole thing."

"There are also cameras throughout the Polar Pavilion that will certainly prove your guilt in this matter," Hoenekker continued. "That's attempted murder. Of a child. You could go away for sixty years. . . ."

"I know!" James exclaimed. "I'm so sorry! It was wrong! I never should have done it!" To my surprise, he started crying. And not merely a few tears. This was full-blown bawling, like a toddler having a meltdown.

Hoenekker seemed surprised by this as well. "Er . . . So you admit to this?"

"Yes!" James was no longer the tough guy who'd threatened me. Instead, he was a blubbering, frightened mess. Rivers of snot were running from his nose.

"Look at him," Mom said in disgust. "He's just like any other bully. Happy to pick on someone smaller than him, but the moment he's in trouble, he shows his true colors."

"I didn't mean to do it!" James wailed. "It was an accident!"

"An accident?" Hoenekker repeated. "How could you throw a boy into the polar bear exhibit by accident?"

"It wasn't planned or anything!" James wailed. "I overheard the kid say he had evidence and I panicked! Please, don't send me to jail! I'm happy to turn over evidence on anyone you need. I kept records! I have names! I'll do anything!" He sank to his knees, sobbing uncontrollably.

Hoenekker frowned. He actually seemed disappointed by how easy James was making this. "Calm down," he said. "Who are you working for?"

"Walter Ogilvy," James replied.

"That low-down, dirty snake!" J.J. exclaimed, loud enough that Hoenekker shot him a warning glance through the window.

James didn't appear to have heard, though. He was making too much noise himself. "He's the guy you want, right? He was the brains of the entire operation. I'll tell you anything you want to know about him. Just don't send me to jail!"

"Whoa," Hoenekker said. "Let's start at the beginning. The more detail you can give me, the better. Was the NFF involved with this at all, or was it only Ogilvy?"

"It was only Ogilvy," James confirmed. "The NFF didn't have anything to do with it. They're a bunch of losers. . . ."

"Really?" Hoenekker asked. "I thought you co-founded the group with Carlos Gomez."

"Yeah, but it was a mistake. Carlos was weak. He only wanted to picket and hand out flyers instead of monkey-wrenching. So a couple months ago, I tried to show him what we could really do. There was a Taco Bell being built right by a wildlife refuge near Houston, so I burned it down." James seemed excited as he told this part. I got the idea that he might have formed the NFF as an excuse to destroy things, rather than to protect wildlife.

"That was you?" Marge asked, and Hoenekker gave her a look that indicated he wasn't pleased by her interruption.

"Yeah," James said proudly. "It wasn't like they'd built too much yet, but I torched what there was. Sent a real good message. Only, Carlos was furious. He chewed me out right in front of a big NFF meeting, called me irresponsible, and kicked me out of the group."

"So you had a grudge against him," Hoenekker stated. "When did Ogilvy approach you?"

"A few weeks later," James replied. "I mean, Ogilvy didn't do it himself, of course. He sent some guys. They tried to keep his name a secret, but they weren't rocket scientists." The story was flowing out of James so quickly now, I got the sense he might have rehearsed it, knowing he might have to turn over evidence. "They made me a cash offer. They wanted help stealing the panda *and* they wanted to frame the NFF for it."

"Which you were happy to do," Hoenekker said.

"Darn straight I was. After how Carlos treated me. So I swiped some envelopes and paper from the NFF that I knew had Carlos's fingerprints on it, and Ogilvy's men used all that to print the fake ransom notes on. I also stole the license plates off Carlos's car, then attached them to a similar model, which we used to dump the vet in the parking lot here."

"And were you involved in the actual theft of the panda?" Hoenekker asked.

"Yes."

"How did that go down?"

"Well, Ogilvy had built this replica trailer, right? Exactly the same as the one the panda was in. So we waited at a rest stop near the border of Texas and New Mexico with it. Ogilvy also had one of the drivers, Juan something or other, on the payroll."

"Juan Velasquez?"

"Yeah. That's the guy."

Summer turned to me, impressed. "Just like you said, Teddy!"

I grinned, feeling proud that my suspicions had turned out to be right. Although at the same time, I was also enraged at James Van Amburg and Walter Ogilvy for everything they had done.

James went on. "That night, Juan and the other driver and you"—he pointed to Marge—"made a pit stop in Las Cruces. Juan bought you a decaf coffee instead of a regular one, and then he spiked it with some sleep medicine too."

"Aha!" Marge exclaimed. "So it wasn't my fault I got drowsy!"

Hoenekker gave her another warning look to keep quiet.

"Then Juan took over the driving," James reported,

"while the other driver went to sleep in the truck. We fell in behind them as they entered Texas." He looked to Marge. "Once you dozed off, Juan pulled over at another rest stop and we all swapped the trailers."

"How long did that take?" Hoenekker asked.

"Less than five minutes," James replied. "We'd been practicing." He looked to Marge again. "You were snoring like a chainsaw the whole time."

Marge turned bright red but didn't say anything.

"What happened after that?" Hoenekker inquired.

"We broke into the trailer and grabbed the vet," James reported. "Some of the guys and I took him while the others took the truck with the panda. They held the vet in a storage unit for a few hours, then dumped him here with the fake note to frame the NFF."

"And meanwhile, you returned to the park in the panda costume," Hoenekker said.

"That's right."

"Why?"

"Ogilvy wanted someone to keep an eye on the investigation. I didn't steal the costume. One of the other guys did that. But they asked me to wear it in the park."

"How'd you get the costume in and out?"

"I didn't. It was stashed in some of the tourist lockers here."

"So you just walked into the park, got it out of the locker, and put it on?"

"Yeah. No one even looked twice at me. There were a lot of freaks dressed up like pandas that day. And once I was wearing it, no one stopped me from going anywhere, even the employee areas. Only, I couldn't get close to the investigation. And then I saw that kid wandering around."

"Teddy? The one you threw into the polar bear exhibit?"

"Yeah. Him. Ogilvy's guys had shown me a picture of the little punk and told me to keep my eyes open for him. They said he once screwed up some attempt to mess up the shark tank or something like that."

At the mention of this, I grew queasy. Walter Ogilvy not only knew who I was, he had specifically ordered a thug to keep an eye on me. As if it wasn't enough that his plotting hadn't already killed me once.

"Anyhow," James was saying, "I saw the kid over by the crime scene, so I decided to follow him around. Sure enough, he eventually went over to the panda exhibit and started asking questions, so I figured I ought to scare him off the case."

"That's when you threatened him outside the dolphin tank?" Hoenekker asked.

"Yeah. I wasn't gonna hurt him or anything. Just make him *think* he could get hurt. But then he pulled some crazy stunt with the dolphin and ran off. So I split and dumped the panda costume in the trash. Ogilvy's guys were still worried about the kid. They said he could still be trouble. So I came back here today, like a normal tourist, then cased the panda exhibit. And the kid showed up again. I don't know what he did inside, but when he came out, I overheard him make a call and say he had important evidence about the crime and, well . . ." For the first time since he'd started talking, James seemed at a loss for words.

"You decided to get rid of him," Hoenekker finished.

"Yeah, but . . ." James's lower lip trembled. It looked like he might start crying again. "Like I said, I wasn't thinking straight. I just panicked. I'm not a murderer. . . ."

"Yes he is!" Summer snapped. "That jerk! He tried to kill Teddy!"

J.J. couldn't contain himself any longer either. Throughout the confession, he'd been trembling, livid at what Ogilvy had plotted against him. Now he sprang from his seat and pressed the microphone button to talk to Hoenekker. "Chief! Find out if that weasel has any evidence to prove Ogilvy's involvement!"

Hoenekker nodded understanding, then spoke calmly to James. "It seems Walter Ogilvy was never directly involved in this crime. Can you prove his connection to it?"

"Definitely," James said. "I'm no dummy. I secretly

recorded all my conversations with his men. His name came up a few times."

"Hot dang!" J.J. crowed, then thought of something else. He pressed the microphone button and asked, "So where's Li Ping now?"

Hoenekker repeated the question to James.

"Um . . . ," James said. "I don't know."

"You don't?" Hoenekker replied doubtfully. "Even though you helped steal her?"

"Like I said, I took the vet, not the panda. I heard Ogilvy had a buyer for her, but no one ever said who it was."

"Do you have any clue who it might have been?" Hoenekker pressed. "Were they in the state? In the country?"

"I've told you everything I know, I swear."

Hoenekker abruptly stood and left the room. Marge followed him.

"Wait!" James called. "Where are you going? I gave you enough information, didn't I? I'm not going to jail, right? Please don't send me to jail!" He started crying like a baby again.

"Don't worry," Dad told me. "It doesn't matter how much information that jerk coughed up. He won't get off easy. He's going away for a long time."

I looked through the window at James. He looked pathetic, clinging to the bars of the jail cell and sobbing. But I didn't feel bad for him at all.

Hoenekker and Marge reentered the observation room.

"Nice work in there," J.J. told him, "but the time has come to hand this over to the feds. We don't have the jurisdiction to go after Ogilvy and they do."

"I know," Hoenekker agreed. "Although I'm still not sure the FBI will be open to hearing us. They've just proclaimed that they've solved the case to the whole world. . . ."

"Now, look . . . ," J.J. began.

"However," Hoenekker continued, "the US State Department has its own law enforcement agency: the Diplomatic Security Service. This falls under their jurisdiction too, and I'll bet they'd be happy to scoop the FBI. I have some friends over there I could call."

"You mean, they could nail Ogilvy *and* make my sister look bad?" Marge asked. "Sounds good to me."

"I don't care who handles it, as long as they can get it done," J.J. said. "We don't have time to fiddle around here. We still need to find that panda."

Hoenekker said, "Unfortunately, that still might take a while."

"How long?" Summer asked, worried.

"I have no idea," Hoenekker admitted. "Days if we're lucky. Weeks if we're not. Maybe even months."

"I don't have months!" J.J. exclaimed.

"Neither does Li Ping," I pointed out. "She only likes

one kind of bamboo, and if whoever got her doesn't have it, she's going to be . . ." I trailed off midsentence, an idea coming to me.

"Dead?" Mom finished.

"Maybe not," I said. "I think I know where she is."

ANIMAL HOUSE

For the second time in two days, a helicopter landed at FunJungle.

However, this time J.J. had requested it himself. It had only taken him a few phone calls to confirm my suspicions about who had Li Ping, after which he'd told Lynda to get him a helicopter. Twenty minutes later, it was touching down behind the veterinary hospital.

J.J., Summer, Dad, and I quickly boarded it. I was invited because J.J. needed me, and Dad was invited because he insisted I ought to have a parent along. Summer simply came because she wanted to, and Summer could be even harder to say no to than J.J. The moment we were buckled in, the pilot lifted off and we raced north over the park.

The helicopter wasn't quite as fast as a private jet, but

it still flew at 130 miles an hour. The rolling mounds of the Hill Country quickly gave way to the flatter plains of central Texas. It took only an hour for us to reach our destination.

It was the biggest house I'd ever seen, even bigger than J.J.'s—and he was a billionaire. I had worried there might not be a place for the helicopter to land, but that turned out to be unfounded: The front lawn was the size of a professional football field. The house itself had blatantly been modeled after the White House, with stately columns, an enormous portico, and symmetrical wings.

That would have been strange enough. Then I noticed the zebras grazing in the backyard.

At first, I thought my eyes were playing tricks on me. The sun was setting, so I figured maybe they were white horses with shadows cast across them. But as we got lower, I could see they were definitely zebras. There were fourteen of them.

There was also a hippopotamus in the swimming pool.

It was only a pygmy hippo, which was significantly smaller than the common hippo, but still, it was odd. The pool itself appeared to be unfit for human use. It was murky brown and there were plants growing in it. A second hippo bobbed to the surface as I watched.

"Holy cow!" Dad exclaimed. "Look at all those cats!"

He was staring out the window on the opposite side of

the helicopter. I joined him and saw a long line of fenced enclosures. Each had a big cat pacing inside it: tigers, lions, panthers, and leopards.

"Jumping Jiminy, she's got even more tigers than Fun-Jungle," J.J. said.

"They don't have much room, though," Summer observed.

It was true. Each cat's pen was only a few yards long. And it seemed unlikely they would ever be let out for exercise, as they'd probably eat some of the other animals.

The helicopter swooped over the house and lowered toward the front yard. A herd of impalas scattered as we touched down.

J.J. sprang out before the rotors even stopped turning and stormed toward the front door.

Dad, Summer, and I scrambled out after him.

A limousine was parked by the front portico. It was peri-winkle blue.

A man in a tuxedo emerged from the house as we came up the front steps. I recognized him as Arthur, the man who had accompanied Flora Hancock on her visit to FunJungle. His face was flushed with anger. "What do you think you're doing?" he yelled. "This is private property! You can't just land your helicopter here!"

"Well, you're not supposed to steal other people's panda

bears, either," J.J. replied. "But your employer doesn't seem to have much of an issue with that."

Arthur recoiled in surprise. His anger instantly became fear. "I don't know what you're talking about," he said, though it was obviously a lie.

"Where's Flora?" J.J. demanded. "I see that god-awful limo of hers is here, so she must be too."

"She's not," Arthur said in a voice on the edge of panic. "She had to go see her sister. I don't know when she'll be back."

As he said this, however, I caught a glimpse of Flora Hancock herself, peeking through the drapes at a window to the right of the front door.

Summer saw her too and pointed accusingly. "She's right there, Daddy!"

Flora quickly ducked away, hiding from sight.

J.J. dodged around Arthur and slipped through the open door behind him. The rest of us did the same. Arthur now appeared completely unsure what to do. "Stop!" he cried impotently, then thought to add, "Please?"

We ignored him, heading straight toward the room where Summer and I had seen Flora. Although I did have to pause briefly to take in the entry foyer.

It was bigger than my entire house. Two enormous staircases swept down the sides, and a gigantic crystal chandelier dangled above our heads. However, the room was in terrible shape. The wood floor and the wallpaper were scarred with thousands of claw marks, while the newels of the banister all appeared to have been gnawed on. Clumps of hair the size of baseballs rolled across the floor like tumbleweeds. And the whole place reeked of animal pee.

J.J. threw open the doors to the next room and marched right in.

It was a formal living room, decorated with extremely fancy furniture, oil paintings, and racks of ancient hunting rifles. It looked straight out of a European castle—except everything here had been sullied by animals as well. There were slashes in the upholstery, the carpets were covered with fur, and the tops of the picture frames were speckled with bird poop.

Flora Hancock sat on a shredded velvet couch, having tea. Even though it was over a hundred degrees outside, she wore a coat and gloves. She was doing her best to act innocent, as though she hadn't seen us through the window—or even heard the helicopter land on her lawn—but she was doing a poor job of it. She was as skittish as one of her impalas.

Two scarlet macaws perched on the couch behind her.

And a young orangutan in a tuxedo stood to her side. It looked to be about five years old. Its tux fit it a lot better than Xavier's had fit him. Given that the orangutan's arms were twice as long as its legs, I had to assume its suit had been custom tailored.

"Why, J.J. McCracken!" Flora cooed, trying to sound natural. "What a delightful surprise! Whatever brings you here?"

"You know exactly why I'm here," J.J. growled. "Where's Li Ping?"

Flora laughed. "Well, how should I know, sugar? I surely don't have her."

"I'm sorry, madam," Arthur apologized, scurrying into the room behind us. "I tried to stop them. . . ."

"It's all right," Flora told him, then shifted her attention to J.J. "Would y'all care for some tea? I'm teaching Suki here to serve it, just like a regular young gentleman."

Suki, the orangutan, held up the teapot, eager to show off his abilities.

"No, I don't want any tea!" J.J. snapped. "I want my panda!"

"Panda!" the macaws echoed. "Panda! Panda! Panda!"

Flora glanced at them nervously, as though they had betrayed her. "Like I said, there is no panda here. How on earth did you ever get such a wild idea?"

J.J. put an arm around me. "Teddy here figured it out. I understand you two met at my park yesterday?"

"Why yes, we did." Flora seemed even more nervous

now, although she was still struggling to maintain composure. "It's a pleasure to see you again, Teddy."

"You too, ma'am," I said, even though that was a lie. It simply seemed like the right thing to say.

Behind Flora's back, Suki stuck the spout of the teapot in his mouth and slurped some tea out of it. Apparently, he wasn't quite as good at serving it as Flora thought.

J.J. sat beside Flora so I could be the center of attention. "Teddy, would you please explain to Flora how you know she has Li Ping?"

I stepped back, surprised to be put on the spot like this. For a moment, I felt a little nervous, wondering if I was actually right.

Dad gave me a reassuring pat on the back. "Go on, Teddy," he said. "Tell her."

I swallowed, then launched into my explanation. "Well, Miss Hancock, I was thinking about the conversation we had at Panda Palace yesterday—"

"Exactly my point," Flora butted in. "Why on earth would I have come down to FunJungle to see Li Ping if she was here?"

"Flora," J.J. said sternly. "I'm sure a woman such as yourself is well aware that it's bad manners to interrupt someone when they're talking. So, if you don't mind, please keep your trap shut until Teddy's finished."

Flora sat back, looking wounded, but she didn't say anything else.

"At first, I figured your being at FunJungle made you innocent," I told Flora. "But then I thought about the timing. Word didn't get out that Li Ping was going to be at FunJungle until yesterday morning. So when exactly did you leave for FunJungle?"

"I suppose around nine a.m. or so," Flora replied. "Isn't that right, Arthur?"

"Er . . . ," Arthur said, surprised to be called on like this. "Yes, ma'am. That's correct."

"Really?" I asked. "Because the news that Li Ping had been kidnapped was reported around ten. You live three hours from FunJungle by car—so you wouldn't have even been a third of the way to FunJungle yet. Why didn't you turn around and go home?"

Flora grew flustered. Her hands began to tremble. "I . . . uh . . . I think I remembered wrong," she stammered. "I believe we left much earlier in the day. Seven o'clock, perhaps."

"Yes!" Arthur agreed. "That's right! It was seven!"

"So then," J.J. said suspiciously, "at seven in the morning, you heard the news about Li Ping and, on the spur of the moment, jumped into the car for a three-plus-hour drive down to my park?"

"Well, I . . . ," Flora began nervously. "I'm not exactly sure when we left. I can't quite recall the timing of the events."

"You can't?" J.J. narrowed his eyes. "It was only yesterday."

Unsettled by this line of questioning, Flora went to put sugar in her tea and knocked the entire bowl off the tea cart. It shattered on the floor. "Oopsie!" she exclaimed.

"Oopsie!" the macaws repeated. "Oopsie! Oopsie! Oopsie!"

"I seem to be all thumbs today," Flora said. "Arthur, could you help me clean this up?" She began to rise from her seat.

I got the impression that Flora had knocked over the sugar on purpose to distract us from our questions.

J.J. seemed to suspect the same thing. He was on his feet before she was. "A little spilled sugar is no big deal. A stolen panda is. So for now, let's forget about the fact that you can't remember the details of yesterday morning. According to Teddy, there's further evidence that you have Li Ping."

"Yes," I said. "Given the weird timing of your visit, Miss Hancock, I started thinking that maybe you'd come down for some reason *besides* seeing Li Ping. Yesterday you admitted yourself that you were listening to me and Chloé Dolkart near Panda Palace, but you didn't approach us until *after* Chloé mentioned that Li Ping only eats one kind of bamboo. However, she hadn't said what that was. So that's when you came over—"

"What kind of evidence is that?" Flora interrupted. "I

was merely interested in what the panda ate. Isn't a lady allowed to be interested in something like that?"

"Sure, if she's got a stolen panda that won't eat," Summer said. She stepped forward, tired of sitting on the sidelines so long. "Here's what *we* think happened, lady. Walter Ogilvy's men stole Li Ping two nights ago and brought her right here to you. Only, you hadn't done your homework and thought you could just give her any old bamboo. No matter what you tried, Li Ping wouldn't eat it. Which was a big problem. Unfortunately, you couldn't just call up FunJungle and ask for help with feeding your stolen panda. So you and Arthur decided to take a road trip. You drove down to FunJungle and lurked around Panda Palace until you overheard Teddy and Chloé talking about what you needed to know. Then you pestered them for details until you learned the right kind of bamboo for Li Ping, raced home, and ordered as much as you could. You got the info you needed—and at the same time gave yourself an alibi, acting like you were all upset and surprised Li Ping wasn't at FunJungle when you'd been involved in her abduction the whole time!"

"I cannot believe this!" Flora exclaimed. She was trying to sound indignant, but she sounded nervous instead. "To think you all would have the audacity to come into my home and accuse me of such a heinous crime!"

"Oh, we're not accusing you," J.J. said. "We have *proof*

you did it. We're merely explaining how Teddy figured it out. You see, Flora, Wolong bamboo, the type Li Ping likes, doesn't grow in Texas. It grows in cold regions, like the ones where pandas live. It's not easy to get. There are only a few places in this country that grow it, and they're all in Colorado. I happen to know them all, since I'm a customer, so I called them up this afternoon. Lo and behold, the second one I tried had just sold their entire shipment . . . to you."

Flora didn't reply. Instead, she sat there, her eyes nervously darting from one of us to the next, like she was trying to figure out what to say.

Suki came to Flora's side, scooped a handful of the spilled sugar off the floor, and dumped it into his mouth.

"All right," Flora said finally, "I admit, I purchased a panda, but I *thought* I was getting one legally. I had no idea that scoundrel Walter Ogilvy was going to steal Li Ping from you until the news broke. . . ."

J.J. groaned. "Flora, that is the biggest load of bull patootie I've ever heard in my life. You know full well there's no way for a private citizen to legally acquire a panda. Emily Sun from the Chinese Consulate says you have approached her about it repeatedly and that she has told you each time that it can't be done."

"Emily Sun knows who you are?" I asked Flora, unable to contain my surprise. "So that's why she looked so angry yesterday at Panda Palace! I thought she was upset at me, but she was really upset to see you!"

Flora lowered her eyes guiltily but didn't say anything.

"Therefore," J.J. went on, "you were either completely aware that you were purchasing a panda illegally—or you have more bats in your belfry than Saint Peter's Cathedral."

Flora's hand went to her chest. "Why, J.J. McCracken! How dare you impugn my honor!"

J.J. said, "If I wanted to impugn your honor, I'd have sent the State Department here instead of coming myself. And by tomorrow, every news channel in the country would be running stories on you. You would instantly become the most hated woman in the world: the thief who willingly participated in the kidnapping of a giant panda—and who allowed an animal rights group to be framed for it."

"The NFF isn't an animal rights group," Flora scoffed. "They're a bunch of hooligans who don't think anyone ought to be allowed to have pets!"

"Have they caused trouble for you before?" my father asked.

"On too many occasions to count." Flora fanned herself with an open palm. "They picket my property! They protest outside my gates! You should hear some of the scurrilous things they've said about me!"

Suki came to my side, holding a teacup and a saucer. The

teacup was upside down and the saucer was filled with tea, possibly regurgitated by the orangutan.

"Er . . . Thanks," I said, trying to be polite.

"So you admit to having a motive against the NFF," J.J. said to Flora. "If I had chosen to let the media in on this story, I'm sure they would have had a field day with that information. But I've kept my mouth shut—so far."

"All right," Flora said, her voice a little harder-edged than it had been before. "I see you do understand the concept of honor."

"I do," J.J. agreed. "And to that end, I'm taking drastic steps to ensure that your name doesn't end up in the news-papers. I had to twist a lot of arms to keep the State Depart-ment and the Chinese government from throwing the book at you. For the time being, they're happy to just prosecute Walter Ogilvy. But if I gave them the green light, they'd come after you, too. And they'd do it fast."

Flora's facade of good humor faded. She stood shakily and led us across the room. "I meant her no harm," she said. "In a sense, I actually protected her. Mr. Ogilvy claimed he had a drug dealer down in Mexico who wanted to buy the panda. Goodness knows how that ruffian would have treated such a delicate creature. But I stepped in and offered more money."

"I'd be willing to bet that's all a load of hooey," J.J. told her. "Ogilvy simply conned you into jacking up the price."

Flora ignored the accusation. "As you can see, I gave Li Ping as good accommodations as anyone could hope for." She opened the door into the next room.

It was a playroom for human children, full of toys and books. But now there was a live panda in it.

I was hit by a cloud of different emotions: pride that I'd found the panda, anger at Flora for helping steal it, and amazement at being so close to such a rare and beautiful creature for the first time. Li Ping was sleeping in the corner. Thankfully, she still looked healthy. Flora had provided lots of bamboo and a tub of water, but hadn't done much else to prepare. The place reeked of panda pee.

The bamboo hadn't been touched. It was browning, the leaves still on the shafts.

"She hasn't eaten anything?" Dad asked, concerned.

"No," Flora admitted, looking ashamed. "Only a bit of fruit salad. I'm afraid the Wolong bamboo I ordered won't arrive until tomorrow."

"We brought some on the chopper," J.J. said. "Not a lot, but enough to tide her over until the truck gets here."

"Truck?" Flora repeated, caught off guard. "What truck?"

"The one I'm sending to collect her," J.J. replied. "It'll be here in a few hours. My people will then remove Li Ping from these premises, and you aren't going to do anything to stop them."

"And in return for that, you'll keep me from being prosecuted?" Miss Hancock asked.

"Oh, I'm just getting started," J.J. told her. "Over the next few weeks, you will begin to transfer your entire collection of animals to FunJungle. I will pay you a fair price for them, and I will give all of them quality care and decent places to live. . . ."

"My pets!" Flora gasped. "You wouldn't dare take them from me!"

"Flora," J.J. said, "I don't doubt that you love these animals and that you're doing your best to tend to them, but the conditions you're keeping some of these creatures in is deplorable. If you really do care about them, then you know what I'm offering you is the right thing to do."

Flora glanced to Summer and me. I got the sense that, if we hadn't been there, she might have thrown a fit. But now she was struggling to maintain a sense of decorum.

"He'll give them a very good home," Summer said.

"And so many other children will get to see them there," I added. "Wouldn't you like to share all these wonderful animals with the public, rather than keeping them all to yourself?"

Flora struggled to keep a smile on her face. It was evident that she *didn't* want to share her animals with the public; if she had, they would have already been in zoos, rather than her house. "I suppose," she said through gritted teeth.

"Very well, then," J.J. said. "After Li Ping is on her way back to me, I'll send up an advance team to catalog all the animals you have here on your property."

At the thought of this, Flora seemed to age twenty years in a second. "Every last one of them?"

"Every last one," J.J. repeated. "I'm sure you can even get along without Suki there. After all, you have a real butler, and pardon me for saying so, but that orangutan sucks eggs when it comes to serving tea."

Suki stuck out his tongue and gave J.J. a raspberry.

J.J. allowed us one last look at Li Ping, then closed the door and ushered us all back toward the front door.

"J.J.," Flora said, looking defeated now. "You indicated a fair price for all the other animals—but you didn't mention one for Li Ping."

"That's because Li Ping is *my* panda," J.J. explained. "You stole her from me."

"*Walter Ogilvy* stole her from you," Flora corrected. "I purchased her from him at a very steep price."

"Well then, that's between you and Walter Ogilvy." J.J. took Flora by the arm and steered her back into the living room. "If you'd like to take this matter up with the authorities, be my guest."

Flora's knees buckled. She sank into a chair. Suki proffered her a teacup that actually had some tea in it.

To my disgust, Flora drank it. Either she was so shaken by events that she didn't realize Suki had gotten orangutan spit in it, or she didn't care.

There was a sudden movement behind me. I spun around, fearing one of the big cats might have gotten into the house, but saw something even more frightening.

Arthur had snatched one of the old hunting rifles off the wall, and with a look of total hatred on his face, he aimed it at J.J. Unfortunately, Summer and I were standing right between them.

I dove, tackling Summer to the floor.

Thankfully, Dad was moving even faster than I was. He broadsided Arthur just as the butler pulled the trigger.

The shot went wide, blasting an old vase to smithereens.

Startled by the noise, the macaws took to the air. Suki leaped onto the tea cart, upsetting what few pieces of china hadn't been broken already, and careened across the room into the wall. A portrait of an old man toppled onto Suki, who tore right through it.

Flora gasped in horror. "Great-grandfather!"

Dad and Arthur were now grappling with the rifle. Despite being much older than Dad, Arthur was surprisingly strong. "You'll never take our animals!" he yelled. "Never!"

Dad socked him in the face hard enough to send his dentures flying. They skittered across the floor one way while the rifle skittered another. Arthur stumbled backward, then took out another vase as he collapsed to the floor.

Dad grabbed the rifle and turned to Summer and me. "Are you guys okay?"

I looked to Summer, who was pale from fright but recovering. "I'm good," she said.

Suki plucked Arthur's dentures off the floor and stuck them in his mouth.

The sight of the little orangutan in the tuxedo triggered something in my mind. I was suddenly struck by a flash of understanding. "Oh wow," I said.

"Look out!" Dad cried.

A Komodo dragon, probably frightened by the gunshot, scurried through the door with a coterie of butlers, cooks, and other servants in pursuit. Suki spit out Arthur's dentures and scrambled up the fireplace mantel in terror. Another painting toppled off the wall and tore, while the dragon knocked over two more vases as it ran about the room.

"Oh wow, what?" Summer asked me. "Like 'Oh wow, this place is crazy'?"

"No," I said. "I mean, it is, but . . . I wasn't thinking about that."

"Then what were you thinking?"

"I just realized who's been swimming with the dolphins."

THE SWIMMER

While J.J., Dad, Summer, and I were at Flora Han-cock's mansion, Chief Hoenekker was calling his contacts at the State Department's Diplomatic Security Service. It turned out the DSS could claim jurisdiction over anything that might impact US relations with a foreign power—and since China was a foreign power, arresting Li Ping's thief counted. Their southern branch was happy to come aboard the investigation, especially when they realized they could make Molly O'Malley look bad in the bargain. Apparently, she'd riled up some DSS agents on a previous case a few years before.

So that night, while the TV news continued mistakenly reporting that the FBI had closed the Li Ping case, James Van Amburg handed over all his evidence to the DSS, which quickly went to work. Within hours, they'd arrested Juan Velasquez and the three other men who'd switched the trailers and stolen the panda. Threatened with long sentences in a federal penitentiary, each coughed up incriminating evidence on Walter Ogilvy.

At 7:00 a.m. the next morning, when Walter Ogilvy walked into his offices at Nautilus headquarters in New York City, the DSS was waiting for him.

By the time I got up for school, the story was out. Every news channel was breathlessly reporting how the FBI had made a huge blunder, while the DSS, working with Fun-Jungle's Security Division, had tracked down the *real* criminal. It would have been a massive story simply because of Li Ping, but Walter Ogilvy had thrown an honest-to-god tantrum as he was being arrested. He'd broken down even worse than James Van Amburg had, sobbing uncontrollably, begging not to go to jail, claiming he'd been framed by everyone from his ex-wife to international terrorists. A disgruntled Nautilus employee had recorded the whole thing and posted it online. The embarrassing footage had trended like crazy; by noon, there were over six million views on the Internet, and Ogilvy had quickly gone from being a respected businessman to a national laughingstock.

Not a single news story mentioned me, however, except to say that one of the criminals involved had accidentally knocked an innocent boy into the polar bear exhibit during an attempt to flee FunJungle Security the day before, and subsequently ruined a parade. Pete Thwacker promptly announced that the Polar Pavilion would be temporarily closed to install better safety railings, and went on to say that the chaos at the parade had all been part of a FunJungle sting operation to catch the criminal. "Our guests were so impressed by the spectacle of our law enforcement agents in action," he added, "that FunJungle is considering adding a permanent stunt-show element to the parade in coming weeks."

I was given many reasons that my name couldn't be revealed as part of the investigation, from protecting my safety to fear that my involvement would harm the credibility of the government's case against Walter Ogilvy. However, Mom and Dad said that it was probably because everyone was embarrassed to admit that a thirteen-year-old boy had cracked the case when no one else had.

It was annoying, but I had another mystery to solve that day as it was.

I waited until lunchtime, then approached the perpetrator in the school cafeteria. "It was you, wasn't it?" I asked.

Xavier Gonzalez looked up from his lunch, startled. "Was what me?"

"The person who lost his bathing suit in the dolphin tank."

"You're joking, right?" Xavier asked, but it was obvious he had a secret. He'd turned bright red and his voice had gone up two octaves. Plus, he was a terrible actor. If I hadn't been convinced he was the culprit before, this proved it.

No one else was at the lunch table with us. I hadn't wanted to accuse Xavier in front of all of them. Dash and Ethan weren't even at school—they had a track and field tournament in Austin—and Summer had kept Violet away by suggesting they eat outside.

I unwrapped my brown bag lunch. Turkey and cheddar on wheat bread. Xavier had a tuna fish sandwich. Now that I thought about it, Xavier almost always had a tuna fish sandwich.

"Yesterday at lunch," I explained, "when I was telling everyone about the dolphins, I only said that they'd been pulling people's bathing suits down. But then *you* said the dolphins had been *stealing* bathing suits. Which you wouldn't have known unless yours had been stolen."

"That's not true!" Xavier said defensively. "You definitely said the dolphins had been stealing suits. I know it."

"I'm pretty sure I didn't," I told him. "And then, there's also the bathing suit itself. It was a FunJungle shark attack suit. Almost every piece of clothing you own is FunJungle merchandise."

Xavier reflexively looked down at his T-shirt. As usual,

it was from FunJungle. Today it read: "Carnivore Canyon Is Awesome—and I'm Not Lion."

"I'll bet lots of people have that bathing suit," he said.

That was probably true, no matter how tacky the suit was. Although there was another piece of evidence against Xavier: The bathing suit had been a men's medium, which had led me to believe a kid couldn't have worn it, especially a short kid like Xavier. But Xavier was overweight and had a much bigger waistline than he should have. I'd realized that when looking at Flora's tuxedo-wearing orangutan. Xavier's own tux hadn't fit right; the arms and legs had been way too long, which meant he'd needed to rent a men's tux so the pants would fit over his belly. It followed, then, that he would wear a men's bathing suit as well.

Only, I didn't feel like bringing this up in front of him. He was sensitive enough about his weight as it was.

In addition to the tuna fish sandwich in his lunch, he also had a soda, a big bag of chips, a homemade cupcake, and two candy bags. Not exactly the healthiest lunch in the world.

"There are cameras all around the dolphin tanks," I said. "FunJungle has footage of you with the dolphins."

This was a lie. There were cameras, but no one had gone through the footage yet. I was just trying to get Xavier to admit to the crime.

It worked. Xavier's eyes went wide in horror. "Footage of me and Violet?" he gasped.

That part was news to me: I hadn't expected Violet to be involved. Luckily, I was much better at hiding my surprise than Xavier had been. "Yes, Violet too," I said.

Xavier slumped over the table, no longer bothering to feign innocence. "How much trouble are we in?"

"I don't know." That was the truth. I hadn't told anyone but Summer about my suspicions yet. I didn't want Xavier to get into trouble, although I didn't know how well I could keep his involvement a secret. Sooner or later, someone probably *was* going to find that footage of him. "It might not be that much trouble if we can claim you weren't going in there to harm the dolphins. . . ."

"Of course we weren't!" Xavier sat up again, offended. "I would *never* harm an animal."

"*I* know you wouldn't. I'm just saying we need to understand what you were doing in there." I took a bite of my sandwich. "So . . . what were you doing in there?"

"Trying to be as cool as you."

I waited for more, but Xavier didn't elaborate. Instead, he kept his eyes on his food, as though afraid to look at me.

"What do you mean?" I asked.

"Your life is so awesome. Your mom's a famous biologist and your father's this amazing photographer and you got to live in Africa as a kid and now you get to live at FunJungle, the most incredible place on earth, and you're dating Summer McCracken, and you get to do all this super cool stuff like going behind the scenes of the exhibits and petting the rhinos and swimming with the dolphins whenever you want. I never get to do anything like that. My life stinks."

This caught me by surprise. I had never considered that anyone might be jealous of my life. After all, I had spent my first ten years living in a tent camp in Africa with a honey bucket instead of a toilet. And now I lived in a mobile home that my family didn't even own. My parents weren't rich; we didn't have a nice car or fancy furniture, and when we ate out, it was almost always at FunJungle, which was usually lousy. Yes, I got to do some cool things with animals, but that was simply what was available to me: I had rarely been able to do many of the things other kids my age did, like go to the movies or play miniature golf or hang out at the mall. I'd never even had a friend my own age until I'd met Xavier, and until recently, Large Marge had been on a crusade to send me to juvenile hall. Plus, I seemed to have a lot of near-death experiences. Most kids didn't get thrown into polar bear exhibits. Or threatened by grown men dressed as pandas.

If anything, I had always been a bit jealous of my fellow students, who'd gotten to have much more normal lives than me.

But out of everything Xavier had said, there was one thing that *really* startled me.

"You know Summer and I are dating?" I asked.

"Of course." Xavier grinned proudly. "You're not the only one with detective skills."

"How'd you figure it out?"

"A bunch of ways. I see how you two look at each other, and how you hold hands when you don't think anyone's watching. And you've been spending a lot more time with her lately instead of me."

"Oh. Does anyone else know?"

"I don't think so. I haven't said anything."

I poked at my sandwich, feeling a little awkward. "Sorry if I haven't been spending as much time with you. . . ."

"I get it. If Summer McCracken wanted me to be her boyfriend, I'd have ditched you in a second. I mean, she's rich and beautiful and cool and her father owns FunJungle. Pretty much the perfect girl." Xavier hung his head again. "It's not fair. She likes you *and* Violet likes you. The two most popular girls at school."

"Violet doesn't like me that way. She only likes me as a friend. The same way she likes you as a friend."

"No, she still likes you the other way. The head cheer-leader. I thought maybe she'd think us sneaking in to swim with the dolphins would be a date. Like, the coolest date ever. But she only came for the dolphins, not me. And then the whole thing turned into a disaster."

"Because the dolphins stole your suit?"

"Yes." Xavier's face turned bright red again.

"What happened?"

Xavier looked around the cafeteria to see if anyone was listening. No one was, but he lowered his voice to a whisper anyhow just to be safe. "Well, you and Summer get to swim with the dolphins all the time, and I wasn't the only one who was jealous of you. Violet was too. We were talking about it one day after school, and I told her I thought I knew how to sneak into the dolphin tank so we could do it too. I wasn't really saying we should actually do it, just that it *could* be done. But then Violet got all excited and said she'd love to go with me . . . and when the head cheerleader says she wants to do something with you, even if it's kind of illegal, you don't say no."

"So how'd you do it?"

"It wasn't that hard. Both of us have annual passes to FunJungle. So I had my older brother drop us off there last Saturday, and then, when the time came for the park to close, Violet and I hid back in the bushes around Shark Encounter."

"Your brother didn't think it was weird you were staying after park hours?"

"No, he knew what we were up to. And he was totally cool with it. I was spending my Saturday night alone with Violet Grace! So he said he'd give us a couple hours after the park closed and then come back for us. He even lied to my parents and said he was taking me to the movies."

"Oh." This was another way in which my life wasn't as cool as other kids': I didn't have an older brother who'd look out for me like that. Or any siblings at all. "So, you just laid low until the coast was clear and then got into the dolphin tank?"

"Pretty much. We had to wait like half an hour after closing time for security to sweep the park, but they weren't much of an issue. Marge came by, but she wasn't really looking for trespassers. She was just swinging her flashlight around like it was a gun and humming the theme from *Mission: Impossible*. Like she was pretending to be a spy or something. Once she was gone, we changed into our bathing suits and snuck into the tank."

This was just what I'd observed about Dolphin Adventure two days before: It was the one exhibit at FunJungle where the animals were out in the open, without any fences or walls or moats. Anyone who was the slightest bit determined could easily get into it. "And no one saw you?"

"I guess the cameras did. But we didn't see anyone else around. We were trying to be quiet, though. We didn't really say much. We only got in and swam. It was pretty amazing, right up until . . ." Xavier trailed off.

"What happened?"

"Well, I wanted to make sure the dolphins came to us. That was the whole point, right? Without dolphins, it would just be like any other pool. I'd watched the trainers a lot, and I'd noticed how they were always rewarding the dolphins with food."

I glanced at Xavier's sandwich, understanding. "So you brought along some fish of your own."

"Right. I really wanted to bring something bigger, like a salmon, but when I went to the supermarket to get one, it was expensive, and I didn't know how to sneak it into the park anyhow. So I thought, maybe tuna would work instead. It's fish, right? And we had a dozen cans at our house. My mom wouldn't miss one. So I put some in the pockets of my swimsuit to lure the dolphins over."

"And that worked?"

"Yeah. It worked *too* well. The dolphins were all nosing around my crotch the whole time we were in the water. They were trying to get at the tuna, but they didn't know how. So they kept nipping at me and tugging at my suit."

I considered this from the dolphins' perspective. As Olivia said, the trainers often gave them puzzles to solve that involved food: It would be placed inside something like a plastic tub or a block of ice and they'd have to deduce how to get it out. They probably would have considered the tuna in Xavier's pockets as something similar: a problem they had to solve, rather than a young boy who'd mistakenly put food in his pants. "And eventually, one of them just yanked your suit off?"

"Yes." I hadn't thought Xavier could turn any more red than before, but now he did. It seemed as though every drop of blood in his body had gone to his face. "I was trying to get the tuna out for them, but they couldn't wait. They were tugging at my suit so much, they actually yanked me under a few times. Finally, the string holding it on came undone and suddenly, I was totally naked. In front of Violet."

"Did she notice?"

"Oh yeah. Right away. The suit was white, so it was the brightest thing in the tank, and she could see it when the dolphin swam off with it. She was like, 'Did that dolphin just steal your suit?' and I was like, 'Maybe,' and then she started laughing so hysterically, she actually had to get out of the water so she didn't drown."

I thought of Violet laughing so hard at lunch the day before, when that soda had come out her nose. I had mentioned that the dolphins were pantsing people, which must have revived memories of her night with Xavier.

"I'm not upset that she laughed," Xavier said. "If it had happened to someone else, I probably would have laughed too. And she was really cool about the whole thing. She got my towel and my dry clothes for me and she gave me time to get dressed, but still . . . The whole dynamic of everything had changed. I wasn't this cool guy who'd gotten her into the dolphin tank anymore. I was a screw-up who lost his bathing suit and wound up totally naked in front of her."

I sighed. "Yeah, I know what that's like."

"No, you don't."

"I do. Because of *you*! The dolphin stole my bathing suit on Sunday because he'd learned how to do it from you." Xavier might not have set out to teach the dolphins to do this, but it made sense that they'd learned it anyhow. They'd performed an activity: stealing the bathing suit—and there had been a reward: tuna fish. So they'd tried it again.

"It wasn't the same," Xavier pointed out. "You had it happen in front of your girlfriend. I had it happen in front of a girl I like—and she's never going to be interested in me now."

He looked so miserable, I decided to tell him the whole story about my experience. "I know Summer said there wasn't anyone else there when I got pantsed, but there was. One of the trainers."

"Oh," Xavier said, then added, "Is she cute?"

"Yes. And yours happened at night, when Violet couldn't see anything. Mine happened in broad daylight."

Xavier laughed, despite himself. Then he tried to hide it. "But you were in the tank, right? So they still couldn't see that much."

"Oh, they saw *everything*. Snickers threw me into the air. Clear out of the water."

"He did?" Xavier couldn't keep the laughter in anymore. He laughed so hard, he started coughing on his tuna fish.

I didn't mind, though. It was embarrassing, but cheering him up was worth it. I even laughed a bit myself. "I must've gone like ten feet up. Buck naked."

"I guess your life's not so perfect after all." Xavier chortled.

Violet and Summer suddenly sat beside us. "What's so funny?" Violet asked.

Xavier gave me a conspiratorial glance, then answered, "Nothing. Teddy was just making a funny face."

"I thought you guys were eating outside today," I said.

"We *were*," Summer told me. "But it's crazy hot out there. Like a sauna. We couldn't take it anymore." She looked at me. "Did you find out what you wanted to know?"

"Yes," I replied.

"What's everyone being so top secret about?" Violet asked.

"Teddy figured out it was us in the dolphin tank," Xavier said.

Violet reacted in surprise, but then nodded knowingly. "I told you he would," she said.

"Hold on," Summer said. "*Both* of you did it?" She looked to me. "I thought you said it was only Xavier."

"I didn't know Violet was there too," I admitted. "Until Xavier ratted her out."

Violet wheeled on Xavier. "You little fink!" she cried, although she obviously wasn't that upset at him.

Xavier pointed at me accusingly. "He tricked me into it! I thought he already knew!"

Violet looked back to me and asked the same question Xavier had. "Are we in trouble?"

"I don't know," I said, then turned to Summer. "They weren't doing anything malicious. Maybe there's a way to square things with your dad?"

"I'll see what I can do," Summer told them.

Violet returned her attention to Xavier and swatted him playfully. "I can't believe you told on me!"

"I didn't mean to!" Xavier raised his hands in surrender, accidentally knocking over his soda. He snatched it up quickly, but it had already left a spot on his shirt. "Look what you made me do," he teased. Now that Violet was around and being friendly with him—and possibly because he'd had a good laugh at my expense—he didn't seem nearly as down on himself as he had before. He headed across the cafeteria to get some napkins.

"Did Xavier explain everything to you?" Violet asked me,

still a bit nervous. "We weren't trying to cause any trouble. We were just jealous of you guys because you get to do stuff like that all the time."

"Yeah, he explained it," I said.

"If you wanted to go in with the dolphins like that, why didn't you just ask?" Summer said.

"We didn't want to take advantage of your friendship," Violet replied.

"It's no big deal," Summer said. "I'd be happy to arrange it."

"Really? That'd be amazing!" Violet exclaimed—and then soured suddenly, noticing something across the room. "Oh no."

The Barksdale twins were making a beeline for Xavier. Poor Xavier didn't see them coming, as he was busily mopping the soda off his shirt. The rest of the student body noticed them, though. And yet, while everyone realized TimJim was looking to cause trouble for Xavier, no one made a move to help him.

"Those jerks," Summer muttered. "The moment Dash and Ethan aren't here to protect Xavier, they go right after him."

"And no one else here is tough enough to stop them," Violet observed.

As she said this, though, an idea came to me. "Maybe we don't have to be tough to stop the bullying."

"What are you talking about?" Summer asked.

So I told them what I had in mind.

Across the room, TimJim grabbed Xavier from behind. "What happened, Tubbo?" one of them asked. "You of all people should know the food goes in your mouth, not on your shirt."

The other one laughed and jiggled Xavier so his belly wobbled in front of the entire school. "Look how fat you are!" he crowed. "It's disgusting!"

"Leave me alone, guys," Xavier pleaded. "I've never done anything to you."

"You exist," TimJim said. "That's bad enough."

They were so busy taunting Xavier, they didn't see Violet and Summer sneaking up on them. They just kept poking and prodding Xavier and saying mean things to him.

And then, Summer and Violet yanked the twins' shorts down to their ankles in front of the entire cafeteria. Both boys were only wearing jockstraps, so everyone had a great view of their bare bottoms.

The whole room burst into laughter.

As I'd recently learned, there's nothing as embarrassing as losing your pants in public.

TimJim paled and instantly forgot about Xavier. They yanked up their shorts and spun around, ready to pummel whoever had pranked them.

When they realized it was the two most popular girls in school, though, they grew even more embarrassed. Which was what I'd been counting on. To be pantsed by a guy would have been cause for retaliation. But to be pantsed by two girls they probably had crushes on was a major blow to their egos. It wasn't merely humiliating; it was also confirmation that the girls didn't respect them.

"That's what happens when you pick on kids who are smaller than you," Summer told them.

"So leave Xavier and everyone else alone," Violet declared.

The entire cafeteria whooped with agreement and burst into applause. Even the teachers who were monitoring our behavior seemed pleased by what had happened.

TimJim fled from the cafeteria.

Summer and Violet took Xavier's arms and raised them above his head, as though he was king of the school.

Everyone cheered for them.

I knew that wouldn't be the end of TimJim. The twins would certainly cause lots more problems for us. But for the first time, I realized there were other ways to handle bullies without needing protection like Dash and Ethan—or using force to fight back.

Besides, now that Marge O'Malley wasn't going to be any more trouble for me, I needed some new targets to play pranks on.

Epilogue

THE DEBUT

The day Li Ping finally went on exhibit, the crowds at FunJungle were the biggest the park had ever experienced.

The story of Li Ping's kidnapping, the FBI's botching of the case, the arrest of Walter Ogilvy, and the panda's triumphant delivery to FunJungle had been a bonanza of free publicity. "Panda-monium" was headline news all over the world, which instantly made Li Ping the most famous panda on earth. (Walter Ogilvy still hadn't gone to trial yet, but the public had already decided he was guilty. He was universally loathed as the jerk who had stolen a panda. Everyone was boycotting his businesses, which were tanking as a result.)

Li Ping's first day on display was the Friday before Memorial Day weekend. After being delivered from Flora Hancock's estate, the panda had spent a month in quarantine, and during that time, Pete Thwacker and the PR department had whipped panda fans everywhere into a frenzy. Advance ticket sales for FunJungle had soared. Every hotel within thirty miles was booked solid for the entire summer. The Texas legislature had given serious thought to declaring Li Ping's debut a state holiday.

It might as well have been. Half my class called in sick so they could go see the panda. So did a good number of teachers. And ours wasn't the only school where that happened. Many businesses reported a severe lack of employees as well. Everyone headed for FunJungle—if they weren't already there: Thousands of people had camped out at the front gates Thursday night so they could be the first in line on Friday. Only half an hour after FunJungle opened, it broke its attendance record.

When Summer and I finally arrived at the park after school, guests were still streaming through the gates, even though it was nearly a hundred degrees. (Central Texas was experiencing record heat, but J.J. wasn't concerned. The hotter it got, the more seven-dollar sodas he'd sell.)

Summer insisted we go directly to Panda Palace. In the past, on a broiling day like that, she would usually have detoured into the Emporium to grab ice cream bars for us, but since our discussion, she'd stopped grabbing food without paying for it. (I had never told her about Marge's plan to use the "evidence" of shoplifting against her; the mere threat of bad publicity had worked well enough.) And if there had ever been a day to skip the lines, that was it. In the heat, the air-conditioned Emporium was mobbed. But Summer barely noticed. She was too determined to see Li Ping.

Despite our connections, we hadn't been able to see the panda while she was quarantined. Even J.J. hadn't been able to. The best we could do was watch her on a closed-circuit camera, but that wasn't much better than people could do on the Internet. Being so close to Li Ping for so long and not getting to see her in person had been kind of torturous, so we'd been awfully excited for this day. And yet, while I'd expected lots of people to come for the panda's debut, I hadn't expected a horde like this.

"Panda Palace is going to be crazy crowded," I warned Summer. "Maybe we should wait until after closing to visit."

"No way," she replied. "I've waited long enough. We're seeing that panda."

I couldn't really argue for anything else to do in the meantime. We'd both seen every exhibit at FunJungle a thousand times, and we couldn't go swim with the dolphins. Dolphin Adventure had reopened to the public—but it was booked solid for the next few months.

Once Summer and I had determined how the dolphins had learned to steal bathing suits, the trainers had quickly taught the dolphins *not* to do it, then reinforced that behavior. Summer had kept her promise to Xavier and Violet; she had convinced J.J. that they'd meant no harm by sneaking into the dolphin tank and shouldn't be prosecuted. Instead, a different punishment had been worked out for them: Each had to do forty hours of volunteer service at FunJungle—although it was up to them to decide where to do it.

Violet had opted for Dolphin Adventure, where she was helping tend the animals. She was working hard but loving it. (She got to swim with them a lot as part of her job.) Not surprisingly, Xavier had chosen Panda Palace. Starting that afternoon, he would be a "junior panda ambassador" at the exhibit, answering guests' questions and dispensing fascinating panda facts. Over the previous weeks, he had spent plenty of time with the panda keepers, learning as much as he could from them. Neither Xavier nor Violet seemed to regard their service as much of a punishment at all.

As Summer and I neared Panda Palace, we spotted Xavier heading that way as well. Despite the heat, he was wearing a tuxedo again, although this one fit him much better than the one he'd worn the day Li Ping had been kidnapped. "Hey guys!" he called to us. "Have you seen Li Ping yet?"

"We're on our way," Summer said.

"If we can get through the lines," I added.

"Don't worry about that," Xavier said smugly. "I'm a

panda ambassador. You won't have to wait in line if you're with me."

"I never have to wait in lines," Summer reminded him. "Seeing as my family owns this place and all."

"Nice tux," I said.

"Like it?" Xavier spun around to model it for us. "Someone in the costume department here found it for me and said I could have it! Cool, huh?"

Summer and I shared a look. In truth, it looked ridiculous, no matter how well it fit him, but we didn't say anything.

We topped a small rise and Panda Palace came into view. The sheer size of the crowd stopped us in our tracks. A massive line filled the entire plaza in front of the exhibit, then disappeared in the direction of Monkey Mountain.

"Jeez," Summer gasped. "That must be two hours long."

"*More,*" Xavier corrected. "I've been told it's nearly three."

I noticed Emily Sun standing in the shade of a jacaranda tree nearby, fanning herself with a FunJungle map. She seemed pleased by the enormous crowd that had turned up to see Li Ping. In fact, she was even wearing a set of Li Ping ears herself. I didn't point her out to Summer, though. Since J.J. had recovered Li Ping, his business interests in China hadn't suffered, but Summer was still annoyed at Emily for threatening her father in the first place.

My friends and I headed on toward Panda Palace. As

we got closer, I spotted Marge O'Malley patrolling the line. After I'd stood up for her, she hadn't been fired—although J.J. and Hoenekker both felt she couldn't work in security anymore. She had caused way too many problems in that department. However, J.J. had cleverly invented another position for Marge that *sounded* like she was still in security, even though she wasn't: director of crowd control operations. The job was perfect for her. It took away the things that had made her a menace—her Taser, her golf cart, her ability to arrest people—but still allowed her to do what she liked to do most: act like an authority and boss people around. At the moment, she was strutting along and barking orders like a drill sergeant. "Once inside the exhibit, no food or drink is allowed. Please deposit all unconsumed food and drinks in the proper receptacles by the entrance. And be aware that, once inside the exhibit, there is to be no flash photography, banging on the glass, or any other pestering of the panda. Violation of any of these regulations will result in your being forcibly removed from the premises."

A velvet rope between two pylons prevented the guests at the front of the line from entering Panda Palace until Marge let them through. A family of four stood just behind the rope; both parents looked exhausted from their prolonged wait, while their two young children—who were covered from head to toe in FunJungle panda merchandise—bounced up and down with excitement, thrilled they were finally about to see Li Ping.

Summer and Xavier headed directly for the entrance, right in front of all the people in line.

"Wait," I warned them. "We probably shouldn't cut right in front of everyone."

"But I want to see Li Ping," Summer told me, "and there's no way I'm waiting in that huge long line." Then she took my hand and dragged me toward the entrance.

As I'd feared, the father at the velvet rope completely flipped out. "Hey!" he shouted at us. "There's a line! Go on back and wait like everyone else!"

Xavier flashed his official FunJungle badge. "I don't have to wait," he said. "I work here."

"Yeah, right," the father snapped. "You're just a kid."

"I'm an official junior panda ambassador," Xavier announced proudly, pointing to the job title on his badge.

The father didn't seem to believe this, but before he could argue any further, Marge hustled over. "What seems to be the problem here, folks?"

"These troublemakers are trying to jump the line," the father explained.

The mother, meanwhile, looked very embarrassed about her husband's behavior. "Just let them go," she said. "They're only kids."

"*We* have kids!" the father exclaimed. "They waited for three hours like good citizens! I'm not about to let some rule-breakers waltz right in before us!"

A month before, Marge probably would have leaped at the chance to bust me for line-jumping. Or anything else she could think of. While Xavier really was a junior panda ambassador and Summer was the owner's daughter, I didn't have any clout to slip through ahead of everyone else. But today Marge turned her attention to the father and put an arm around me. "Sir, this boy is no rule-breaker. In fact, there wouldn't even *be* a panda here right now if it wasn't for him. When Li Ping was stolen, Teddy here figured out who'd taken her."

The two children looked at me, wide-eyed in amazement, as did a few other people in line. However, the father didn't buy it. "Him?" he scoffed. "Then how come I didn't hear anything about it on the news?"

Marge gave the guy the type of withering stare she used to reserve for me. "You really think the government's going to admit that a kid figured out who stole the panda when none of their agents could? The FBI would still be grilling the wrong people if Teddy hadn't come along."

Xavier gaped at Marge, shocked she was giving me praise like this. I was a bit surprised myself, even though I knew the reason behind it. Molly O'Malley, who'd been so dismissive and disdainful of us, had received a ton of bad press as the agent who botched the big panda case. Marge had been thrilled to see her sister screw up in such a huge way—although I'd never expected her to give me credit for helping make it happen. And in public, no less.

The father backed down, cowed by Marge's defense of me—and probably aware that his wife would be very annoyed with him if he pushed things further. As it was, the wife seemed very impressed by what Marge had said about me. "Did you hear that?" she asked her children. "This young boy helped rescue the panda!"

"Wow!" exclaimed her son.

"Thanks for saving Li Ping!" said her daughter.

Summer teasingly threw her arms around me and cooed, "My hero!"

The children giggled at this.

"Just hang tight a few more minutes," Xavier told them. "Soon you're going to see one of the most amazing animals on earth!"

Marge ushered us toward the entrance. "Right this way, kids."

Xavier and Summer headed into the exhibit. But before I could follow them, Marge grabbed my arm and held me back. "Hold on there, Teddy."

For a moment, I thought she might reveal that I really

was in trouble after all. Instead, she pulled me aside and whispered, "I never got to say it, but . . . thank you. I owe you big for how you stood up for me with the top brass."

"Well, you did save my life with the polar bear."

"Yeah, but I was also a major pain-in-the-rear to you all last year. You could've gotten rid of me for good, but you looked out for me instead. *And* you helped me show up my sister. I saw her at our parents' house last weekend. The FBI's really peeved at her because of this whole panda fiasco. They're relocating her to some department way out in the sticks. It's a major demotion. You should've seen how devastated she was! It was hilarious!" Marge broke into laughter thinking about it.

Summer peeked back out of Panda Palace, wondering what was holding me up. I signaled I'd be right there and that she could go on ahead. She eagerly slipped back inside.

I returned my attention to Marge. "If you really owe me big, then I need a favor."

"Name it."

"You know those recordings you have of Summer shoplifting stuff? Destroy them."

Marge frowned, as though she wasn't pleased I'd thought of this. But then, she sighed and gave in. "Done."

"Really?"

"One thing you should know about me, Theodore. I'm

good on my word." Marge gave me a pat on the back and an honest-to-god smile.

The sounds of a ruckus came from the line. Some teenagers were trying to cut. Marge vigilantly turned that way. "Looks like we've got a situation," she announced. "Don't worry, folks. I've got this." Then she hiked up her belt and strode over to handle the trouble.

I hurried inside Panda Palace.

Li Ping was in the first viewing area, although I couldn't see her right away. Even though Marge was limiting the number of visitors inside Panda Palace, the room was still packed. People were stacked four deep against the glass, oohing and aahing with delight.

Xavier had already taken his place at a small podium, where he was professionally relating information to the crowd. "All of you are very lucky," he was saying, "as Li Ping is wide-awake and in a playful mood right now."

I spotted Summer at the glass, riveted to the panda, and wove my way through the crowd toward her.

"She's perfectly happy in there all by herself," Xavier went on. "In the wild, pandas are extremely solitary, only meeting up with other pandas for a few days a year, if that. So when our male panda arrives here, the two of them won't share an enclosure. Instead, Shen Ju will be on display in the exhibit next door."

I squeezed in beside Summer.

In the exhibit, Li Ping was playing with a large plastic ball, rolling it around with her front paws.

"Look at her," Summer said. "Isn't she the cutest thing ever?"

Li Ping's ball got away and rolled right in front of us. The panda bounded over to it, so we were only inches away from her on the other side of the glass, close enough to see right into her dark brown eyes.

"She's beautiful," I agreed.

Summer turned to me, her smile shifting to a look of concern. "What was all that about with Marge?"

"She just wanted to thank me again for helping keep her job."

Summer kept staring at me shrewdly, as her father often did, like she knew there was something more to the story. "She wasn't upset at you?"

"Nope."

"So everything's cool?"

"Yeah," I said, taking her hand. Standing there with my girlfriend, watching one of the most amazing animals on earth, it didn't seem that life could get much better. "Everything's perfect."

Li Ping Is Not the Only Panda in Danger!

The giant panda is the most endangered member of the bear family. There are fewer than 2,500 of them alive on earth.

Thankfully, over the past few decades, the Chinese government has been extremely aggressive with panda conservation. According to the World Wildlife Fund, the most recent National Giant Panda Survey revealed a 16.8 percent increase in wild panda numbers over the past decade (up to 1,864 estimated individuals), as well as an 11.8 percent increase in the panda's geographic range, with the addition of twenty-seven new panda reserves.

But even though these numbers are encouraging, giant pandas still need our help. Hunting and habitat loss are still threats to pandas who live outside conservation areas. Furthermore, when you protect giant panda habitats, you also end up protecting many other, less well-known (but equally fascinating) animals that share those places: creatures like the takin, the serow, the red panda, and the awesomely named golden snub-nosed monkey.

If you want to help, a good place to start is with the World Wildlife Fund (whose mascot is a panda) at www.worldwildlife.org. Or you could go to www.panda.org.cn to learn about the Chengdu Panda Research Base in China and how you can support their work there.

The World Wildlife Fund also does a lot of work to confront the serious issue of animal trafficking. As I indicated in this book, the illegal wildlife trade is decimating animal populations all over the world—and the United States is one of the top importers. Every year, traffickers sell thousands of live animals that have been illegally taken from the wild—as well as parts of larger animals, which have been killed for them, like ivory from elephant tusks or rhino horns. You can help by refusing to buy any products made from endangered animals—and if you're in the market for an exotic pet, make sure you're buying one that has been bred or obtained legally. (I know you're probably not buying a panda or a tiger, but even buying a bird, reptile, or fish that has been illegally taken from its habitat can have drastic effects on those species.) Ask dealers if they can provide paperwork to prove where their animals have come from—or see if their company has a sustainability plan. If they don't, you might want to take your business elsewhere.

If you're concerned about trafficking and want to know what you can do to help stop it, visit www.worldwildlife.org /pages/stop-wildlife-crime or www.traffic.org.

Finally, here's a list of other organizations that do great work protecting endangered species and habitats:

The Nature Conservancy: nature.org

The Center for Biological Diversity: biologicaldiversity.org

Greenpeace: greenpeace.org

Thanks!

Stuart Gibbs

Acknowledgments

I am indebted to many people for their help with researching this book.

Rachelle Marcon at the San Diego Zoo gave me a wonderful behind-the-scenes tour of the zoo and the panda exhibit, while Julie Breslow, Larry Hanauer, and C.J. Hanauer did the same for me at the National Zoo in Washington, DC. On the dolphin front, the fine folks at DolphinQuest on the Big Island of Hawaii introduced me to a few of these wonderful animals and answered all my questions about them. My intern, Emma Soren, dug up a lot of fascinating and incredibly useful panda facts for me. Greg Lesser offered great insight into how jurisdiction might work in a case like this. Giavanna Grein, who specializes in fighting illegal animal trafficking at the WWF, didn't merely advise me; she also brought me in to meet with a lot of incredibly impressive people in the WWF's animal crimes division. I offer huge thanks to Ben Freitas, Bas Huijbregts, Nilanga Jayasinghe, John Probert, Rachel Kramer, Crawford Allan,

Robin Sawyer, and panda conservation specialist Karen Baragona for their insight—and for the amazing work they do every day to protect wildlife.

On the publishing front, my editor, Kristin Ostby, provided incisive notes, my designer, Lucy Cummins, knocked it out of the park (as usual), and my agent, Jennifer Joel, got me this whole career writing these books in the first place. Finally, thanks to my favorite junior editors, the real Dashiell and Violet, for their encouragement, and my incredible wife, Suzanne, for her unending support.